Isla Dewar is a regular contributor to Scottish newspapers and works with her husband, a cartoonist, on a strip in the *Scottish Field*. She lives in Fife.

KEEPING UP WITH MAGDA is Isla Dewar's first novel and her second, WOMEN TALKING DIRTY, is also available from Headline.

Keeping up
with Magda

Isla Dewar

First published in 1995
by HEADLINE BOOK PUBLISHING

First published in paperback in 1996
by HEADLINE BOOK PUBLISHING

A HEADLINE REVIEW paperback

10 9 8 7 6 5 4

ISBN 0 7472 5112 6

Printed and bound in Great Britain by
Clays Ltd, St Ives plc

HEADLINE BOOK PUBLISHING
A division of Hodder Headline PLC
338 Euston Road
London NW1 3BH

With love and thanks to Nadia Carlotto
who taught me to cook.

Chapter One

When she first came to Mareth it seemed to Jessie that she had come to live in Toy Town. Toy Town with sex. Nothing, absolutely nothing could break the air of frenetic unreality. It was a huddled place on the edge of the world, only the ancient harbour wall between it and the grubby grey and swelling sea. Next stop – who knew where? The streets were kitchen clean. It had that languid air of permanent procrastination. Tourists and other strangers thought that nothing ever went on there. But they were wrong. There was more to life in Mareth than a resigned journey from birth to menopause then death. It seethed. Everything that ever could happen happened there.

Every morning, seven-thirty, regular as clockwork, Jessie was woken by the solid click click clicking of Magda Horn's six-inch stilettos storming up the pavement. Lying in bed, hand between her thighs – a solitary indulgence to check she was really real – unwillingly awake, Jessie would curse the woman in the street below for her noisy footwear. A tangle-haired forty-something hooligan with the brattish way of someone half her age. Oh yes, Jessie had the mark of Magda Horn.

Mareth dawns were exquisite; the sun slid up over the horizon and hung, a glowing red globe, above the harbour. Gulls woke and rose in shrieking, tumbling squalls to claim their space in the day. The first people of the morning, the workers at the quay, the bin men, Magda Horn appeared. Everyone swore. Not a curse, more a rude awakening. Junk language, highly seasoned, quick and easy to use for people who were

1

glad to find the world the way they left it, and who were claiming their space in the day.

Rattling a great clutch of keys and cursing, Magda opened the Ocean Café just below Jessie's window and daily exchanged raw morning banter with the men working on the quay across the road. She swore. And, swift as a nod and a wink, back would come their merry quips, 'Fuck. Fuck. Fucky. Fuck.'

Jessie, moaning on her pillow, reached for her first cigarette of the day, lit it, coughed and complained to the empty room, 'These people can communicate volumes using only one word. What are they all on about? Is that all they can think of to say?'

Granny Moran, known in her heyday as Greasy Mae, came out from the house next door, voluminous tartan dressing gown drawn round her as she shuffled swollen-footed in worn and ancient pink slippers over the road to the harbour's edge to spread breadcrumbs and bacon rinds on the ground. Seagulls took hysterics, came squabbling and crying, fighting each other and the wind, to swoop for food.

'Hey Mae,' a swearer on the quay called, 'cold enough for you?'

'Fine healthy weather,' Jessie heard Granny Moran's cracked and over-used voice reply. 'Kills all them bloody germs. An' watch yer bloody tongue when you bloody speak. I hear you swearing every morning. I've heard enough of that language to do me all ma days. Besides I knew yer granny.'

'I thought you *were* his granny,' another swearer joined in. 'The way you carried on, thought you were everybody's granny.' Granny Moran would never escape her raunchy past. The old lady sucked her gums and stared through the freezing January fog at the thickly anoraked gathering on the quay. Muttering fiercely, she turned back to her front door. It seemed to Jessie that when Granny Moran spoke to herself, her language was as monstrous and vivid as everyone else's.

The swearers, who always enjoyed their own jokes hugely, roared and laughed. A seagull screeching wildly soared past Jessie's window, splattering shit on her little white Peugeot parked below. And she swore. This language was catching.

In the café below, the first rock'n'roll of the day started. The Rolling Stones; bass thudded through the ceiling, rattling the windows. 'Soul Survivor', Jessie heard Jagger holler, and stiffened. The din worsened. Pots clattered, crockery crunched, cutlery rattled. Magda made the same thunderous noises every morning. Jessie wondered vaguely if she knew she was still in bed and made a din deliberately to irritate her. The life's philosophy of such a strident personality could only be: I am up therefore everybody should be up. Then she started on the children.

Every day she brought trailing behind her a brood of six or seven luminous infants, assorted sizes in multi-coloured shellsuits and back to front baseball caps, like pick'n'mix kids. Jessie could never decide if morning to morning it was the same six or seven straggling along the harbour swinging schoolbags, kicking stones and discarded coke tins, yelling taunts and laughing insults. Once inside the café, Magda fed them breakfast and a stream of abuse. 'Are you going to eat that or are you going to sit there doing your junior James Dean act?' Clatter of pots, bang of door, rattle and crunch of crockery, babble of voices and laughter. And Jagger's howl.

'Well, I'm not havin' any adolescent crap here. Bugger off and be moody somewhere else. Come back when your hormones have settled down.'

Slam, blam, crash. The smell of bacon wafted from the outlet ducts at the back of the café. Cereal rattled into bowls. Jessie lay tense with the strain of listening to other people's lives. She imagined everyone down there in the cheery warm café busy eating cornflakes and being young.

'The bloody noise and mess, a bit of child abuse would do the lot of you some good,' Magda's voice cut through the din.

'Oh God,' a communal groan. 'That old threat.'

Despite herself, Jessie smiled.

Seeking solace after the life she had sought to make perfect had taken a vicious turn, Jessie had come to the noisiest, rudest place in the world.

The first time Magda Horn ever spoke to Jessie Tate, Jessie

was standing at the harbour's edge staring out to sea. The wind was whipping her hair about her face and she had tears in her eyes. From her window she had seen porpoises swimming by and had rushed out clutching her binoculars to get closer to them. There they were sloping and dipping, effortlessly through the freezing grey swell only yards from the pier end. Oh God.

Jessie spent hours at the window of her flat above the Ocean Café looking through her binoculars. It was addictive. Sometimes it hurt. She spent so long staring into the dazzle, sun on water, that when she turned back into the room the light had blinded her and it was a while before she could see properly again. She watched gulls squalling and bickering. Eiders busying by, dowdy ladies, gaudy males. Boats came and went, churning trails of frothing water behind them. Mostly, however, she watched the sea. The hugeness, bulk and constancy of it fascinated her.

That day a strange shape loomed, grey against the light. Just a small triangle in the midst of all that sea. Then it was gone. She watched. It loomed again. And again. More and more of them. She gasped. Porpoises. Her heart tumbled. Crying in triumph at her find she ran out of her flat, down the stairs and over the road to the harbour's edge. She had to get closer to them. They were so beautiful. It was an effort stopping herself diving in and swimming after them. Foolish in March.

'What's that you're seeing then?'

Magda stood behind her, looking quizzically out to sea. She had seen Jessie standing shivering in T-shirt and jeans as close to the water as a person could get and, fearing the loony woman upstairs was about to do something silly, had rushed out of the café to stop her.

'Porpoises,' Jessie's voice cracked; she couldn't contain her joy. 'Have you seen them out there?'

Magda smiled. 'They sometimes come by. Means good weather. So they say. Haven't noticed it myself.'

Jessie pointed to where she had seen the porpoises. Tears streamed down her face. 'They're beautiful,' she said, 'so incredibly beautiful.'

'Yes,' said Magda flatly. She had lived here all her life, had seen porpoises before. But then, these days Magda felt she had seen everything before.

'No,' Jessie insisted, barely able to focus. She was weeping openly, tears streaming damply down her face, nose running, upper lip quite out of control, 'you don't understand. The porpoises. They're wonderful.' Her face crumpled into full hormonal blubbering.

Magda nodded, 'Of course they are.' She shivered. In skimpy black skirt and gaudy pink shirt, she too was inadequately dressed. Also she felt undermined by Jessie's sophisticated thinness. And could hate her for it. One of Magda's many many theories was that a woman's life was written on her hips and stomach. Hers told a tale of surfeits: alcohol, food, sex and children. Hers were hips of excesses. Jessie's said control. One swift eye flick and Magda knew she was in the company of a woman who could casually refuse pudding or place an abstemious hand over the top of her glass before it was refilled. Here was a woman who could say no and think nothing of it. Magda recognised the mixture of envy, respect and loathing she felt when she met someone like Jessie. Though, that same swift eyeflick had also registered a certain slackness round the belly. A recent indulgence, Magda thought. Life has caught up with her. She returned to the café, picked up a cloth and feverishly wiped the bar.

'See that new woman upstairs?' she said to Edie. 'Well I thought I was bad come the time of the month. But by God she's totally off her head. There's a woman seriously in need of a cup of hot chocolate and a whipped cream doughnut. She's awash with hormones.'

It was their first meeting though they had been watching each other for months.

Chapter Two

The baby died. Jessie lay back in the delivery room eyes fixed on the ceiling. She was aware of mumbling white-coated strangers moving near her. An embarrassed rustle, nobody spoke. Dr Davies stood at the end of the delivery table, 'I'm so sorry, Mrs Tate,' he said, smiling apologetically. 'We'll have an autopsy, find out what went wrong. Now we'll get you to the ward so you can rest.' He patted her. Professionally sad. 'Never mind. You're young. In a few weeks you can try again. Think of all the fun you'll have.' In shock, sweat-drenched, hair matted after thirteen hours in labour, Jessie stared at him dumbly and nodded. 'My baby,' she thought, 'baby boy. He would have been mine.'

Four months, two weeks, six days later it came to Jessie what she should have said. 'Piss off.'

She had risen from her sleep screaming, 'You bastard. How dare you?' Alex had only momentarily opened his eyes to look at her. He'd got used to her rantings. Loony time, he told himself mildly, pulling a pillow over his head to obliterate the ravings.

'Piss off, Dr Davies. I'm coming to get you, Dr Davies. Think of all the fun I'll have.'

It had been going on for some time, Jessie's insanity. It was a hum in her head, a tunnel she was in. Alone. She had been going to have a baby. Death had not occurred to her. 'Dead,' she would say. 'Dead. Dead,' trying to imagine the numbness of it. The finality. Her baby, tiny corpse, white and perfect, lifeless alone in the depth of the earth. She kept conjuring up

7

images, torturing herself. Couldn't help it. A million avenging hormones coursing through her urged her on. Equipped and ready to nurture, she didn't know how to handle grief. 'Dead. Dead. Dead.' A mournful monotone.

'Stop it.' Alex spoke from the depths of irritation. Tired and lonely, he wanted some comfort. He wished the demented recluse he was currently sharing his bed with would go away and his real wife would come back. His real wife, the one with pale painted toenails, who wore a silk ivory teddy in bed and shared Sunday morning champagne picnics under the duvet, warm bagels filled with scrambled eggs and smoked salmon, Nina Simone being sultry on the bedroom CD player. Of course all he had to do was shop for bagels, eggs and smoked salmon and do it. But shopping had been Jessie's part of the deal. He loved that life. This is how we live, he often said. This is who we are. So, he ached for Jessie's return, and if this one didn't come soon, he was sorely tempted to find her elsewhere.

'I think you're enjoying the pain.' She considered this. Perhaps he was right. Perhaps she had to have pain. Needed the hurt. It was, after all, her fault. Guilt consumed her. Nights she lay awake staring into the dark, reliving the pregnancy minute by minute, trying to pinpoint the actual moment of blame. She hadn't taken her iron tablets. Had she? She couldn't remember. She'd drunk too much. She should not have worked past the sixth month. She should have stopped as soon as she knew a baby was on the way. She'd developed a passion for tomatoes, too much acidity. It was all her fault. She had walked too much. Stayed up too late. Not drunk enough milk. Worn too tight clothing when she saw how huge she was getting. Stopped the proper circulation getting to the infant. Nights she tossed and turned, rolled her head on the pillow trying to stop the ache. The guilt. The guilt. The guilt.

She was haunted by the child she was sure she had killed. She imagined him, a dark-haired, sombre little one, staring at her, wide brown eyes. She stood in the nursery they'd prepared for him, gently fingering the clothes he'd never wear. She thought about him as he might have been: A toddler stumbling after her in the park, laughing, hair blown behind him, chubby fingers stretched out to reach her. Would he have been bright? Her child? Of course he would have been.

She recalled the little life she had plotted for him as she stroked her swollen belly, felt him kick and move within her. Now he wouldn't learn to play the piano. Wouldn't ride a bike. Wouldn't go on holiday to Cornwall every year as she'd done. Wouldn't sit on his grandfather's knee listening to the stories she listened to before him. Wouldn't. Wouldn't. Wouldn't. The wouldn'ts went on and on. She listed them, brought them out to heighten her hurt. The pain got too much to bear. She was alone in her tunnel of grief, beyond the comfort that Alex or her friends offered.

It was a long slow sink into the black. When she first got back from hospital she seemed to be coping. Her doctor called, his young face creased with concern. 'I'm so sorry, Mrs Tate. How are you?' She sat palely, legs curled, on her sofa smiling slightly. 'I'm fine,' she said. Absurdly, he believed her. The local health visitor called in several times during Jessie's first fortnight at home. Jessie would see her car drawing up outside and swiftly add some blusher and lipstick to her brave face. She hated the bustling intrusion. The health visitor, however, didn't intrude for long. There were people who were actually sick or old to tend, and mothers who had actual babies; besides, Jessie seemed so sane.

When her chums and late-night drinking companions, Trish and Lou, called to see her bringing vodka, white chrysanthemums and sympathy, Jessie cracked a few weak jokes and mustered some enthusiasm for Lou's new car.

'She seems all right,' Trish said as they drove away.

But Lou said, 'Hmmm. You never know with Jessie.'

After five weeks, Jessie went back to the office, far too soon. She worked as an editor in a small publishing firm. She sat at her desk desperately trying to concentrate. Tears flowed down her cheeks and fell on the typescript she was reading. 'What's the point?' she said. 'What's the point?' It was all she could say, all she could think. Someone called Alex who came, wrapped his coat round her, and led her out to his car. She never went back.

She gave up her job, and lay in her bed late in the mornings, television on. She watched it glumly, her face rarely registering an expression. She stopped cooking, stopped dressing. Roamed the house all day in jeans and a torn sweatshirt. A slow sticky mess gathered in the kitchen, in the bathroom, dishes in the sink, dust and crumbs on the floor, scum in the bath, brown stains in the lavatory, bins overflowed. There were damp towels, the laundry smelled, the grill-pan reeked of stale fat. She didn't change the bed. Newspapers piled in the living room. Ashtrays overflowed. Alex found some willing comfort in a girl at work called Annie, a replica Jessie. He came home late, sometimes not at all. Jessie hardly noticed. She did not deserve a husband. Her body had failed him. She had killed his child, her child.

She walked to the corner shop every morning, bought a pack of Marlboro and five bars of chocolate. She ate, smoked, drank coffee, no milk, no sugar. Numb, cocooned in guilt, she would stand at the window for hours, staring out at the garden eating peanut butter straight from the jar, letting the silence and her shame roar inside her head. She fooled herself she was enduring. But she was in hell.

She did not emerge suddenly. It just occurred to her one morning that her car had been lying neglected for weeks. She rammed her spoon into her Sunpat jar, put it down on the windowsill and went to the garage. She did not expect the car to start. But it did. Perhaps, then, she thought, she ought to go somewhere.

She went back into the house to fetch a jacket, her chequebook, some loose change, and was filled with a rush of urgency. Her heart thudded, panic moved wildly within her. She must go now. She must get out of the house this minute swiftly before the phone rang, Alex turned up unexpectedly, before something – anything – happened to stop her. She ran out of the door. She drove blinking at the world. Everything was still there as it had been before she renounced it. Traffic rumbled.

Cars jostled from lane to lane. Billboards jarred, slick and gaudy messages. Skinny-faced youths leant on traffic barricades, meanly watching her go. Watching everybody go. Radios blared. Life was so noisy. Overhead a crane heaved. She leaned down on the steering wheel, watching it, flooded with fear. What if it fell? I do not want to die, she whispered. On pavements people ratted to and fro carrying briefcases, bags, books. On a whim, it seemed, they left their safe runs to dash free-fall through the cars. Women pushed prams. An old man in a brown hat waited by a tree, patient whilst his dog sniffed and peed. Bikes weaved through the traffic lanes. Everything was moving. Everything was busy. All that life out here, minutes from her front door. And she had forgotten about it. She clacked through the pile of tapes beside the gearstick, selected Van Morrison, found her sunglasses then, signalling, shifted down to three, put her foot flat to the floor and shot forward through the traffic, weaving in front of less decisive cars and into the fast lane and down the Queensferry Road and out of Edinburgh. She didn't know where she was going. Just out of town.

She headed north. At the Forth Bridge she paid her toll and came out from the barrier at speed. She was with other cars doing the get-into-the-fast-lane-first dash. She hated bridges. She always gripped the wheel and stared grimly ahead in a headlong rush to make it to land again. What if it broke in two whilst she was driving across it? She'd plummet into the sea. But today she felt jubilant to be so high above the water. She allowed herself swift sidelong glances at the river weaving and widely gleaming.

The rhythm of driving returned to her. Once learned, like riding a bike or making love, never forgotten. She hummed along in top gear, easily overtaking everything that appeared before her. Van sang, she joined in. Badly. She hammered up the motorway, then on a whim signalled into a slip road and headed for the coast. The scenery changed. More sky. Light and cloud. She drove and didn't think, didn't contemplate her loss, didn't wonder what might have been if . . . and if . . . and if; even Alex didn't occur to her. The tape ended and a sign loomed before her. Tourist Trail. She took it. The road twisted and looped, seemed to turn back on itself. She couldn't decide what to play next. Mozart, *The Marriage of Figaro*. Chorus, orchestra, tenor, soprano eased exquisitely from her speakers. She passed fields and, poised at the foot of little hills, little houses like children's drawings with perfect smoke curling from perfect little chimneys. All those weeks, days, hours she had been tucked away this had been out here carrying on as if tragedy never happened. She crested a hill, and gasped. The sea was before her, glistening and moving, spreading to the horizon and beyond. She snapped the cassette out of the player.

The road along the coast was straight and flat. She found her favourite Billie Holiday. That still and mournful voice slid out: 'April in Paris'. She made it seem like the saddest place on earth. Villages were strung out a mile or so apart. Little places, cobbled streets, pantiled roofs. They were built sloping up from the sea. The old houses clustered round the harbour, moving up through the centuries to the Victorian houses at the top of the hill, and modern bungalows on the main road. She stopped at Mareth on the road between Largo and Shell Bay. She had not until now known this place existed.

It seemed to Jessie that this was the place to be. Nothing could happen to you here. It was sleepy and slow. The air smelled of coal fires and sea. There were seventeenth-century, teeny-windowed houses on one side of the road, on the other the shore and a small harbour. Buildings were painted different colours: blue, pink, dark red. This place sparkled. A row of well-spaced, ancient trees lined the narrow pavement.

Even then Jessie noticed the Ocean Café. It was small, windows steamed, temptingly seedy. She heard some blues playing inside. People would be having fun in there.

The terraces were separated at intervals by a series of tiny, cobbled, evocatively-named lanes: Tolbooth Wynd, Peep'o'Day Lane, Water Wynd, that sloped steeply to the High Street. Jessie chose Peep'o'Day Lane, couldn't resist it. It was so narrow that she could touch each side with arms outstretched. The stones on the walls were old, old, worn, touched by three hundred years of passers-by.

The High Street was also painted, shops and more houses. A pub, fronted with tubs overflowing ivy, a betting shop, an ironmonger's, a butcher's and a Spar grocery store. There was a car park hidden behind a row of giant trees, probably more ancient than the village. Jessie wandered about, staring into shop windows. Children played in the street, trundling up and down on trikes. Jessie stared: when had she last seen that? This place was safe.

Young and Neil, Solicitors and Estate Agents, were set back off the High Street, down a steep wynd that led back to the harbour. Jessie read the properties for sale advertised in the window. Immaculate residence, must be seen, spacious, open outlook, well-stocked garden – estate-agent-speak broke all colloquial boundaries. Wherever you were you understood exactly what they were on about. On impulse she went in. She stood nervously at the desk.

'Yes?' a young blonde receptionist smiled at her. She wore pink, everything pink.

'I was wondering . . .' Jessie spoke softly, uncertain. Until this moment she hadn't known she was going to do this. '. . . If you had anything to rent about here.'

'I'll get Mr Young.'

Pretty in Pink disappeared, came back seconds later with a Suit wringing his hands, smiling weakly. Striped shirt, polka-dot tie, hair waved back, he peered at her through wire specs. This could be Alex. Alexes were everywhere, smitten with style, aching for wealth.

Thinking of him now she realised that Alex didn't have a life, he had a masterplan. He mapped out his days like an old campaigner spending time each evening putting the final touches to the blueprint of the day ahead. He rose each morning, showered, shaved, moisturised his skin and scented the body he worked hard to preserve in peak condition. He spent some time laying out clothes on the bed: shirt, tie, jacket, trousers, choosing the right combination to suit both his mood and the world he was about to face. He would leave the house before eight and come home some time after nine. He was a resources manager with a video company that produced films for advertising agencies. He was a busy busy man.

'I have to be there,' he said. But that wasn't it. He had to be seen to be there. Jessie sighed. 'You are present at the job from seven in the morning, till seven at night, and the job is present in you all the bloody time.'

Looking at this man in front of her now, noting a small stain on his tie and the way he ran his fingers over his chin, she realised that beneath the veneer there was a certain uncertainty. 'This man is as insecure as I am,' she thought then, realising the truth behind her husband's meticulous routine and design for living, 'as Alex is.'

'Something to rent?' said the Suit. There was The Steadings. A converted stable block just out of town. Five bdrms, gym, kitchen with Aga, two baths, spacious living rm, dining with french windows to patio. He smiled at Jessie, scrutinising her. Old jeans, baseball boots, torn sweatshirt, no make-up; when had that hair last seen a comb? Ah, no. He didn't think so.

'I'm sorry,' he said, 'not at the moment. If you'd like to leave your name—'

'There's that flat on the shore. Above Magda's . . .' Pretty in Pink chipped in.

Derek Young paused.

'The shore,' Jessie brightened. That sounded just right.

'It's a bit of a mess, I'm afraid.'

Jessie shrugged. So what was a mess to her? A mess? She could take this man home, show him a real mess if he wanted messes.

'It sounds perfect,' she said. Regretted right away that she sounded so keen. 'How much is it?'

'Ah . . .' Derek Young had had enough time to reconsider his initial judgement. The hair – beneath that tangle – was very expensively cut. The filthy jeans had cost a bit too. He couldn't see the label on the jacket, but the sunglasses were Armani. He knew, he had the same pair.

'Four hundred . . . and – ' dared he risk it? – 'fort . . . um . . . fifty a month.'

'I'll take it.'

'You should see it first.'
'Fine. I'll see it. Then I'll take it.'

Chapter Three

Jessie moved to Mareth. She bought food at the local Spar, posted mail at the post office, and went for daily walks round the harbour, stepping over heaped nets and ropes. She stood at the pier end staring at the horizon. Several times a week she walked along the shore, past the last few houses on West Way that led down to the sand. Jumping from rock to rock, carefully keeping the salt water from her precious Timberlands, she would make her way to the foot of the cliff path. Puffing, she'd climb the overgrown muddied way to the top. The wind would push her hair from her face, whip her breath away. She would stare down to where the grassy slope turned sheer. Far below the sea churned and frothed white over jagged rocks. Fulmars gathered noisily, clumsily on the cliff face. She would stand for hours watching them career absurdly in, making sometimes two or three runs before they managed a landing. It surprised her. She always thought birds and animals managed their lives perfectly. There was something cheering about these birds and their duff attempts at coming in to land. 'It isn't just me that screws up, then.'

The aloneness exhilarated her one day, saddened her the next. But she could not find the deepening silence she sought. The rattle and hum from the Ocean Café downstairs reminded her constantly that there were other people in the world, all of them having a better time than she was.

She had thought that if she could spend some time speaking to nobody, a stranger in a strange place, the turmoil in her head might cease. She might find some peace. But after only a short

17

time in Mareth she stopped being a stranger. She became 'that funny woman that lives above the Ocean Café. Who is she anyway? And what's she doing moving into a place like that, this time of the year?'

Here in Mareth everyone knew everyone. They knew everything there was to know about each other. And what they didn't know they assumed. Their assumptions were passed on in conversations and gossip in shops, kitchens, living rooms and bars until distorted by time, speculation and rumour, the assumptions became facts. And who would meddle with facts? Certainly nobody in Mareth, where the crack was so beloved it was the stuff of life itself. There was nothing better than a good rumour. People here were prepared to believe and in time heartily narrate the assumptions even about themselves that had passed into local folklore. They were their own myths and legends. And proud of it.

People started to nod to her when they met her in the street. It was a curt, uncomfortable nod, with a 'ynumph' sort of a greeting. A shy acknowledgement that she was in the same world, country, village, street as the nodder and it didn't seem right not to say something about it. Ynumph fitted the bill, or sometimes nyoink. Jessie hadn't mastered the sound effects and said a crisp and distant g'morning, or gd'afternoon. They nodded because she had been discussed, dissected and decided upon. So now the nodders felt that they knew all about her and were therefore obliged to say hello, or as near to hello as they could get.

Jessica Tate was thirty-four years old and living separately from her husband. Everyone knew that. Derek Young had extracted the information whilst preparing the lease on No. 38 The Shore, the flat Jessie rented from his partnership, and Pretty in Pink, Shona Kerr, who was now into powder blue, had passed it on. Jessie was tallish, thinnish, had dark hair and no visible bloke to replace her husband. In whispered discussions in the Anchor and Crown it was being speculated that the broken marriage left her bitter and hating all men; likely, perhaps, even to be turning into a lesbian. But the Ocean Café rejected this notion. It was the café opinion that she was just recovering from some sort of break-up and in no need of a new relationship.

Jessie had a lot of books. What did she want with all them books? Ruby at the Spar mini-market wanted to know. Had she a lot of reading to do? Or had she read them all? If so, why bother carting about a lot of books you've already read? They'd just clutter up the shelves when you could have a few nice ornaments and a pot plant. Jessie bought macaroni and spaghetti, which she called pasta, tins of tomatoes, onions, wholemeal bread, Alta Rica coffee and bars of fruit and nut chocolate when she shopped. Everybody knew that. Ruby told them.

Jessie had red knickers, black knickers and silky green camiknickers. They'd been spotted on her washing line. But so far no bra. She'd not need a bra with them wee tits, Woody at the Anchor and Crown said. Jack, his barman, agreed. Besides, them bull dykes don't wear bras. Do they?

Jessie wore 501 jeans and boots and a soft, all-enveloping jersey. The boots were tan leather and cost a bomb, everyone thought. But they didn't cost as much as the dark burgundy jersey which came from one of them designer shops and was probably cashmere. And though it had come from Benetton and cost twenty-five pounds, the guessing on its price was two hundred pounds and rising. Of course Jessie had other clothes: striped silk pyjamas, a patterned robe, a navy nightdress which wasn't as nice as the pyjamas but probably warmer these cold nights. Especially for someone who slept alone. Jessie wore a leather jacket sometimes, and sometimes a long black coat. When she wore her long black coat, Mareth decided she was mourning her long-lost lover. Mareth had a romantic heart.

Jessie drove a three-year-old Peugeot that needed a new exhaust. Freddie Kilpatrick who owned the local garage knew this because one night on the way home from the Ocean Café he had lain on the road and slid under it. Ah, he had smiled, knew it. When he got home his wife looked at his back and said scathingly, 'Have you been looking under cars again?'

Lying under Jessie's Peugeot, he'd figured out his business

plan. Didn't Crumbly Al have just such an exhaust lying in his scrapyard. He could swap the Fiat gearbox he had in the back of his workshop for a couple of central-heating radiators Joe Roberts the plumber had lying in his yard. And swap Crumbly Al the radiators for his exhaust. He could have it ready when Jessie brought the car down to him in about a couple of weeks. She'd not get much more out of that thing, he reckoned. He fished some string from his pocket and tied Jessie's ailing exhaust up. He couldn't risk her breaking down somewhere else after all the trouble and bartering he'd have to do to get the right part for her motor.

Jessie didn't get much mail. 'Only stuff about her credit card, and bank statements,' Duncan the postie said. And though her phone rang a fair bit she rarely answered it. Granny Moran knew this. She mentioned it when she was at the post office picking up her pension. 'She's avoiding somebody,' she said. Could it be she was on the run from the police?

Magda at the Ocean Café laughed out loud. 'That one,' she said squeakily, rubbing a peephole in the café's steamy window to watch Jessie stump round the harbour, 'is only on the run from herself.' Remembering a couple of mornings ago when she had come face to face with a tearstained Jessie at the café door, added knowingly, 'Look at her go. Striding about all hours speaking to nobody, leaving the phone ringing, all weepy and eating chocolate. It can only be one thing . . .' The café held its breath. When Magda spoke, an opinion worth hearing and discussing was on the go.

'It's hormones,' she said, nodding at her own wisdom. 'It's purely hormonal.' Several faces joined Magda's peering through the peephole at the hormonally stricken Jessie. Word spread. And so when men met Jessie in the street they said ynumph or nyoink, making a wide berth. Hormones, especially female ones, were to be avoided. Women, however, stared at her piercingly, trying to fathom the depth of Jessie's woes. Hormones; they knew about hormones.

The flat was miserable. Even Jessie in her doldrums could see that. It smelt not just of damp but as if dozens of unwashed agoraphobics had lived here, cramped and refusing to go out. It had two rooms, a bedroom and a living room with cupboard-size kitchen off. It has potential, Jessie told herself as she unpacked. I can make something of this. I can make a statement about me. Just me and nobody else. This is a wonderful opportunity. I can be happy.

As the little world outside speculated about her she painted the bedroom a pale smoky blue, the living room and kitchen white, and the bathroom a sagey green. She put up pictures, installed a small sofa, but left the carpet which was so vile she found something comforting about it. She liked to imagine the cosy mores of the person who would choose such a thing.

This is me, she thought. In the blue and sweary chilly mornings she lay listening to the ribaldry outside and felt almost at home. In the evenings young bloods would come duding out of the Ocean Café, hollering. Their raw voices cut through the night, and if Jessie was foolish enough to come to the window to watch the goings-on they would shout up to her.

'Hello darlin',' drunken voices, 'show us yer tits.' They'd wiggle their hips at her, uninhibited sexual motion, 'C'mon down. Look at this,' and someone would moon at her. White bottom gleaming under the streetlights. 'Let's see *your* arse, darlin'.'

Jessie would gaze sadly down. 'Not a bad bum,' she'd think. 'Seen better.' Then she'd go back to her fireside, turn up her Mahler and try to read.

The streetlamp mooners started to come by every Saturday night. They would call her name. 'Hey, Long Coat, come an' see this.' Mareth's fascination with Jessie's manic strides round the harbour in her long black coat had gained her the nickname. Foolishly she would go to the window to look at them. After one particularly raucous evening there was a whole row of bums shining in the night for her to view.

'Good heavens,' she breathed, staring down mesmerised. She hadn't the gumption to pull her curtains and declare her disinterest. There were fat bums and medium bums and tight little nubby bums with cute little side indents that a person could certainly consider giving a second glance. Jessie did. And as she did, Magda Horn came out, keys in hand, to lock up for the night. She did not shriek; scarcely noticed the row of exposed cheeks. Jessie was impressed.

Magda looked up at her. 'So what do you think,' she called, pointing to the first bum. 'A five probably. And this,' she indicated the next arse, 'a two. A seven. A three, an eight. Oh Lipless, you're only a one: you'll have to start some serious bum workouts.'

Lipless rose indignantly, heaving up his pants. 'It's not that bad, Magda. You'll go a long way before you see an arse as magnificent as mine.'

Magda hooted. 'As long as you think so, Lipless. I'd hate you to get some sort of complex about what you've been bringing along behind you all these years.'

Lipless slapped his rear, 'Me and my arse get along just fine, Magda.'

'I have the same thing going with mine,' Magda said, bustling past them.

'Ah Magda,' Lipless said, shaking his head in admiration, 'you've a great arse on you.'

'I know,' she said, walking off down the street, well aware the mooners were now all upright and staring at her bum.

'Enjoy,' she called. 'This is as close as any of youse will get to it.'

The mooners below moved off mumbling. And Jessie, returning to her sofa, hurt her back trying to look over her shoulder at her own backside. It was the first time she had thought about herself, her appearance in months. Perhaps she was getting better.

Chapter Four

The bum incident happened only a couple of days after the porpoise incident. Jessie now considered she just about knew Magda Horn and could therefore go into the Ocean Café. She had been under its steamy spell ever since she'd arrived. Mornings the thick aroma of coffee spread through the chill air, evenings the boozy wafts and babble were almost irresistible. But only almost. Jessie was astute enough to know that Mareth was not the sort of place that welcomed unaccompanied female strangers into its drinking establishments.

The first time she went into the Ocean Café she stood nervously at the door. Was this the right thing to do? To come in here? Conversation slowed, stopped. Heads turned. What does she want? It was a horrible moment. Magda broke it.

'What can I get you?'

'Coffee,' Jessie spoke weakly, taking a seat by the window, far from where the in-crowd sat. The chair scraped loudly on the floor as she pulled it back, wood against wood, a long farty noise. 'Sorry,' she said, mostly to the chair.

'Black? White? What sort of coffee?'

'Black, please. Strong.'

Magda brought it. She smelled of musk. She laid Jessie's coffee on the table and alongside it a chocolate croissant.

'I didn't ask for that,' Jessie pointed at the plate.

'You didn't have to.' Magda sounded snippy. If she decided you wanted a chocolate croissant, you wanted a chocolate croissant. And, staring in surprise at the delicacy in front of her, Jessie found that she wanted it. She started to eat slowly, picking bits off and putting them carefully into her mouth. Conversation started up again as the bar accustomed itself to her sudden presence.

There were four men at the bar, workmen from the quay. Jessie recognised them. Three were drinking coffee and eating bacon rolls. The fourth thumped the bar with his fist, demanding whisky.

'Not from me you'll not get that at this time in the morning,' Magda shook her head. 'Not you anyway.'

'Why not me?'

'You and your liver are shrivelling visibly, Lipless. If you want whisky, go and shrivel your liver somewhere else. You can have soup.'

'Soup, Christ. Soup. I hate soup. Soup's just a cheap way of disguising mushed-up vegetables. There's something sneaky about that.'

Magda stared at him stonily. Lipless continued, 'What's this you have about feeding people anyway? Offering me soup. Giving her,' he jerked his thumb towards Jessie, 'that chocolate thing.'

'That's hormones,' Magda explained.

'Christ, Lipless,' another of the workmen whined, 'now look what you've done. She's going to start on about hormones. Can't you just eat some soup?'

'No. I hate soup.'

'See,' said Magda, 'some people say love or money makes the world go round. Rubbish. It's hormones.'

'Eat your fucking soup.' One of the workmen yanked the plate in front of Lipless.

'It only just came to me the other day that hormones were at the root of all our triumphs and tragedies. I mean, a hormoneless person is one of those bland sorts. You know, beige cardy harmless. If everyone was like that there'd be no wars. No passion. But where does that get you?'

Nobody answered. Lipless sucked at his soup. His workmates shifted uneasily, chewing their food. They had a gnawing feeling that any moment Magda was going to start talking about periods and other female atrocities. 'Don't start, Magda. Please,' one of them pleaded.

'Oh, but I've started. So I'll finish,' Magda grinned. There was nothing more enjoyable than making men squirm. Once in full flow she was unstoppable. 'Us women can get all hot and bothered. We start stroking our men saying we want a baby.'

'That happens to me all the time,' said Lipless sadly. 'Every night.' He continued eating his soup.

'It's nuts. Babies. I ask you, who wants them?'

'Wimmin,' said someone. 'Babies are not a man's idea.'

'It's nothing to do with women. It's hormones. Women say they want a baby but in the depth of them they know it's the end of them. Once you've had a baby that's it, you'll never go out again. You'll be in for the next ten – fifteen years. And what are you to a baby anyway? The face behind the spoon till you become the face behind the chequebook. They start needing money to sate the demands of their own leaping hormones.' She leant on the bar, holding her coffee cup, addressing nobody in particular. Not caring that everybody was pretending not to listen. She was working out her thoughts. Jessie watched, intrigued.

'Don't you agree?' Magda suddenly asked her.

She shrugged, 'I suppose if I could have a hormonectomy, I would.'

'Time for us to get back to work,' Lipless shoved his empty soup bowl across the bar. 'Look, I ate it.'

'And wasn't it good?' Magda demanded.

'Yes. As a matter of fact it was. Don't tell me what it was. I'd rather not know. There was garlic and funny stuff in it. And I don't eat that kind of thing. And now I have to go back to work and it's all your fault, Magda Horn.'

'My fault?' Magda pointed at herself, eyes wide. Innocence.

'Yes, your fault. If you didn't keep feeding me instead of letting me drink I'd've died long ago and I wouldn't have to go out in the cold and work.'

'Oh, blame me,' Magda said mildly. 'Everything's my fault.'

He left, heaving himself into his faded navy jacket, rasping insults and self-loathing.

'You know you're really alone when you don't have someone to blame,' Magda shrugged to Jessie. Crumbling slow pieces from her croissant and carefully placing them into her mouth, Jessie considered this. She must be truly alone then. For who had she to blame? Herself and only herself. Magda, however, knew who she had to blame for the absurd path her life had taken. Her mother. Every so often Magda was consumed with rage against her mother. Calling her by her full name, Mary Lomax, as if she was miscalling her best school-chum and not the woman who gave birth to her, she would throw cutlery and plates the length of the Ocean Café shouting, 'Bugger you, Mary Lomax.'

Everyone near to her knew of this rage and hatred: Little Jim Horn, whose name she had taken, father of her four children, her four children and Edie who worked beside her in the café. The only person it seemed who did not know about Magda's fury was Mary Lomax.

The rages completely swamped Magda, seeming to well up within her from nowhere. A thought, a song, a smell; anything that brought back past times could set it off. Once it had been more than that. Once the rage had been constantly with her. That it had now been reduced to sudden maddening outbursts, steaming blood pressure and a few bits of broken crockery pleased Magda. She considered she was getting better. She was coming to terms with her inadequacies. And, in particular, that one inadequacy that loomed large every single day of her life. Magda Horn could neither read nor write. She had been a difficult child. That one has always been a trial, her mother would say, shaking her head. She remembered those years before Magda started school as being the worst, noisiest in her life. She remembered spending them rushing around bent double, arms outstretched, trying to keep up with her exuberant daughter. 'Children are fine right up until they can move about on their own,' she expounded over gin and tonic at the Anchor and Crown. 'After that it's hell. The best thing you could say about our Magda was that she left me so shagged out I was too knackered to do anything about having another baby. She was the most effective contraceptive ever.'

At Mareth Academy it was decided that Magda had limited learning capabilities. She couldn't concentrate. Her books were a mess. They were actually so filthy that disgusted teachers held them in horror between thumb and forefinger at arm's length, as if they could catch something nasty from them. Her handwriting scrawled illegibly. Erratic, her reports said. And, work this year has proved once again beyond Magda's comprehension. And, this child is uncontrollable. The more she was criticised, the wilder she got. During her first seven or eight years in school Magda sat in front of the sort of teachers who thought the way to reach Magda's brain was up through her backside. She was beaten daily.

In time she discovered that teachers are cowards. Or at least the ones who taught her were. They had an inbuilt loathing of violence when it was turned against them. Magda bit and kicked and scratched and howled and they stopped hitting her. The headmaster, a quiet man called Harvey Scott, suggested she be sent to a special school, but Mareth looked after its own. When Granny Moran took to wandering round the harbour in her nightgown looking for her long-dead husband, whoever found her took her home, put her to bed and locked the door. When Gordon Masters drowned, the whole village went quiet for weeks, curtains were kept drawn, children told not to shout in the streets till it was decided by some silent mutual agreement that the period of mourning was over. When Freda Bishop, after watching one too many dismaying documentaries on the gruelling miseries of post-holocaust life, and convincing herself that the day of reckoning was nigh and the bomb about to be dropped, decided to camp on her roof so that she would see the plane coming in over the sea, nobody minded, really. They took her thermos flasks of soup and cheese sandwiches and called soothingly from the street below that the bomb wasn't coming and if it did they'd all go together and wasn't that the best way?

The suggestion, then, to send Magda to a special school wasn't favoured. She was Mareth born and bred. In Mareth she would stay. Stay she did, in a constant state of outrage. Taking tantrums, shouting, swearing, banging her desk lid, jumping on her seat, chattering to her friends in class – when she went to class.

Magda was fourteen when Alice Barnes came to Mareth to teach English. The girl interested her. Here was a highly intelligent, outstandingly outrageous pupil who could barely read. Dyslexia occurred to her.

'What,' Mary Lomax had sighed when Magda's condition was finally diagnosed, 'in the name is that?'

'Word blindness,' Alice Barnes said slowly. She was used to incensed parents. 'And more than that. They think it's to do with both sides of the brain being the same size.'

Mary Lomax had eagerly seized upon this piece of information. 'I always knew she was loony.' She pointed dismissively at Magda, 'Typical of you to have a weird brain.'

'On the contrary,' Miss Barnes remained calm. 'I'd say your daughter was very remarkable. It's hardly surprising she behaves the way she does. She's had years of frustration. But she has got through school scarcely able to read, using only her memory. She seems to be able to commit great tracts of information to her mind after only one hearing. It's amazing.'

Magda's young heart had leapt. She wasn't the silly stupid erratic worthless child she was constantly being told she was. She was amazing. She had always suspected that. Mary Lomax, however, was not one to praise children. It didn't do to tell them they were amazing. They'd get above themselves.

'Well, she isn't all that amazing to me,' she said harshly. 'Is this dyslexia thing hereditary?'

Miss Barnes nodded, 'Can be.'

'Ah.' All was clear to Magda's mum. 'In that case she got it from her father.'

Alice Barnes ignored this remark. 'Thing is, most dyslexics are highly intelligent. Talented one way or another.'

This professional declaration that she was not vastly stupid came in time, just, to save Magda's sanity, but was too late for her self-esteem. The humiliation of being permanently bottom of the class, of having her school-mates snigger when her marks were read out, left its mark. Atrocious, despicable, try harder, unreadable, you are a thoroughly stupid child, see me: phrases from her education that Magda would run through her head, torturing herself. Everybody else looked at a page of print and read stories. She looked and saw rivers of white running through black type. Enlightenment, the things that people knew, would never be hers. She had stumbled through her school years bedevilled by bewilderment. She was alone, looking in on life, never taking part. The rage started.

She discovered rock'n'roll. There was a beat to her fury, a rhythm. And when it wasn't actually playing, it was playing in her head. The Stones, Dylan, Lou Reed, Aretha Franklin, The Who. She never switched them off. She woke to them, cooked to them, fucked to them. Sometimes it seemed that there were folks out there who were even angrier than she was. Maybe she wasn't quite as alone as she thought.

On her truant afternoons, Magda would sit out on the point, letting rip the rhythms in her head. Thinking. She wasn't part of the world. Nobody would let her join in. Things were a mystery to her. What were people on about? She couldn't understand anything. It seemed to her that there was a smug society of women who understood the mysteries of life: knitting patterns, how to bake scones, why it was necessary to put white cloths over the back of sofas and chairs, how to change a baby, how to put rollers in your hair, how to arrange flowers, the correct way to wipe a sink, all that and oh, a whole load of other stuff that she didn't understand. For some reason women who joined the smug society, the society of always being right, didn't like her. She worried them. Furthermore, she was scared stiff of becoming one of them. Alice Barnes spoke to the Mastertons, owners of the Captain's Table, a four-star restaurant along the coast where she and her husband often ate. They gave Magda a job waiting tables. It didn't work. She was slow, could barely write down the orders, could not contain her rage. When customers laughed at her obvious failings, she tossed down cutlery before them. She whipped menus away before diners had finished reading them, tutted and sighed at those who took too long to choose what they wanted to eat. She was out of her depth. These glossy diners who knew a Beaune from a Margaux and what was a good year for Chardonnay, who knew without asking what fillet of sole veronique was and how monkfish should be roasted and how to serve crêpes more than scared her. They chipped away at the edges of her already low self-esteem. Her inadequacies reached howling point. She knew herself well. She was a slow, shiny-faced, shovel-handed, large-hipped waitress whose stupidity was written all over her face. She knew nothing of the gleamy candlelit world of gourmet dining. She was hurting and it showed. How it showed when a long established customer crisply demanded bisque homard with a decently chilled Sancerre and, as Magda struggled to wind her uneducated tongue round the order, raised an amused eyebrow to his co-diners who all sniggered. Oh it showed then.

Magda, unable to contain any more humiliation, threw her order pad across the dining room, picked up a fork and held it threateningly under the eyebrow-raiser's nose calling him a 'Bastard . . . bastard – ' she struggled here for the ultimate insult – 'man,' she screamed. The room silenced. The discreet clatter of upmarket cutlery, the chink of plush crockery, the dulcet babble of mock élitist conversation stopped, all stopped. Well, well, well. This was hardly the stuff of a civilised evening out. Secretly though, the only thing everybody in the room felt was relief that this hadn't happened to them. They were, after all, the bourgeoisie. Every eyebrow in the room was raised. By rights Magda should have been fired for her outburst. But George the chef pleaded her case. He had been watching her. Magda had been hanging about in the kitchen even on her days off. Food intrigued her. It was George's idea to move the absurd and gawky girl to the kitchen, a stroke of genius. Magda's salvation. Magda could cook. She was a natural. Those large hands that could not properly grip a pen could slice and chop and mix with ease. The girl that had turned in filthy and illegible schoolwork could turn out the most delicate of pastries, the most exquisite of sauces. Outside in the world, Magda was still Magda: enraged, unmanageable. In the kitchen she was turning into a queen. A goddess.

And oh, the thirst for knowledge. Every day a new culinary term. One day Madga came home and asked her mother what a marinade was. George had mentioned making one and she hadn't a clue what it was.

'A whatinade?' Mary Lomax said, instantly dismissing anything that was new to her. 'Never heard of such a thing.'

Next day, Mary asked Granny Moran, who sucked her gums, shook her head, and doubted there was such a thing.

'Have you ever heard of a marinade?' Granny Moran asked Lipless, who worked on the pier. Lipless curled his lip. 'If y' can't drink it I won't know about it.' Still, he asked Ruby at the Spar mini-market who didn't know but at lunchtime asked Woody at the Anchor and Crown but he didn't know either. After a couple of days it was established that nobody in Mareth knew what a marinade was. But Magda came home and told her mother it was just a mixture – oil and wine maybe with some herbs and garlic – that you soaked meat in.

'Why would you do that?' Mary wanted to know.

'So it'll taste better.'

'Doesn't it already taste fine? Don't they buy quality meat at the Captain's Table?'

'Yes, of course they do. Just a marinade sort of changes the taste. Makes it more complex, deeper.'

'What's wrong with meat tasting of meat? Good plain food, that's what you want.'

Sighing, Magda realised there was nothing she could say on the subject of marinades, or anything else really. But the word went round Mareth that the oh so posh Captain's Table bought meat that was so bad they had to doctor it with garlic and herbs and such like fancy stuff to make it edible. Local custom at the restaurant dipped for a while. But picked up again as there was nowhere else to go that was special for anniversaries and birthdays and well, it was agreed that if they did marinade their meat it certainly made it tasty. An interest in wines and olive oil began to slowly spread through the village. At the mini-market Ruby added a couple of bottles of Beaujolais to the three bottles of sherry, half-dozen cans of lager and two bottles of whisky that made up her booze section. She also put a small packet of mixed herbs next to the salt and pepper, her seasonings section and some garlic appeared alongside the fruit and veg. Though Ruby folded her arms disapprovingly and expounded on the subject of garlic. 'I can't be workin' with the likes of that,' she said.

Magda meantime was gaining a reputation as something of a cook. People would come to her door, or stop her in the street and ask for culinary advice. What should they make for tea tonight? Tagliatelle was all very well, but how did you actually cook it? Were there any quick puddings you didn't need to actually cook, you could just, well, sort of make? What was an interesting thing to do with haddock?

'Put it in a cheese sauce. Smoked haddock and fresh makes it better. Y'know, tasty. Just slice up the fish and put it in. It'll do in no time in the oven. I dunno, maybe one side of "Exile on Main Street". Or maybe the whole of "Sad-Eyed Lady of the Lowlands". And you can mix cheeses as well. For a spot of piquancy. Know what I mean?' She would have mentioned adding grapes or a splash of white wine or scattering some pine nuts over the top, but was well aware of her neighbours' culinary limits. Some folks bought a jar of mixed herbs and it did them for ten years, maybe more. At the word piquancy, Magda would make a small circle with her middle finger and thumb. But nobody in Mareth really minded this little flash of gourmet upmanship. They knew she wasn't getting above herself. She was just getting her act together. Surviving.

Magda worked at the Captain's Table for ten years. Tears and tantrums, rage and flying cutlery. But something started to happen, to slowly happen. There was a drift of new faces appearing mostly at the weekends. They would sit in quiet raptures over the food that was placed before them, leaning towards each other exchanging forkfuls.

'Taste this, carrots and mushrooms sort of sliced up and cooked together.'

'No, look. Have some of these little potatoey things. What's in them, d'you think?'

People would ask for recipes and would send their compliments to the cook. But the Mastertons knew better than to bring Magda out to meet her fans. Her loathing of the people she fed still showed. 'Posh fucks,' she would say as she poured an apricot and brandy sauce over pork fillets. 'And why do they have to eat in French? They don't fart in French, they don't snore in sodding French, or belch in French.' She would steam about the kitchen waving her hands in the air, smacking her forehead, nutting the air, imagining no doubt that some snotty diner was the victim of her assault. 'Prats oohing and aahing over some food, as if they ate anything other than instant chips all week. Sitting in their catalogue clothes out for the evening talking shite, pretending to be nice people.'

Hands on hips, she would gaze witheringly through the screen door at the diners. 'Nice,' she would say, 'who wants to be nice? Where did nice ever get you?' She held the concept of nice in contempt. She loathed nice. It seemed to her that her mother had squandered her whole life pursuing the notion of nice. 'That's not a very nice thing to say, Magda.' 'Don't do that, Magda, that's not nice.' 'Nice people don't go out dressed like tramps, Magda. Cover yourself up.'

'Nice, nice, nice, nice. To hell with nice,' was Magda's conclusion. Nice got you nowhere.

Mary Lomax's ambition to live the nice life faded every Friday night when she would go down to the Anchor and Crown. She would without fail drink too many vodka and cokes and end up imitating Elvis. She would pull her hair down over her eyes, deepen her voice and run through her repertoire of The King's greatest hits. Her cronies would root for her, clap and shriek as she strutted across the floor, wiggling stiffly her sixty-four-year-old bum, thrusting her groin. She would wave her arms above her head and holler 'Jailhouse Rock' and 'Heartbreak Hotel' in her sandpaper voice. Sometimes she would abandon Elvis for Roy Orbison but it wasn't the same with Roy, too much angst.

But oh the reckoning from her conscience on Saturday morning. Sitting in a heap of pink velour dressing gown, she would clutch her sex'n'chocolate mug, swigging hot tea, chastising herself, 'Oh, I don't think I was very nice last night. Never again. Remind me to stay away from the vodka in future.'

But of course she never did. Come next Friday she was in need of another bout of sleaze. Magda could never decide if she preferred her mother when she was living her neat and tidy behind-net-curtains nice life or when she was out pubbing, being bawdy. Either way she was embarrassing.

Chapter Five

Money had never really occurred to Jessie. She had always had it. Until today when she'd put her card in the cash machine and found her account empty. Panic prickled and flushed through her. What to do?

This was a new dilemma. For the first time in her life there were no incoming funds to replace the break in her cash-flow. Her parents had supported her through her lean student years, but no way could she contact them for help now. This escape was hers, and she would see it through on her own, her way.

She walked slowly back down the cobbled wynd to her flat, reviewing her situation. Her bastard husband must have cleaned out their account. Another move in their game of marital chess. Checkmate, she thought. She had very little cash left, but enough food to do for the rest of the week. And then what? Starvation? According to Freddie Kilpatrick at the garage, her car needed a new exhaust. How was she to pay for it? Also the rent was due in a couple of weeks. She'd be cold, hungry, homeless and without transport. Life sucked. She wearily climbed the stairs to her flat. She shut the door behind her and threw herself on the sofa.

Below, the Ocean Café was operating full throttle. Rock'n'roll, songs of freedom that people had been writing and singing and jumping up and down to whilst she was tucked away, cocooned in her perfect life. She heard Magda join in, and knew she'd be in the kitchen moving in time, hips swaying, jiving on the spot as she chopped onions and celery. She was making pasta, the smell came up through the vent. It smelled more desirable than ever to Jessie now she couldn't afford it. She sighed. Moved into a depression. A deepening thoughtless black, a mood that started, it seemed, in the pit of her stomach and spread through her. There was no logic involved. She lay back and let the despair roll.

Late afternoon, as the room darkened, she reached for the phone and dialled Alex's number. He'd be at the office. Better to get him with eavesdroppers around, then he couldn't swear back at her.

'Alex, you bastard,' she said as soon as she heard his voice on the other end.

'Jessie? Is that you?' It was strange to hear him. He sounded unsure of himself. Guilt, no doubt.

'Yes it's me, you bastard. Who else do you think it would be? Are you such a bastard everybody who phones you calls you a bastard?'

'No,' he said flatly.

'You shit, you emptied our account. I've no money.'

'What else was I to do? How else was I to find out where you were? Jessie, I've been worried sick. Where are you anyway?'

'Mind your own business.'

He heaved a tired sigh. 'Grow up, Jessie. We've things to sort out. Tell me where you are.'

'Mareth,' she told him. This wasn't right. This wasn't what she wanted to do. She wanted to scream and shout at him. She wanted to hurt him. She wanted him down where she was.

'Mareth? Where's that and what are you doing there?'

'Up the coast. And just living . . .' Then, an afterthought. 'In poverty.'

Downstairs, Magda's cooking shifted gear. The Stones started up. Jessie imagined Magda boogying round, tossing chillies into a pot from across the kitchen as she had once seen her do when she'd been having coffee and her now regular morning chocolate croissant. Magda and Edie had been jiving about, chopping, singing along, slapping each other's hands high in the air, moving in natural harmony, having a good time. Jessie had watched sadly. Life and friendships had never been like that for her. Of course there was Trish and Lou and others, but all they did was speak.

Alex had always been jealous of her women friends. Especially Trish and Lou. 'They'll lead you astray,' he said.

'If anyone is going to lead me anywhere, astray is where I choose,' Jessie told him.

'When are you coming back?' he asked her now.

'I'm not,' she said surprising herself. 'I'm never coming back.'

'For Christ's sake, Jessie. What are you doing there?'

'The hell's it got to do with you. And some of that money you emptied out of our account is mine. Put it back.'

He hung up. She lay listening to the dialling tone till its hum and the darkness filled the room. She had a horrible feeling that no good was going to come of that call. 'I should not have told him where I am.'

The rock'n'roll din had stopped. It was so easy now to let her depression flow. She could slip effortlessly into it. A hollowness. God, she could almost hear it. She stretched out to feel the full benefit of this gloom. Her hand fell to the floor. She could feel the rough of the patterned fireside rug against it. The room smelled of yesterday's coal fire, and her perfume. There was no noise, only her breathing. Outside a slow car rolled carefully along the shore, engine humming. Someone called, 'Hey,' a raw and primal call, deeply male, it cut through the evening. 'He-eey pal.' Boys should get voice licences before their balls are allowed to drop, Jessie thought. The Ocean Café was coming to life, that meandering drone of alcoholic conversation.

'I am enduring,' she said. The words hung in the air.

'I ... AM ... ENDURING,' she said again, listening carefully to herself. She sounded sad, addicted to sadness. 'Oh, no. I'm not.' She rose. Took the last of her cash from the table where she'd spread it before her to despondently consider. And went downstairs.

She slapped her hand on the café counter and demanded a large whisky. 'A single malt,' she said. 'A double.'

Magda waved her arm towards the large selection of malts on her upper shelf. 'What'll it be?'

'Lagavulin. A huge Lagavulin with very little water and no ice.'

Magda placed it in front of her. She lifted the glass and breathed in the fumes. A deep whiff of Scottish gorgeousness, the whole of life caught in glass. Peat and earth, sweetness and wind. Fire to the throat. If she listened to it she'd hear eagles call and if she could look into the depth of it she'd see hills purpling into the distance and mountain streams, perfect water. The longing it set up in her, she was intoxicated already.

'Are you going to drink it, then?' This prolonged savouring was beginning to irritate Magda.

'In a minute,' Jessie said. 'I want to enjoy this. I can't afford it. Booze you can't afford is the best booze.'

'Thought you had plenty of money.'

Jessie smiled, 'So did I. But there you go . . .' She didn't feel like giving out explanations right now.

'So what are you going to do?'

'Dunno. Find work, I suppose.' Jessie took her first fiery sip. And coughed.

'What do you do?' This is what Magda had always wanted to know.

'After I graduated I worked in PR for a while – a couple of years, I think. Then I switched to publishing. I headed a department that did literary textbooks. We were working on a series where we invited critics to write concise, accessible books on the works of renowned writers.'

'You'll not get a lot of call for that here,' Magda said.

'No. I didn't think so,' Jessie readily agreed with her. 'I also used to freelance, writing occasional articles for women's magazines.'

Across the bar, Lipless stopped eavesdropping to remark that he'd read an article in a woman's magazine in the dentist's waiting room and it was all about orgasms. 'What a thing to write about. Who'd want to read that?'

'You did,' Magda scarcely interrupted speaking to Jessie to tell him.

'Yes, me. But that was only because I was having root canal work.'

Jessie and Magda stared at him.

'I needed something to take my mind off it.' He pursed his mouth, raised his eyebrows. What fools wimmen were that they did not see that.

'We were just bringing out a book about Virginia Woolf when I left,' Jessie spoke slowly. She didn't know whether or not she missed work. 'Then we were talking about expanding our range to music, critics writing about musicians. Not just, you know, Wagner and Mahler, but Bessie Smith and Charlie Parker. Maybe even Zappa and Van Morrison ... it could be fascinating ...'

'Yes,' said Magda. Bessie Smith, Van Morrison, she'd heard of them. Now they had a mutual point of reference, Jessie was slightly less different. The distance between her and Magda narrowed. Perhaps she was just a person after all.

'Y'know young Shona works up at Young's the solicitors?' Lipless asked.

Magda nodded and asked Jessie if she was going to go back to finish her musician project thing. Jessie shook her head. 'No. No.'

Till this moment she hadn't realised how distasteful returning to her old life had become to her. She really wanted to hear about Shona who worked up at Young's the solicitors. She remembered Shona, Pretty in Pink, who had suggested the grotty flat above the Ocean Café. She remembered well the day she'd been so desperate she'd accepted the flat unseen, and agreed to the ludicrous rent.

'Well ...' Unconcerned with Jessie's conversation with Magda, Lipless continued his gossip. 'Shona stole a magazine that she'd been reading in the dentist when he called her in. She was getting one of her back teeth filled. And did a competition in it. And she won a car.'

'Did she?' said Magda. 'I never knew that. That red car she drives about in?'

Lipless nodded, 'A boxy thing with brown seats. I never liked it.'

'No,' said Jessie, 'I think I'd like to stay here.'

'It was the brown seats,' said Lipless. 'They were pale, the colour of sick.'

'You're just jealous. You've never had a new car in your life.'

'Rubbish. It was a crisps competition. Some crisp company, and along with the magazine entry form she had to send in six empty packets and a slogan on why she liked chilli'n'cheese potato snax.'

'Well, there you go. She worked for it.'

'Did she buggery.' Lipless was incensed. 'It was her wee brother said they were cheesily the chilliest potato snax ever. And she got the bags from us one lunchtime. And the dentist provided the magazine. What did she do?'

'Had the gumption to put it all together?' suggested Magda.

'She bought the stamp to send it all in?' suggested Jessie.

'That car should've been sold and the money divided equally between us all. If you ask me. Fair's fair after all.' Lipless drove his finger into the bar, emphasising his point.

'Here is a bitter man,' Magda said to Jessie.

'Well, the dentist could have got something. At least we all got the crisps.'

'How bloody trivial can you get?' Magda wanted to know.

'Oh, a lot more trivial. It takes years. Years and years. A truly trivial mind is a wonder to behold,' Lipless boasted.

'So it is,' said Jessie.

'Is it triviality you're after?' Magda asked.

'Yes. I think, perhaps, it is. Why not?'

'I can give you that. I'll be needing help for the summer. Some hard mindless waitressing, graft.'

'And the pay?'

'The pay!' Magda roared. 'The pay sucks. You're in Mareth, baby. But we'll feed you.'

'Oh, righto.' Unused to such directness, Jessie succumbed.

Lipless suddenly confessed that he supposed he really did like reading about women's orgasms. Orgasms, he said the word gruffly. Plainly he did not trust pleasure. It would take its toll of you in the end.

'I suppose women fascinate me more than anything. I mean,

who the hell are they? And what do they think about? And why don't they let me into their secret?'

'What secret?' asked Jessie.

'Exactly,' said Lipless. 'What secret.'

'You wouldn't think,' said Magda watching him go, 'that man had a degree in philosophy.'

'My God,' Jessie gasped. 'No, you wouldn't.'

'That's because he hasn't,' said Magda. 'Jessie, you've got to stop believing all you're told. In fact, I'd advise you not to believe anything you're told. But that's just me.'

Outside, Lipless was moving slowly through a gathering guffawing throng of women.

'Actually,' said Magda, 'it's sad really. Since his wife died, Lipless doesn't live life. He just copes.'

'What happened to his face?'

'He was standing on his boat going out to check his creels. As he went out someone fishing off the harbour wall cast out and the hook caught his upper lip and pulled it off.'

Jessie's hands flew to her face. 'Oh horrible. Oh ghastly.' Then, gazing up from her squeamishness, 'Is that true?'

'Oh yes,' said Magda.

'Isn't it a bit cruel to call him Lipless?'

'Yes. I suppose. Ain't life a bitch? It just sort of started. He's used to it. Signs his Christmas cards Lipless.'

Outside, the throng got noisier, a rising shriek.

'What's going on out there?'

'The lady regulars at the Anchor and Crown have hired a coach. They're off to London to see *Cats*.'

Through the hazed window – early evening the café hadn't hit full steam – Magda pointed at a small, thin woman with tightly permed hair who was loudly supervising the loading of a vast amount of alcohol on to the bus. She was pointing and waving and hooting with bawdy laughter. A deep howl, the throaty ravages of booze and fags.

'That's my mother,' said Magda.

But Jessie did not look where Magda directed. She was watching with horror a man pushing his way through the crowd. He was clutching his jacket, painfully protecting its perfect cut from the jostle and throng.

'Oh God no,' Jessie wept. 'That's my husband.'

Chapter Six

Ginny Howard was one of the élite. It wasn't hard for her. Some are born to it, she said, and some have to strive for it. She was born to it. It came naturally. Though, as she always said, she had a deal of respect for those who set about civilising themselves. 'Always a worthwhile pursuit,' she maintained, nodding vigorously at her unquestionable rightness.

She was committed and committeed. 'There are people who turn up everywhere,' Magda said. Ginny Howard turned up everywhere. She was the insistent and highly vocal chairwoman of MIG, Mareth Improvement Group. She was once seen striding the length of Mareth counting the litter bins. 'There are not nearly enough of them,' she complained to the council, writing crisply on MIG headed notepaper. 'No wonder our streets are plagued by crisp bags and cola tins.'

The doings of the MIG were despicably worthy. Ginny Howard's sudden appearance on the street made people duck into doorways, dive for cover. She had a vile knack of making people do what she wished them to do: bake pancakes for Children in Need, collect money for the local lifeboat, take a stall at the church fête, no matter how they felt about it themselves. She had a look that defied resistance, an emotional bully. She would thrust out her bosom, heave herself up to her full and electrifying five foot three and glare. It was generally felt she was wasted chairing the Mareth Improvement Group; such a woman could sort out the Middle East, or at least get the ozone layer patched up. Though considering her two pressed and shiny children, Judith and Brian – their cowed please and thank-you ways and shrill, sanctimoniously weepy passion for whales and tigers, and their embarrassing clothes (their gloves were sewn to their sleeves) – it was unanimously agreed that the Middle East would be more content with its turmoil than anything Ginny Howard might inflict on it.

Her success was, of course, in knowing her limitations. She never, at least publicly, took on someone who would get the better of her. From that simple rule had grown her reputation for invincibility. Only Magda had seen her off. And at that it hadn't been the confrontation the villagers had hoped for. It was a simple exchange of opinions. Magda's had been the riper.

At a wedding where the bride had been deliciously pregnant, bulging in eight months' bloom out of her bridal gown as she waddled down the aisle, Ginny Howard had bristled disapproval. She looked Magda grimly in the eye. 'I can't say I like today's modern relationships. Call me old-fashioned, but I simply don't believe in sex before marriage. Do you?'

To the surprise of surrounding eavesdroppers, Magda agreed. 'Absolutely,' she said. 'It rumples your wedding frock and your veil goes all askew.'

Lovely. Ginny Howard nil, Magda one. It was a score Ginny secretly vowed to settle.

Alex looked round Jessie's flat. He did not bother to conceal his horror. 'You live here?'

Perhaps there was some mistake. She was joking, surely. Any moment she would remove him from this small place with its dubious smells and reveal to him her real home. But she didn't. Instead she spread her arms and smiled. 'Isn't it wonderful? Don't you just love it?'

'No.'

Jessie wasn't undermined by his lack of enthusiasm. 'I love the smallness of it. Cosy, don't you think?'

'No.' He twitched. She had him. A glimmer of triumph sparked within her. She went for the kill.

'Yes, cosy.'

'Cosy?' The word came icily to his lips. Cosy, he loathed cosy. Detested its cloying ethos.

'Cosy and comfy,' she crowed. Ha ha, the glee of it.

'God's sake, Jessie.'

'What?' She turned her gaze on him. Innocence. This was the man who loved space, Nordic sparseness. He was driven to distraction by anything – a discarded training shoe, an abandoned half-read newspaper, a jacket yanked off and left over the back of a chair – anything that disrupted the flow of light and space of his perfect décor. He loved the home they shared. Its polished floors, matching sofas, Persian rugs filled him with pride every time he came back to it. On days off he would pad through it barefoot, listening to Maria Callas.

He bought the right paperbacks and CDs. He drank the right wines. He was a man who worked hard at his lifestyle. A zeitgeist kind of guy, who would always be right about everything, because he kept redefining the meaning of right. He made sure his definition of right was always ahead of the game. When, for example, he noticed that the local supermarket stocked his favourite green and gold hexagonal coffee cups, he knew they had to go. He dropped them off at Oxfam the next day and bought something plain, Parisian and café-style to suit his mood of the moment.

'What?' she said again.

He turned on her, 'You know perfectly well what. How could you live like this? In this rathole. Jessie, I hate to see you in a place like this.'

'Rathole.' A shrill protest. 'Rathole!' Even shriller. 'This is my home.'

'I thought your home was our home.' A sincerely delivered and effective sermonette. She felt the regulation rush of guilt, almost said sorry.

'Leave me alone, Alex. This is what I want.'

'Why?'

'I don't know. Don't ask me that.'

'What can I ask you?'

'I don't know. Leave me alone.'

She couldn't collect her thoughts, didn't want to collect her thoughts. For the last few weeks since leaving Alex she had been cruising on instinct and was, she considered, doing fine.

But plainly he was not going to leave her alone. He stood before her, hands thrust into his pockets, head slightly bowed. She could read this man, she knew his every gesture. Language? This body was a book she'd read over and over. He was going to make a pass. He wanted to fuck.

'Don't,' she said before he even moved to touch her. His hands were still deep in his pockets.'

'Don't what?'

'You know what.'

'No I don't. What?'

'You want to go to bed, don't you?'

'No.'

'Of course you do. I know you, Alex. That's your answer to everything. We have a baby and it dies and you want to get into my knickers as if that would've made it all better.'

'It might have helped. It might have kept us together.'

'Sod off,' she dismissed him. 'I have never felt so bad. I realise now that nothing bad had ever happened to me before that. I got into the university I wanted, the course I wanted, the degree I wanted, the job I wanted. I had never failed at anything. Failure just never crossed my mind.'

'You didn't fail.'

'Tell my body that. I feel like I failed, Alex. I couldn't come to terms with it.'

'So you left.'

She shrugged. Surely that was obvious. 'I rather think you left long before me.'

'What do you mean by that?'

'You were never there. You went back to work as soon as I got back from hospital. I needed somebody, Alex. I needed you.'

He looked at his feet and sighed. Jessie waited for an answer, an explanation. 'I didn't know what to say,' he said. He was no more used to failure than she was.

'Listen to us,' said Jessie. 'How could such a brittle relationship have survived tragedy and trauma?'

'When are you coming back?' He didn't want an analysis of his marriage, he wanted everything back the way it was. He was fighting for the life he'd worked hard to construct.

'What happened to your girlfriend? Has she dumped you, too?' Jessie only now realised how deeply she was hurt by his affair.

He shook his head. 'You don't understand. It was just a fling. It didn't mean anything. I needed somebody, Jessie. I needed someone to hold me. I was hurting too, you know. I shouldn't have done it. I'm sorry.' He looked repentant. He loved Jessie and though he'd strayed often enough in his head, he'd only actually physically been unfaithful once before. With Trish, Jessie's friend. He just didn't rate monogamy as highly as she did. He wanted this to be over, and was irritated that Jessie wasn't responding in the way he imagined she would when he worked through this scene on his drive to Mareth.

'Are you coming back?'

'I don't know.'

'Don't know. Don't know. That's all you say. Do you know anything? Let's work on what you do know.'

'I don't know what I know any more.' Jessie was tired of all this. His arguments were so clinical. He made logic of every-thing. And she was beyond logic. She existed now on feelings. Her actions were based on messages from her gut. She no longer trusted clear thinking. She knew he would push her and push her till he got the answer he wanted. Why didn't he leave her alone?

'Oh God,' she burst out, 'it's over Alex. I'm not coming back. I don't miss you. And I don't miss your tired little dick pressing against me at night.'

Alex hadn't till this moment realised how much he loved her, how deeply she could hurt him. Even when he'd discovered her gone he hadn't acknowledged his pain. He could fix this. He could talk her into coming back to him. He had been always able to talk Jessie into doing whatever he wanted her to do. She was his. He was stunned by this vile blow. There were tears in his eyes.

Jessie hadn't really meant to hurt him. She just wanted him down where she was. She felt suddenly awful, suddenly shamed and suddenly, and for the first time in her life, utterly utterly powerful.

Magda got out of bed, 'You should sleep on the damp side.'

'Sorry,' Jim had arranged his body ready for sleep but rolled over to look at her.

'It should be part of the wedding vows. Stuff all this love, honour and cherish rubbish. It ought to be, do you James Migilvary Horn take this Magda for your lawful wedded wife and promise always to sleep on the damp side, never to toss your dirty socks under the bed, and to hang up the towels properly after you've used them? That'd half the divorce rate.'

'Christ, Magda, will you shut up?'

'No.' She was striding out of the room now. Jim raised himself on one elbow, 'Anyway, we're not married. Is this a proposal?'

'No. But when I do get married that's the ceremony I want. But I don't want a husband. You're just a sex object to me.'

'Suits me.' Jim heaved himself back into his favourite sleeping position.

Magda went downstairs to the kitchen. Lately sleeping had been a problem. She made some tea and sat at the table.

'Darkly whining,' she muttered to herself. 'I spend my nights darkly whining.' She liked the phrase. She liked words. Her inability to decipher them written down meant that they came to her aurally, and each time they came to her they came afresh. In her head she strung them together in her own way. At the moment darkly and whining were her two favourite words. She turned them over and over, muttered them during the day as she stirred her sauces and made incisions in chicken breasts ready to insert slivers of garlic and ginger.

Darkly whining. Darkly whining. Darkly whining. Forever darkly whining. She had been aware recently that repeating darkly whining was beginning to replace her rages.

For the last few days she had been filled with foreboding about her mother's trip to London. She couldn't fathom why. Her mother had been away on coach trips before and had come home safely. Even if she didn't come home safely, Magda didn't know what degree of concern she could muster. But there it was: a flutter of nerves in her stomach whenever she thought of her mother. Jim had come to dread Magda's feelings. He who scoffed at religion and superstition had come to respect, even dread, the flutterings in the pit of his lady's stomach.

With virtually no education, instincts were all she had. She paid them heed. Sitting now at her kitchen table, doing nothing to counter the early spring splintered chill, she let her feelings roll.

Here she was, forty-three years old, a man in her bed, four children all healthy and reasonably sane; she owned – well, sort of owned – a café; she made money, had her own house – well Jim's house, car, television, stereo, everything she could want she had. And yet. Big sigh, Yes but.

'Life's yes-buts, are a bitch. Yes but. Yeah but. Yeah but. Yeahbut. Yeabut. Yeabut. Yeabut. Yeabut. What we have to contend with is the yeabut factor.'

Her tea was cold. She drank it anyway. So what was her yeabut factor? Magda was used to the night. A long-time insomniac, she knew it well. Could tell the time by the shade of grey filtering past the edges of her curtains. She knew the rhythms of her home as it creaked and shifted through the dark. The kitchen looked out on to the sea and she could hear the surf heaving on to the shore not far from her front door. She pulled the curtains. The world outside was exquisite. Too beautiful by far, she thought. She did not trust beauty. A huge moon lit the bay and spread a path rippling over the water. A fishing boat chugged out to sea, masts lit.

'You don't fool me pretty picture postcard scene,' Magda said. 'There's shit in these waters. And that's the Johnston brothers going out. They'll be below with a crate of lager watching skin-flicks on their video.'

She was a cynic. Her constant refusal to commit depressed Jim. She gave him and their children her furious love, but considered nothing else merited it. A beautiful landscape was a beautiful landscape, yeabut. Yeabut there would be no doubt stray used condoms lying just out of view, and noisy jets screaming overhead. It was the same with everything. There was always a yeabut. 'Couldn't you just relax and like something?' Jim would sigh.

But Magda said nope. She couldn't. Wouldn't. If she just relaxed she felt she would lose her edge, the diabolical lippiness would go. And that would be the end of her.

Lately, though, when she wasn't expounding life's yeabuts, Magda would fall profoundly silent. She would sink deep into her own quietness, her mobile face falling into a sulk. Sometimes she would say nothing for hours. She might bite her lower lip or twist the silver snake ring on her left hand, but she would say nothing.

'God, you're so silent. Are you in mourning or what?' Jim, unable to bear her silence, let loose his frustration. And Magda stared at him in surprise, still saying nothing. Jim threw his newspaper at her before storming from the room.

'I think you're right,' Magda said to him in bed. 'I think I am in mourning.'

'Who's died?'

'Me.'

'What sort of garbage is that?'

'Not garbage. I don't actually think I've died. I just haven't lived.'

'Oh, don't give me that. I can't stand that stuff. Have you been reading the Californian dictionary of Clichéd Crap?'

'No,' Magda told him stiffly. 'I haven't been reading anything, have I? That's what I'm in mourning for. What might have been. If things had been different.'

Jim said nothing. He wasn't going to pursue this conversation. Why didn't people just accept what was? He lay waiting for one of Magda's smart remarks and when it didn't come put his hand on her back. She turned to him. He pulled her head down to kiss her and ran his fingers across her tits. Twenty-odd years together, she should be used to this. He shouldn't still excite her. But he did. She loved the soft just inside his mouth, would trace it with her tongue. And his face, steady calculating eyes, cherubic lips firmly pursed beneath his cropped dark beard.

And when she went down on him. The taste of him was always the same. An indefinable mix of salt, always salt, the sea, oil and Palmolive he lathered himself with every night before he came to bed. She would stroke the inside of his thighs, then draw her nails round his bum, and down to where it set him moaning. Far away above her she would hear him. He would be fraying at the edges, losing control, giving in to her. She would hear him gasp and would stop to watch him. Oh don't, he'd say, don't stop, holding her head, pushing it back down. Don't. Stop. She would look at his face folding, unfolding with pleasure. She would purse her lips and grin. She could get him, every time she could get him.

She never tired of him and sometimes she resented it. She wished there was a cure for him, a potion she could take that would make her immune to him and his moods. She would no longer try to assess from the way he came down the stairs in the morning, and the way he slammed the door when he came home at night, how he was feeling on a day-to-day basis. She wished he didn't have such an effect on her. With Jim she wasn't in control and that unnerved and annoyed her.

In her direst moments she cursed the debt she thought she owed him. He had rescued her from herself. When she was at full teenage wildness he had taken her in. One night at the Anchor and Crown, after he had finished drinking, he put his empty glass down on the bar, walked across to where Magda was making a lot of noise drinking with her friends, looked directly at her, extended an inviting hand and said, 'Coming?'

She got up from her seat leaving a half-drunk vodka and coke – she always remembered that vodka and coke – and went with him. Just like that, like a scene from a bad B-movie. She'd gone to his house and had lived there ever since. After a year she ceased to be Magda Lomax and became Magda Horn. At the time it surprised nobody really, and was only a topic of gossip in Mareth for a couple of days. There was something natural and right about it, the tempestuous girl and the self-possessed fisherman. He was a match for her. At last Magda was removed from Mareth's conscience. Nobody worried that an outrageous and uncontrolled intelligence had been left ignored. And Magda? Life, Magda told Jim, would be a synch if it wasn't for feelings.

Downstairs she made tea and sat, as she did most nights, staring out of her kitchen window. She ran through the people she'd been to school with. Most of them had long left Mareth. Where were those little people with their bony knees and scrubby hair and the seething squabbling playground life they'd led.

'Where are you, little zoo?'

Gone to become photocopy-machine salesmen, a florist, a marine, a dental mechanic and what else? Wasn't that nose picky smelly Carstairs boy an art historian? Little fart. And where could she go? She laid her cheek on her hand. If only she could cry, that would help. But crying was a treat she'd long grown out of.

'Oh, bugger this,' she said, 'where does wondering get you?'

But wondering was part of Magda's life. It's my hobby, she said, wondering about other folks, women especially. Magda mentally divided women into groups. There was the divine sisterhood of rightness who belonged to the holy church of Tupperware. There was the group of incomers in trendy clothes who all had some connection with the university ten miles up the coast. They wore long skirts and big boots, jeans and baggy shirts, waved their arms about and said um and ah a lot when they spoke. They came to the Ocean Café and drank wine or pints of beer. They spoke about books and films and relationships. What so-and-so did with so-and-so and who was sleeping with whom. What did whossname really meant when he said such and such. It was a complex, judgemental world of intense friendships and, as far as Magda could tell, faked orgasms.

Did all women fake it? Did they tell each other about faking it, how to do it? Ostracised at school except for Edie, Magda had never had a close female friend. And her mother had never discussed anything with her, from the keeping of a bank account to coping with her periods. They had come as a complete surprise to her. A boyfriend had told her about sanitary towels. The same boy had told her about sex. Chat with her mother, then, about faking orgasms had been out.

Orgasms. Magda had been having them for years before she knew that's what they were called.

She wondered if individual women stumbled across making mock moans of delight, lying on their backs waiting soullessly for the humping to be over. Did the divine sisters of rightness from the holy church of Tupperware fake orgasms? Did they ever have sex? If so, would they remove their sensible shoes, cosy anoraks and neat little strings of pearls? Magda doubted it.

'Magda,' small voice wailed from upstairs. 'Magda. I can't sleep.' All her children called her by name.

'OK, Rosie,' she said, 'I'm coming.'

The child was already halfway down the stairs.

'Back to bed,' Magda ordered. 'School tomorrow.'

'I hate school.'

'No you don't, you love it. And you're going tomorrow.' She took Rosie's hand and led her back towards her bedroom.

'Tell me a story, then,' the child wheedled.

Magda looked down at her daughter. Rosie, seven years old, her youngest child, with her sallow complexion and mane of unmanageable hair was a replica Magda. When she looked at her other children, Magda saw Jim; when she looked at Rosie she saw herself. And her heart went out to her. Poor little bugger, she thought.

'All right.' She watched Rosie clamber back into bed and pulled the covers over her.

'Twice upon a time there was a frog . . .' she said, gently moving the hair from the child's forehead.

'Twice. You only get upon a time once.'

'Not if you're reincarnated. Then you get twice.'

'If you're reincarnated,' Rossie crisply corrected, 'you don't get to be a frog twice. Only once, then you move on.'

'Yeabut,' said Magda. 'This was a bad frog. He had to do his frog time over to get it right.'

'Ah,' said Rosie. 'It'd be like you. Darkly whining. That's what you're always saying.'

'There you go,' Magda grinned in surprise. She had no idea she said the thing out loud.

'You'll have to be Magda twice upon a time, just like the frog.'

'Oh goodness,' Magda said. 'There's something to darkly whine about.'

Mary Lomax didn't trust London. There were too many people. Looking each one in the eye in passing exhausted her. Furthermore, nobody said hello. In Mareth people always said hello if you knew them or not. It was just manners, wasn't it? It was gritty here, smelly. She had London in her eyes, and London up her nose.

'Oh,' she declared to her friends in the bar of their hotel, 'I wouldn't live here if you paid me.' She sipped her sherry and heartily agreed with herself. Sherry because she didn't trust herself with her usual vodka. It didn't do to get legless and sing old Elvis numbers when there were strangers about. She hunched herself against the city. Held her stomach in, kept her face straight and tried not to think about the red dress.

But it was there. It had wormed its way into her soul. And she could not sleep or eat for thinking about it. She had given her heart to it.

She had arrived in London at six o'clock in the morning, crumpled and sweaty. All the others on the coach had gone into their hotel to bathe, or snooze till breakfast, but Mary had been too excited to do that. She wanted to sightsee right away. Urgently now in case this wasn't really happening, in case all the sights to see suddenly disappeared. She walked through empty streets, listening to the lonely clicking of her high heels and was overwhelmed.

As the morning went on, the city gathered speed. By eight it was going full hurtle. Thrumming traffic, a rush of people, people wearing breathing-masks riding mountain bikes, blank faces, weird hairdos, fabulous clothes, dreadful clothes. She was swimming against the tide here. All those people, and everybody looked at her, a swift eyeflick, but nobody registered recognition. Not a nod to let her know she was alive and in

the same world as they were. She didn't know what was going
on, had the urge to find a back street café to hide in. She was
engulfed by her smallness, thinness and the cheapness of her
clothes. She wanted desperately to apologise to someone, everyone. Everybody that walked down these streets had somewhere
to go, and she hadn't. She felt lost. All these people around
here knew some sophisticated secret about living she didn't.
She was an open-faced fool, the hurtling crowds could all, she
was sure, at a swift, dismissive glance see that.

But she was really overwhelmed by the shops. The shops,
the shops, so many shops. Turn a corner, a new street full of
shops; walk the street, turn a corner – another street, another
long line of shops. In Mareth there was one street with six
shops in it. There you could buy almost anything and be home
in time for the four o'clock soap. You would never have thought
there was so much to spend your money on. No wonder people
got into debt. That was what was so good about Mareth, you
couldn't really overspend there. There was nothing you really
really wanted. A loaf of bread, a tin of beans, you wouldn't
lose your soul to anything like that.

She saw the dress in a window tucked in the heart of Kensing-
ton. One look and the desire to own it consumed her. For her
entire London trip, Mary thought of nothing else. All through
the performance of *Cats* she dreamed of the red dress. What
would she look like in it? Where could she wear a frock like
that? Could she even put it in her wardrobe? All her other
clothes seemed suddenly tawdry. Oh, what was the matter
with her? She couldn't afford it. Couldn't afford it, pah, what
difference did that make? She couldn't go into a shop like that.
Posh folks went there, rich folks; they'd spot her for the bump-
kin she was right away. No, it was not for the likes of her.

Still she lusted. It wasn't red exactly. Not obviously red like
your ordinary cheap catalogue red dress. This red was deep
and rich and lasting; reds in her life so far had been innocent
paintbox colours. This red you could bury your face in. You'd
have to put moisturising cream on your shoulders and shave
your armpits for a red like this. Oh, she wanted that dress.

Looking at it she was a child again, living on the outside, nose pressed against the window. And looking at it she knew what the city was about. It was about having the savvy to buy the right thing and go to the right places. It was about thinking on your feet. Worrying what Ruby at the Spar was saying about you behind your back had nothing to do with it.

The shop was expensive. Everything about it said expensive: the dark green paintwork and gold lettering, the striped canopy, the swirling gold leaf that wound round the doorpost. Everything. Mary could not enter. She was sixty-four years old and worked three mornings a week cleaning Dr MacKintyre's surgery. She had only been to London once before. What did she know? All the words to 'Jailhouse Rock' and 'Hound Dog' for goodness sake. People who wore a dress like that never admitted to knowing such songs. And yet. Why shouldn't she have it? Her money was as good as any. 'I'm gonna have it. I'm gonna have it,' she promised herself over and over. Over and over. I am going to have that red dress.

The bus home was leaving at three in the afternoon. At twenty to two, Mary found herself walking to the shop. She hummed 'Blue Suede Shoes', a belligerent sort of a song, as she walked. Concentrating on it took her mind off her fear. She walked into the shop and imagined a hush. People were looking at her.

A woman stepped forward. 'Can I help?' Rounded, educated vowels. Mary felt as if she was gasping for breath, she was swamped by her inadequacy. This woman was thin, as Mary was. But anyone could see it was a different kind of thin. Mary's was natural. It came from lack of food when she was young. This woman's was acquired. This was the proper kind of thin.

'How much is that dress in the window?' Mary wanted this over as quickly as possible. She wanted out.

'The red one? Nine hundred and twenty-seven pounds.'

Mary flinched. What? Nine hundred and twenty-seven pounds. Her car cost less than that. She fought to hide her astonishment.

'Do you take credit cards?'

'Yes. I'll have to phone.'

'I'll take it,' Mary said.

'Don't you want to try it on? It may need altering.'

'No,' Mary waved her arms in dismay. No. No changing rooms, no fuss. Just let her out of here.

'No, I have to catch a bus. I have to get home to Mareth. I'll take the dress.' She instantly regretted admitting to the bus and Mareth. Now they had verbal evidence that she was not one of them.

She handed over her card and hoped to sink unnoticed into a corner whilst all the fussing, phoning and wrapping went on. She hoped to be unnoticed lest they shoo her out, as she shooed schoolboys and old men from the surgery with a flap of her duster when they trod on her clean shiny floor. She wanted out of here. She didn't know what to do. Did she stand back, arms folded? Or did she stay at the counter and chat? No chatting was out. She wanted to tell them she liked the paint outside. It looked velvety. But thought if she mentioned this they would laugh at her. I am a fool, she thought. These people can see I'm a fool.

In silence she watched the dress being spread on the counter, then folded, wrapped in tissue paper. Not white tissue paper, but dark navy pulled from a drawer in perfect sheets. When she got home she would iron that tissue. She would keep everything perfect.

Still she was scared. What if they decided she was not good enough to buy the dress? Not quite the sort of person they wanted to sell it to?

The saleswoman put down the phone and smiled at her. 'That's fine,' she said.

Still Mary panicked. Maybe her money wasn't good enough. Maybe they wanted rich money, not cleaning-lady money. There was a difference.

When she finally got the dress it was swathed in tissue and placed in a thick cardboard bag with two long dark red cord handles. She wanted to thank the saleswoman profusely, invite her to look in should she ever find herself in Mareth. But refrained. She humbly took her parcel and walked back to her hotel and the bus home. Her heart pounded, she was flushed with triumph. I have seen the other side, she breathed. She felt like a stormtrooper who, armed only with a red patent handbag and a plastic rainhat, had accomplished a successful raid on the enemy. If they'd spotted her they hadn't let on.

'I've got it. I've got it. I've got it.'

Triumph buzzed through her. As she walked from the shop her mincing, high-heeled steps quickened. She had to be away before they discovered the mistake, before they rushed after her, demanding the dress be returned to them. They could not possibly have meant to sell such a frock to the likes of her.

Chapter Seven

Jessie never knew if she was shocked or delighted at Magda's OC scheme. It was cheeky, rude even, utterly wrong, and, she had to admit, very satisfying. When she first saw the special red-bordered OC bills she had thought the initials stood for Ocean Café. But they didn't. They were for Over Charge. Magda vented the rage certain customers brought out in her by bumping up their bills. The amount varied according to how much she had been irritated. It hadn't been an organised decision, this OCing of people. It had just happened. Magda drifted into it.

When she first took over the Ocean Café she was filled with a mix of enthusiasm and rage. She loved the place. Had always loved it. From the first time she had ever come to it as a child she loved it. The old mahogany counter, the sturdy wooden tables and solidly comforting ladder-back chairs with intricate flower patterns on faded velvet cushions. The walls were wood-panelled halfway up, then there was a layer of dark-red deco tiling and after that some ancient faded wallpaper. And on the far wall, ridiculously out of place, an Alpine scene. She had moved silently about the bar, stroking it, whispering, 'Mine. Mine. Mine.' Then, a realist always added, 'Well, not actually mine. Mine and Edie's and Jim's. But mostly mine . . .'

The Ocean Café brought her joy. The customers caused her rage. She tried to get along with most of them but finally settled into a role of bawdy, bossy cook and barkeeper. She discovered that people accepted being bossed, even liked it. She chipped people for their dietary deficiencies. Made grown seafaring men eat their greens. Involved the unlikeliest people in culinary debates. But she never could come to terms with serving people she didn't like.

Her old primary school teacher, Miss Clarkson, had come in for some lunch and had beamed at her, patronisingly remarking, 'Well, Magda, who'd have thought it? You've made something of yourself. The girl least likely . . .' And she'd laughed heartily. Magda seethed. She'd hated this woman for years, remembered with biting bitterness the beatings she'd received for her constant inability to master basic literacy. The humiliation haunted her yet.

'You, Magda, come out here. Look at this work. Messy, messy, messy. You're such a grubby child.' That fiendish face would be thrust close to hers. Magda could see the wiry hairs sprouting untamed on her chin. 'Your work's atrocious. Do you know what you are, Magda? Lazy.' On an authoritarian high, she would whirl Magda round, lift her skirt and, taking her ruler from her desk, whack her backside. 'Lazy. Lazy. Lazy.' Whack. Whack. Whack. The watching rows of children, unable to control their fear that this horror might happen to them, dissolved into alarmed sniggers.

This had been an almost daily occurrence in Magda's early school days. For her education had not been an enlightening of her spirit or opening of her mind. Education had been a sore bum. Keen to keep her pupils in a state of fear, when there had been no naughty children to chastise, Miss Clarkson would give her desk a sound thrashing, 'This is what I do to those who don't work.'

Her teaching methods had a profound effect on her pupils. She would point at a child and demand, 'You there, six sevens. NOW.' Her stubby finger, the finger from hell, jabbed with such ferocity that little minds numbed, throats seized, the blood chilled. The only functioning organ was the lower bowel. Her classroom reeked constantly with the farty smell of fear.

Standing in the Ocean Café years later, confronted by that same ogre, Magda realised how little she had recovered from the humiliation. She flushed deeply, couldn't meet the old lady's watery eye and dropped the cup she was holding.

'Ha ha,' her teacher scolded triumphantly. 'The same old Magda.' She pointed across the room, 'I'll have the chicken in ginger and honey and I'll have it over here.' She sat down by the window. Magda disappeared into the kitchen. For some minutes she stood staring out into the restaurant. Then she turned and slowly started to wash some dishes. She would never serve that old cow. Never. Never. Never.

'Christ, Edie,' she hissed. 'When you meet one of your old teachers, pacifism flies out the window, you realise what violence is for. Nut the bastards. Do some damage to the arseholes who damaged you.'

The dragon sat for some time before she realised she was not going to be served. Other people arrived, ordered, ate and left. Still she sat.

'What's happened to the service around here?' she called. 'I've been waiting for hours. A person could starve.' Nothing happened. In the kitchen nothing stirred.

'I will not serve that old bag,' Magda said, tears in her eyes. 'I will not carry food out to her. I will not.'

'Spell school for me, child,' the beast had demanded, shoving her crumpled ancient face close to Magda's. Terror. No six-year-old bladder could cope. There was a sudden hot pool at Magda's feet, her shoes were horribly damp. Magda never forgave that degradation. Never forgave. She hid in the kitchen, skulked by the sink. Tutting, sighing and muttering, typical and, what else could you expect from a girl like that, Miss Clarkson left.

Magda regularly refused to serve people she did not like. To the embarrassment of other customers the hated ones were left sitting looking sheepish, or howling dissatisfaction at the service.

'For heaven's sake,' Jim told her, 'you're in business. You can't choose who's going to eat your pasta and who isn't. You're not here to judge personalities. You're out to make money.' He emphasised this last by jabbing at her chest with his blackened oily finger. Magda watched it, cross-eyed. He was right, of course. Wasn't he always? God she could hate him for that.

'But I hate these people,' she protested as her latest bunch of rejected lunchers walked, baffled, across the road to their car. They had committed the unpardonable sin of being patronising. Had spoken to Magda in ringing, rounded tones, expressing disbelief in the likelihood of anyone in such an unsophisticated part of the world having heard of balsamic vinegar.

'They're such wankers.'

'Wankers with cash. When they go they take their cash with them instead of leaving it in your till.'

Their voices drifted back. 'Extraordinary.' 'I can't believe it.'

'Take their cash, Mags. Take it for the poor and the meek. Strike a blow for the misunderstood. Avenge the child you were, the infant with the constantly sore bum. And if you don't take it for any other reason, take it so you can pay the lease on your café.'

Not long after that, Magda had devised her OC method of charging. She put extra money on the bills of those customers she found hateful, patronising, or who had wronged her in her turbulent youth.

When the dreaded Miss Clarkson returned for a second attempt at sampling Magda's chicken with ginger and honey sauce, she had been OC'd. And how. The meal had been excellent and, expressing some surprise at Magda's ability to do anything well, she had paid up willingly. The excess money had been put aside in a jar. With Edie's help, Magda had in time found a home for it that she was convinced Miss Clarkson would find distasteful. The Lesbians in Wheelchairs Encounter Group had received the money.

A woman with Magda's rage soon accumulated quite a bit of OC money. The rule was that the charity must truly horrify the OC'd one. Dishonest though it was, OCing people did a lot to soothe Magda's childhood humiliations. And it made wiping up after and serving obnoxious people almost pleasurable.

'It's better than therapy,' she confessed to Jim. 'And it isn't costing a thing.' She was delighted with herself.

At first Jessie had protested. OCing people she said was

immoral. You couldn't charge people some phenomenal sum just because you didn't like them. You couldn't send other people's hard-earned money off to outré causes. It wasn't on. Magda stared at her. She was wondering what outré meant but knew this wasn't the moment to ask.

But that was before Jessie had her first hateful encounter. A bulky boozy-faced man had summonsed her across the room with an officious flick of his hand, complaining loudly that there were only six croutons on his soup. Jessie had fetched some more and, as she turned to go he said, thanks girlie and patted her bum. Oh, the rush of loathing. Jessie's eyes glowed momentarily red. She'd a swift flash of herself crashing her tray down on the arse-patter's head whilst shoving his soup-hot spoon up his nose. She swallowed. And returned to the kitchen.

'Did you see that?' she fumed. 'That arsehole. The shit... Jesus, who does he think he is? My bum's mine.'

Magda went to the kitchen and peered out. 'Oh, look at him. Right-wing hetero with macho problems. I think he could send a little contribution to Gay Poets for Socialism, a wee something to help fund their next leaflet. What d'you think, Edie?'

'Oh yes. Poor old sod. Give him an extra potato with his duck. Keep his strength up.'

It was some time before Magda saw the dress. She knew it was in her mother's house, she had seen the carrier bag and the beloved tissue wrapping. But Mary was reluctant to take it out. Several times a day she went through to her bedroom to examine and cherish her purchase. She would run her hand over the bag and peer into it. She had bought an entry into a new world. This was the sort of thing real people had in their wardrobes.

John Lomax, her husband, sighed every time he came across the bag in the bedroom. 'I'm tripping over that thing,' he complained. Though he wasn't. The dress hadn't been two days in the house and he hated it already. It was dresses like this that made husbands disappear into sheds at bottom of the garden, or hide behind newspapers. He knew his life was about to be disrupted. This dress gave him indigestion.

'When are we actually going to see it?' Magda asked. 'You can't keep it wrapped up for ever.'

Mary knew this. It wasn't that she didn't want to unwrap the dress. She just wanted to preserve the whole package. Besides, if she removed the dress from its bag she would have to face the challenge of wearing it. Eventually, though, she did carefully ease it out of the bag more tenderly than she ever treated any infant. She unfolded the precious tissue wrapping and, breathless with awe, lifted the dress and held it to her face. It was wonderful. The smell of it. The unsullied newness of it. No sags at the bum or creasing round the thighs. No stains.

'Oh, I love you,' she told it, putting it on her special padded green velvet hangar and hooking it on to the back of the door. Then she gently smoothed out the tissue and laid it in a drawer. The knowledge that the dress was here in the house filled her heart, she did not want to leave it. Took regular trips through to the bedroom to say hello to it.

'Hello, frock. How are you hanging there?' For heaven's sake, she cursed herself, she was talking to a dress. She couldn't help it.

She hadn't felt like this since she'd been fifteen and wildly and totally in love with Lawrence Kemp who sat across from her in the French class. She had forgotten this thrill. Now it came flooding back. The way her heart pounded when he leaned over and asked if he could borrow her pencil. And how she held it close after he handed it back; it was still warm where he'd held it. Her fingers curled round the very spot his fingers had curled round. Was there ever a thrill like that? Secretly, in bed that night, she had put it to her lips. Lawrence, she whispered his name. He never found out about the crush she had on him.

The suddenness of this memory shook her. She sank on to the bed. She felt as if she held her life before her. It was clear, she could see everything. She had wanted to be a nurse but her parents had considered her too young to leave Mareth.

'I could have gone,' she said. 'I was not too young.'

She had stayed home. Worked at the fish shed filleting cod and haddock before she met and married John. Lawrence had become a surveyor.

'I didn't know,' she said again, surprised at the sound of her voice in the empty room. 'I didn't know.' She stared sadly at the floor, red and gold patterned carpet. 'I didn't know I was going to get old.' A tear slid down her cheek. 'It's over, all over. I won't ever be a nurse. My God,' an almost violent revelation, 'I'm going to die one day.'

Jessie enjoyed waiting tables. When she got home after a night's work she would flop exhausted on to her bed. There was something virtuous about the ache, the stiffness in every muscle and every bone she felt when she tried to get up in the morning. For a while she contemplated a change of image: glossier lipstick, dramatic layerings of mascara, more cleavage – though she didn't actually have any cleavage – jaws in nonchalant motion with gum, a teetering, stilettoed walk; but could she ever power-mince like Magda? She decided she couldn't keep it up. She was just beginning to realise how exhausting the business of being female could be.

Mareth was waiting, little village poised and still, for the visitors to arrive. They came every year, droves of them, to wander round the harbour, lick ice-creams, chatter and stare. At last a first few hardy souls in Barbours braved the spring storms, high tides, driving winds to walk, bent horizontal, faces scrunged against the weather, coats flapping, along the shore. They watched the waves, white horses, galloping in, ran backwards as the surf chased their shoes. They wondered at the ancientness of it all: timeless stones, cobbled streets, houses with steps up to the front door, lace curtains hanging on twelve-paned windows.

'It's all so dinky,' they would say. They were wrong, of course.

They came into the café bringing in the cold clinging to their clothes. They would order Magda's tiny onion soup, tiny onions glazed and golden in a thick tomatoey stock with pasta and ham, topped with freshly grated parmesan. It was garlicky and filling. It made diners aglow with such well-being they wanted to go on and on eating. And they usually did. They oozed anticipation at Magda's duckling with baby turnips, or smoked fish omelettes or pesto-topped baked salmon. And they ended with Magda's bread-and-butter pudding, buttered brioche spread with bitter marmalade dipped in fresh orange juice and baked in a creamy vanilla custard. Flushed and replete, the eaters would go smiling into the soft Mareth night watched by Magda and Edie.

'I think the shellfish and courgette risotto and the lamb stew are definitely on tonight. Fact, I don't think they're going to make it home. Look at them. Look at his hands.'

'Ooooh.' Edie craned up to watch the lovers' progress to the BMW they'd parked on the harbour. 'More fun than I'm going to have when I get home.'

'Do you ever get lonely, Edie?' Magda asked.

'Oh, I used to. But after you've lived alone for a while you come to quite like it. I get home after midnight most nights and I don't feel like talking to anybody. After a day in here all I want to do is lie down. I have a bath, pour a wee whisky . . .' she indicated with two abstemious fingers the size of the whisky.

Magda made the same gesture, indicating a much larger measure. 'A wee whisky,' she mocked. Then, 'Still, you do get a bed to yourself. I'd love that.'

'Magda Horn,' Edie scoffed. 'You'd hate to have a bed to yourself. You wouldn't know where to put yourself.'

Then an afterthought, Magda said, 'Have you ever faked it, Edie?'

Edie looked at her. Every time she told herself that Magda could never again surprise her, Magda surprised her.

'Well,' she shrugged, shook her head, flustered. 'As a matter of fact. Yes. Yes, I have.' Jessie, carrying a couple of truffle tortes, stopped to listen, fascinated. She found it hard to imagine thin little, shy little Edie doing it, far less faking it.

'Have you?' Magda turned to her.

Jessie reddened, 'Um, well, yes. Yes. Me too. I have.'

'How did you know to do that? Who told you about faking it?'

Jessie and Edie exchanged baffled looks. 'Just came to me one night when I was with Fred. He was taking ages. You know,' Edie shrugged, embarrassed at this confession.

'No, I don't know,' Magda looked hurt. 'Nobody tells me anything.'

Lipless, leaning on the bar clutching a pint, bent forward. 'I'll tell you something, Magda. I've never faked it.'

Magda stared at him bitterly, 'Well, you wouldn't would you? Don't have to. You'd only be fooling yourself.'

The dining room silenced, everyone stopped eating and looked at Lipless. 'There was no need for that,' he said. 'That was a bit rude.'

'So it was,' said Magda. 'Never mind.' She went into the kitchen and put on James Brown.

'Very rude indeed,' Lipless complained into his beer. 'Even if it is true. How did she know.'

The silence evaporated. Cutlery began to chink again. The eating started up. Life went on.

Jessie loved her new life. This work was restorative. It was, she told herself, honest. She served tables. She mastered new skills, carrying half a dozen plates at a time whilst kicking open the kitchen door. She ironed tablecloths and napkins, laid table, wiped, shouted orders, joined the steamy clamour in the kitchen and went home to bed. She didn't fret about what other people said or what they might be doing behind her back. She did not lie awake at night worrying about the long-term implications of remarks she had not properly registered when they were made to her.

She carried food to hungry people and, as she laid their plates before them, she could eavesdrop. She had fascinating fleeting glimpses of other people's lives. Best of all, she could watch Magda. All her life she had fought for what she thought she wanted: a degree, a job, a relationship. Now she wanted none of that. She wanted to be able to cook like Magda, wear absurd shoes like Magda, move around the kitchen like Magda.

'Hey boogie,' Magda would shout, waving her spoon in a moment of culinary joy. 'Don't take three steps when fifteen and a wiggle of the hips will do.' And The Rolling Stones would play. And Jessie wanted to be able to make rude remarks like Magda. She wanted to be Magda.

Billing and ordering at the Ocean Café were intriguing. The menu, small and daily handwritten by Edie, consisted of three choices of starter, main course and pudding. Each item was given a colour. On the kitchen wall was a diagram of the table layout. Orders were taken and, instead of writing them down, magnetised coloured tokens matching the colours of the daily dishes were stuck on the diagram. As dishes were taken to the tables the tokens were removed. Jessie found it very confusing.

'Why can't I just give you a note?' she wanted to know.

Edie shifted her feet uneasily. Magda sniffed. 'I have my methods. They work for me.' She turned back to the carrots she was noisily shoving into her food processor.

'But,' ignoring the restrained atmosphere, Jessie persisted, 'yesterday I served someone a tarragon chicken that had a yellow token in it.'

'Yellow for chicken, that's right,' Magda nodded. Her scheme obviously worked. She vigorously scraped her mass of grated carrots into a dark blue bowl and started on the dressing.

'This restaurant is run oddly if you ask me,' said Jessie.

'Well nobody's asking you.' Magda turned her back on her and poured some runny honey into a mixing bowl.

'Well,' Jessie only wanted to make things more organised and remove the worry of small metal tokens finding their way into the food, 'also last week there was a white token in the brown bread ice-cream.'

'Oh,' Edie shrugged.

'Shouldn't that be brown? I mean in the brown bread ice-cream?' Magda looked quizzically at Edie.

'No,' Edie raised a soothing hand to calm the rising angst. Angst that Jessie seemed unaware of. Magda spooned balsamic vinegar into the honey.

'How much of that do you add?' Jessie had recently become

keen to learn some of Magda's recipes. And her carrot salad seemed a good place to start. Everyone liked it.

'It is my aim,' Magda confided, 'to make everyone in Mareth eat this. I'll make the bastards healthy. And that old shite optician Carter'll go out of business.'

'So how much honey and how much vinegar do you add?' Jessie loomed over her shoulder.

Magda looked slightly alarmed at the question, 'Just some. You can feel it. I mean, sometimes the carrots are drier, woodier. It all depends.' She waved her hands. Precision irritated her. 'You can just tell,' she said. 'Then there's the olive oil and some salt and pepper. Then you can drop in a spot of walnut oil, and coriander. It's not always the same. See,' returning to her original theme, 'carrots. They're good for the eyes, aren't they?'

'No,' said Edie. 'I think that's just a bad joke about never seeing a rabbit wearing glasses.'

'Why isn't it always the same?' Jessie said. 'Surely people want the carrot salad to be the same every time they order it.'

Magda found it hard to pass on her skills. Many had asked and were usually sent scurrying from the kitchen. 'Questions, questions, questions. Don't ask. Just look. Take it in. Breathe it. Be it. Do it. That's how to learn.'

'Ah,' Jessie nodded. 'Only I seem to need some point of reference.'

'Rubbish. You just make it.'

'But how do you make it the same if you don't have a recipe?'

'It isn't the same. Is anything that's worth knowing the same every time? Is sex the same?' She started vigorously mixing her dressing. 'No. Sometimes it's wild, or passionate or cruel or comforting. Well . . .' she spread her hands. Jessie was tempted to point out that it was only a carrot salad and was it really likely to be cruel or passionate or wild? But she could see Magda's temper rising. Something was bothering her. She returned to the tokens.

'Yes. I see,' she said. 'I just thought writing the orders down would speed things up. Would make things easier. Cleaner . . .' She tailed off.

Magda turned suddenly furious. 'Can't you see I don't want a new method? I don't want efficiency. I want my tokens. I like my tokens. They're my tokens and they work for me.'

'I just . . .' Jessie spread her arms weakly.

Magda glared at her. Jessie wilted. Angry, Magda was more than formidable. She was terrifying. She seemed to fill the kitchen. Edie looked to be getting smaller. She was backing towards the door.

'God dammit,' Magda yelled. 'Can't you tell? Can't you sense there's something wrong. Isn't it obvious that I have to have the tokens because I can't fucking read or write. I'm illiterate. I'm a great big illiterate fool. That's what. That's me. Sod it . . . and dammit . . . and . . .'

She took her bowl of carrots and threw them across the kitchen. It smashed fabulously against the wall, splattering gratings everywhere. It was surprising how far they flew.

'Now look what you've done,' Edie tutted.

'And I really liked that bowl.' Magda kicked a stray bit of broken crockery. Jessie didn't know what to do. 'I would never have guessed,' she said quietly. 'You're such a good cook.'

'That's it for me,' Magda said. 'Cooking's what I do. Cooking. Fucking and having babies. That's all.'

Jessie stared at her. All? By God it was more than she could do. She couldn't even decently lose her temper. Well, not like that anyway. Common sense would have prevailed. She would have had the bowl in her hand, then at the last minute, considering the consequences, put it down. She wished she could throw things about like that.

'Well,' Magda relieved the tension, 'peel some more carrots.'

Chapter Eight

June. The full gaudy parade was on. Jessie could hardly push her way along the street. It was a time of ice-cream lickers and starers. Multi-coloured shell-suits on the move, shuffling slowly along the shore filling the litter bins, dragging vast bulging bags of beach stuff – rugs, buckets, spades, hats, balls, inflatable dinghies, booze, food, stuff – along the West Way to Mareth's small scrap of sandy beach. Locals knew the best swimming beaches along the coast but rarely told tourists about them.

Magda got ready to make the bulk of her annual income. The café filled. Days crowded in one against the other. Jessie moved into an exhausted haze. Even when she was away from the café she could smell chips. The backs of her legs ached. Someone asked if they could have tomato ketchup to put on their chicken with button mushrooms and Jessie whirled round and snapped, 'No. No you can't.' And had been shocked at herself. But not shocked enough to apologise.

The kitchen hit hyper-steam. Bunty, who came in at weekends to wash dishes and had a hygiene problem, came in every evening and had a heightened hygiene problem. Even when she wasn't at the café, when she was at the end of the harbour breathing in huge gulps of fresh air, Jessie thought she could smell her. She would discreetly try to sniff her own armpits, checking that the problems weren't catching. Odours from Magda's kitchen clung to all her clothes. When she stared in the mirror she saw a strange face looming back. Hair dishevelled, pores opening round new wrinkles on her face. She had bags under her eyes. Sometimes, lying on her bed, she would remember fondly the office she had once inhabited. Plants on the windowsill, constant fresh coffee, the soothing whir of her Apple Mac, pleasant voices, accents she understood. Why was she doing this? She was aware that sometimes a whole week would pass without her once thinking of her little son, Dr Davies and her guilt. She knew though that this was no real way to cure the blues. She soothed herself body and soul, listening to Mozart. She thought she must by now know a lot of things she didn't know before. If only she could put her finger on what they might be.

'I see Non-existent Dave's back,' Magda said, nodding towards the bar.

Edie coyly stuck her head through the kitchen door and greeted him, 'Hi Dave.'

'Edie,' he acknowledged her. She ducked back.

Of course Magda had affairs. These affairs were mostly with people passing through. She didn't want complications. But of all her illicit lovers, Non-existent Dave was the one she couldn't put out of her mind. It had the tingle factor, she supposed. The swiftness, wildness, wrongness of what they did, mostly in the kitchen, was thrilling. She caught her breath remembering.

'You serve him, Jessie,' she said.

'Non-existent Dave?' Jessie couldn't believe some of the nick-names. 'Sounds existential.'

'Existential,' Magda silently mouthed the word to Edie behind her back. And they both went, ooooh. And laughed.

'What the hell is existential?' Magda asked.

'It's a philosophy,' Jessie told her. 'Um . . .' she waved her hands about, '. . . um . . . to do with existence. Jean Paul Sartre. Um . . . it's like the future doesn't exist . . . and . . .'

Edie was carrying the big soup pot into the kitchen, through from the dishwashing area. It seemed to make her even smaller. Magda had her hands in a sinkful of cold water scrubbing mussels.

'Well . . .' Jessie wished she hadn't started this, since she was beginning to realise she didn't properly understand it herself.

'See, he questioned things like existence ... or he questioned our view of existence, our experience of it ...' Edie and Magda watched her.

'This Sartre bloke,' Magda said, 'he got paid for this?'

Edie heaved the soup pot on to the stove. Magda wiped her chilled hands on her apron.

'So he said we couldn't be sure things existed or not? Is that not just like a man,' Magda roared. 'Christ, don't tell Jim about that. Take the bins out, will you? No. How can I? We can't be sure they exist.' She nudged Edie. 'That's the best one yet.'

'And he got paid for it,' Edie reminded her. 'What are we doing slaving here?'

Jessie went to serve Non-existent Dave.

The name came from his great scheme. A computer ace, whilst working with the district council he'd wiped himself and his house from their records thereby freeing himself from local taxes. He had also removed all evidence of himself from the filing system. He'd emptied and closed his bank account. The council wanted to fire him for not coming to work. But there was nothing to fire. His plan was to hack into the computers of his credit card companies and remove himself from their records. He wondered if it was possible to wipe himself from the Inland Revenue records.

His great scheme had been that for a fee he would, using his home computer, hack into any system necessary to remove his clients from the face of the earth. He'd even offered to remove all evidence of Mareth itself. But discussions in the Spar and the post office supported the notion that someone would notice. There was hardly anyone in the village that hadn't been tempted. In the end all Dave did was fix the records that the harbour constantly needed repair. They'd been repairing the same bit of harbour wall for the past two years. It was good for Lipless and his work gang. And it was good for Lipless's liver. Magda kept him fed and refused him alcohol before noon. But they all knew that in the end someone would notice.

Dave's fate since he became non-existent confirmed Magda's passionate belief in irony. She believed in little else. She still prayed the same prayer she had been offering to whoever was up there since she was ten years old, hiding in her head from the sick slap-on-the-side-of-the-head philosophy of her Sunday school teachers, 'God help me please, and bless me. Keep me sane and safe from the Church of Scotland. Amen.'

Magda believed there was irony and only irony. People would all get what was coming to them in the end. And Non-existent Dave's fate proved her point. Not long after his wiping himself from the face of the earth, his wife left him for an ostentatiously rich builder. Then his nineteen-year-old son disappeared. He'd set off along the beach after drinking a vodka laced with acid one fabulously hot summer afternoon wearing only cut-offs and canvas deck shoes, walking walking past the shimmer till he was gone. He'd never been seen again. Searches found nothing. No washed-up body, no clothing nothing. Dave even became briefly existent again, registering his son as a missing person. But nothing. After that Dave started drifting. He disappeared from Mareth sometimes for months at a time, sometimes years.

'There,' Magda said when Dave first disappeared. 'Told you so. It's irony, that's what it is. Everybody gets what's coming to them in the end.'

'Oh boy. It really is a religion with you. I can just see you,' Jim amused himself, 'standing in the pulpit belting out your hymns, gospel style. You got what was comin' to ya babe. You had it comin' all along. Oh lordy lord.'

Magda didn't reply. What was coming to her then? Considering her relationship with Non-existent Dave? Her best affair ever. The heated rush and whispered urgency of it. The freedom when he slipped off her bra and the air hit her tits. His hands on her, his skin, skin on skin. It was like being teenage again. That first fuck when you first discover the wonders of fucking. Magda had been on the table and all she could say was, 'Do it. Do it. Do it.'

She plunged her hands back in the icy water, started feverishly scraping a mussel. 'It's been a while,' she said. That familiar longing started deep deep inside her. 'I have to go,' she said, a sudden urgent statement. She threw the mussel she was working on back into the water and left. Wiping her hands on her apron, ridiculous heels echoing on the cobbles, she hurried along the shore to Jim's yard, just past the harbour.

It was empty, silent and empty. The office was locked up. She looked round. She never felt she belonged here. She knew, standing amidst the bits of engine leaning on the *Sad-Eyed Lady*, his boat, she was out of place. She was wearing a short skirt and denim shirt tied around the waist, and her shoes were patent and pointy. In the evening when cooking she would dress like a cook, as the environmental health regulations demanded. A cook in a baseball cap, the only thing she could bear to wear on her head. But in the afternoons when she had also to wait tables she didn't bother. A breeze came in from the sea and above her swallows shrilled and cried. Something was wrong.

She hurried back along the shore past the Ocean Café to their house on the West Way. Jim, sitting at the kitchen table, was surprised to see her. Magda looked at him and knew this was not the moment to say she got horny scraping mussels and had come to find him, you know, just in case he might be persuaded to share her mood. Something was wrong.

'What is it?' she asked.

He shrugged. Spread his palms. 'That's it,' he said.

'What's it?'

'My yard. It's over. Isn't it?'

She watched him. His face was grey. 'Bank's called in the loan. And I can't pay my taxes. I'm bust, Magda. Bankrupt.'

'You can't be,' she protested. 'How can you be?' Which really meant how can you be when I know nothing about it? She sank into a chair opposite him. How could she have missed this? Something as big as this. She opened her mouth to ask all the questions crowding into her mind, but not a sound came out.

Jim shrugged and sniffed, 'There you go,' he said. 'The house is safe, I think. They'll take the yard. Sell off everything.' He did not look at her, did not meet her eyes. 'Bastards,' he said.

'Why. How could this happen?'

'Somebody didn't pay me so I couldn't pay somebody else. In my case the somebody elses I couldn't pay were the bank and the Inland Revenue. That'll do it every time. They'll see you off.'

'How long has this been going on? You didn't tell me.' Magda couldn't grasp what she was being told.

'Months. Months and months.' He put his hand over his eyes. He didn't want to look at her. 'I know I didn't tell you. I thought I could handle it. I thought.' He took a deep breath, adjusting his nerves. 'I think I thought if I ignored it, it would go away. I couldn't face it. I didn't tell anybody.'

She came to him. Took his head in her hands and held him against her. He clung to her. He was falling. He sank his face deep into her, breathing her. She smelled fishy. Her hands were cold. Still he clung and she touched the top of his head with her lips. He pushed up her skirt, ripped at her knickers, 'Wait,' she pulled them off. And he brought her down on top of him.

'No. No. This isn't right.' He shoved her off. Gripping his trousers he shoved her towards the bedroom. But they only made the stairs. Uncomfortable love. The edge of a step at the base of her spine cut into her. She wanted him to stop and didn't want him to stop. But he was far away, he was working out his ache. Pounding and crying. And when he came it was the nearest to screaming Magda had ever heard him.

She went to wash herself. When she came back and he was still lying spread out on the stairs, 'This is me then. Lying on my back with my trousers at my ankles,' he said.

Magda scarcely looked at him, 'Always liked you best like that,' she said. 'Defenceless.' She stepped over him and through into the kitchen.

Jim rose, slowly heaved his trousers up as if they were extraordinarily heavy, and followed her. 'I don't know why men wear trousers,' he said. 'The only good part of any day is when you take them off.'

'Life isn't that bad,' Magda assured him crisply as she made coffee.

'Yes it is. It's worse.'

She was rumpled when she returned to her kitchen. Her skirt was tellingly wrinkled round her arse, and she hadn't buttoned herself up properly.

'Where have you been?' Edie wanted to know. Though she knew very well.

'Just out,' said Magda. 'I had to see Jim about something.'

Edie turned to Jessie and they both mouthed, oooooh, behind her back.

'I see you,' Magda grunted. 'I see you both.'

And out at the bar, Non-existent Dave yelled that there was no service here and what did a man have to do to get a drink?

'Oh piss off,' Magda called back. Damn staircase. She was going to have a hell of a bruise on her bum tomorrow, and as far as she was concerned it was all Dave's fault.

The frock hung on the back of the bedroom door. Mary hadn't faced the trauma of trying it on. As yet it was enough to look at it, to own it. Mary would lie in bed at night and admire it. Even in the dark she knew it was there. And was thrilled.

'That thing's been there weeks now,' John said, yanking at it. 'Are you going to wear it or what?'

'Mind your own business,' Mary said. 'And take yer grubby hands off my dress.'

John belched. That frock did terrible things to his digestive system. He went out to his car and drove to the cliff. He had to get away. His heart burned with badly digested food. He could still taste the hamburger and chips he'd had for lunch. It'd be with him for a couple of days yet. Why did he eat that stuff? Warm from the sun streaming through his windscreen, safely away from his wife's neurosis, he would sleep. Everyone in Mareth knew this was his habit, nobody disturbed him. Locals out taking the air or walking their dogs tiptoed by. Ssssh . . . John was sleeping. And he needed his sleep. They all knew why, Mary snored something awful. Had done ever since her menopause.

Back in her bedroom, Mary pulled the curtains and stood a moment in the soothing dark. Then she slipped out of her frilly blue afternoon blouse and dark brown skirt. In stockinged soles she padded through to the bathroom and washed. She put on fresh make-up, carefully lining her eyelids and taking off the excess lipstick on a bit of toilet paper. Back in her bedroom she took her Christmas bottle of Chanel from her underwear drawer and scented her wrists and behind her ears.

'Now. The dress,' she muttered, plucking up her courage. This was the moment. It had come.

Nervously she removed the dress from the green velvet hanger and laid it on the bed. She slid down the zip. Then at last she stepped into it and gently gently pulled it up. It fitted. It fitted perfectly. She smoothed her hands over her hips. Not a sag, not a bulge. Over the shoulders, perfect. Under the arms, perfect. She could hardly breathe for the pleasure of it. Tears misted her eyes. 'Oh my. Thank you, God.'

She walked stiffly across to the mirror and looked at herself. The dress was wonderful, she could see that. There was nothing wrong with the dress. Oh no. It was her that was wrong. Her face was old and wrinkled and had a slightly surprised look on it. How had that happened to it? Her face was letting the frock down.

Four Harrys lived in the yard at the back of the Ocean Café. There was Black Harry, White Harry, Orange Harry and Stripy Harry, assorted cats, assorted sexes all called Harry because one name was enough. Harry, Magda would call out the back door, and the cats would appear rushing through the dark. They were gourmet beasts, no tinned cat food for them. And though Magda had them all neutered so that they wouldn't stray, there was no chance any of them would move away. Life outside the Ocean Café was too sweet.

'Still,' Magda said. 'It'll stop them breeding. There's too much breeding going on around here anyway.' Harrys would drape themselves on her windowsill and Harrys would lie along the yard wall idly watching, waiting for tasty bits. They all knew better than to follow Magda home.

'You're not worming your way to my fireside,' she told them firmly as they lined up for their trout-in-red-wine leftovers.

Sleek and glossy, weaving through her legs, purring.

Recently, however, Black Harry had taken to sitting mournfully on Jessie's doorstep, yowling plaintively to be let in.

'He knows a sucker when he sees one,' Magda said. The betting in the café was three to one that the cat would be on Jessie's bed by the end of the week.

'Nuts.' Magda knew a sucker when she saw one, too. 'She's desperate for a cuddle, that one. She won't hold out past tomorrow.' She was right. Black Harry's desperate pleas were too much for Jessie to bear. She let him in. Magda pocketed her winnings, ten pounds.

'He'll see you all right,' Magda said, nodding at the cat. 'He'll help cure whatever it is that ails you that you're not telling anybody about.'

'What ails me?' Jessie looked at her.

'What ails you.' Magda gave her a serious bit of eye contact.

'What makes you think something ails me?' Jessie said slowly.

'When people are all you read, you read them very well,' Magda told her.

So Black Harry moved in, spent nights purring on Jessie's bed and days draped on the windowsill beside the geraniums.

Geraniums. Geraniums in the window by the sea, that's for me, Jessie thought. She had been passing Frankie's Ironmongery at the time. A shop that defied every modern sales technique. The window displays were so messy, ·they could have been a definitive piece of anti-design. There was a lavatory and three clay pots in one, and a scattering of ancient boxes of nails in the other. Locals knew that the windows had been like that for years and years. Occasionally tourists would stop and wonder. Did this mean something? Was this some kind of minimalist statement?

It was one of Mareth's long-standing rumours that Frankie was a millionaire. But Jessie doubted it. Though he did have a unique method of pricing his goods.

The clay pots reminded Jessie of trips to Provence and Italy. She would buy a couple and have them in the window overflowing with geraniums.

'I'll have a couple of clay pots,' she pointed to the leaning tower of various-sized pots precariously placed in the corner. Frankie moved stiffly over to it.

'Size?' he asked. The conversation here was minimalist also.

'Oh, medium.'

He moved stiffly back with two pots and charged her eight pounds.

'That's a terrible price for two pots,' Jessie complained.

Frankie readily agreed, 'It is that.'

The customer standing behind her joined in, 'I'll have a couple of them too, Frankie.'

'That'll be three pounds,' Frankie said.

Jessie was incensed. 'How come it's eight pounds for me and only three for him?'

The question seemed so absurd Frankie almost didn't answer. He leaned forward, pointed to the other customer. 'He's local,' he said.

'So am I,' Jessie told him.

'You live here?'

'Yes.'

'You're not just on holiday?'

'No.'

'Where do you live?'

'On the shore just above the Ocean Café.'

Frankie put his face close to hers, 'And are you renting or buying?'

'Renting.'

'And what are you going to be doing with the pots?'

'Planting geraniums,' Jessie replied, surprised that she was actually putting up with this.

Hmm, a scraping sound – Frankie rubbing his unshaven chin. 'All right. That'll be five pounds then.'

'That's still two pounds more than him.'

'Ah yes,' Frankie nodded. 'But I haven't known you all my life.'

Chapter Nine

'It's my face,' Mary whined, 'it's ruining my new dress.'

John didn't quite know what to say. 'Why don't you go down the pub?' he countered. 'It's been weeks since you went. A few drinks and a spot of Elvis'll fix you.'

'Don't be silly,' Mary cried. 'I can't afford any of that. I have to get my hair done. I have to buy new shoes. I have to get new face cream and pluck my eyebrows. And ... oh ... you don't know what a dress like that needs. I mean, even the bedroom looks drab with it hanging there. I was thinking we could get some new wallpaper at the weekend, and you ...'

She didn't need to finish. John sank into his chair and stared glumly down at the criss-cross pattern on his jersey. He felt his face crumple. His discontent and bewilderment showed constantly. He was lonely. A better man than me, he thought, would go through and cut that frock to shreds. A piece of clothing had got the better of him. A strident bit of cloth that glowed triumphantly at him as he lay in bed. Oh, he hated that dress.

Mareth youth was wild. Always had been. Shore boys and their cars along the harbour, screech of wheels, handbrake swiftly on and they would spin. Even in the direst weather they wore only T-shirts, Marlboro packs tucked into the sleeve. They leaned out of their car windows, banging the roof with the flat of their hands and yelling. Yeeha. Yeeha.

They were the yeeha generation. And their music would play. Howling through the night, thudding from deep inside their motors. In summer they took to the water. They skidded speed-boats round and round the bay, still hollering.

Granny Moran sometimes came slowly to the front of the building to watch them and shake her head, sadly. 'Too much wildness,' she'd say. 'They've got more life in them than they know what to do with. It's the fishing. They're brought up wild to go out to the fishing. But now it's all gone. They've nothing to do with their wildness.' And she'd shuffle back indoors.

There were casualties. Tom Bailey drank fifteen cans of Becks and a bottle of vodka and spun his car right off the harbour and drowned. Emily Brown got raped at a party. Woody at the Anchor and Crown refused to serve Little Weasel on account of he looked fourteen and had done since he turned twenty. Before that he looked twelve. Weasel, in a fury, had put on a balaclava and returned to the pub waving his father's gun. He'd shot the chandelier and his own left leg. 'Always hated that thing anyway,' said Woody, sweeping up the shattered glass. He claimed two thousand pounds damage from his insurance company and happily settled for eight hundred. It had only cost him a tenner in a car-boot sale.

Younger yeehas emptied half the contents from a two-litre coke bottle and refilled it with vodka or cider, sometimes vodka and cider. They would drink at the end of the harbour till reeling with alcohol and angst they would come yelling and vomiting back into the world where they'd unleash their yearn-ings and rage upon litter bins, parked cars and the bus shelter. And when Jessie passed, moving swiftly from the Ocean Café to her own front door they'd yell, 'Fancy shagging that?' Or, 'Great tits on that thing.' More like no tits on that thing, she thought. But she didn't know how to cope. Magda would get the better of them. They seemed like subterraneans lost in their own little world of hopelessness and anger.

'There's not many insurance men and accountants in the making yelling out there,' Magda said.

'They're so wild,' Jessie complained. 'So full of wildness.'

Magda nodded. 'Still,' she said. 'Best time for it. Get all the vomiting and howling over with when your digestive system is young enough to cope.'

Her own two older children, Janis and Joe, were among the shouters and vomiters.

'It's our own fault,' she told Jim. 'We shouldn't have given them these silly names. They went through their young childhood sounding like something from a sickly kiddie's television programme.'

'We had to give them something to rebel against,' Jim decided. 'They'll thank us for it yet.'

The naming of children was always a problem in Mareth. Jim came from a long succession of Jims. It was something of a scandal, though a small scandal by Mareth standards, that he'd broken the mould and called his own son Joe. But, as he said, 'How many Jims can you take?' His father had been Jim, his grandfather therefore had been Big Jim, making him Little Jim. When his own son was born he would have become plain Jim had he not been called Joe. In the complex system of Jims it seemed to Jim that if you were born plain Jim you were all right. But if you were born to be a Little Jim you remained a Little Jim all your days, no matter how big you actually grew.

And the Jim-ing of Mareth went further than that. There were more families of Jims than just the Horns. Jims became known for their jobs – Postie Jim – or nicknames – Haddock Jim – or after the boats they had sailed on – Bountiful Jim; and when they had sons there was Big Bountiful Jim and Little Bountiful Jim. It was an intricate business that was just the nature of things in Mareth. But Jim had had enough of it.

'This pecking order of Jims has to stop,' he decreed. The naming of Joe caused a storm in his family. His mother hadn't spoken to him for two years. Magda was the same. She came from a long line of Marys. Her mother had broken the line because her husband John was not Magda's real father.

Though she had never mentioned this to either Magda or John. Magda after Mary Magdalene seemed more than appropriate. And Magda didn't mind. In fact she often said, 'My name's the only thing I really like about me.'

Joe's break from tradition did nothing to stop the wildness though. He had done the full drunken thing: stolen a car, driven foot to the floor beyond its capabilities, crashed it out on the coast road and walked footsore and sorry for himself fourteen miles home, where Magda and Jim were sitting at the kitchen table waiting for him.

They knew all about it. The whole village knew all about it. But nobody called the police. They didn't use police in Mareth if they could help it. Best to sort out your troubles yourself.

'What did we do wrong, Magda?' Jim asked, running his fingers through his hair.

'Had children,' Magda said. 'It could've been worse. He could've taken up religion.'

In fact she found it easy to forgive Joe. He had her heart. And he had been so filled with guilt and shame he'd put his head in his hands and wept. 'Will you stop that?' Magda said, tears streaming down her face. Didn't matter what her child had done, she couldn't bear to see him hurting. 'How can I do dreadful things to you when you cry?' Which made him cry harder.

Joe sorted out, they now had Janis to keep them awake at nights. She had stopped eating. Daily, before her mother's eyes, she was getting thinner and thinner. Magda knew better than to nag, except nagging was what she was best at.

'Will you please eat. Just something. A tomato. Some melon. It doesn't have to be fattening. Just eat.'

Janis had stared at her palely and slowly put a sliver of melon into her mouth, and let it lie there. She would not chew. She glared at her mother with passionate defiance.

'God dammit child, will you eat? What's wrong with you?'

Janis spat out the melon. 'It's you. It's fucking you, you fat slag. I don't want to look like you.'

Shocked and deeply hurt, Magda put her hand to her face. 'Well, congratulations, Janis. At last we agree on something. I don't want to look like me either.'

Lying in bed Saturday morning, Jessie saw the seagulls come

yammering in. They swirled and jostled outside her window and she heard the loud splat, splat, splat as they shat all over her car. It was too much. Too much.

'That's it. Damn birds,' she swore and leapt from bed. Time to do something about this. She pulled on a T-shirt and a pair of knickers and swiftly ran out of her flat. She had to catch Granny Moran in the act of actually feeding the birds to get her to stop. Confrontation, that's what any decent therapist would tell her to do.

'Confrontation. Confrontation. Confrontation,' she muttered as she hurtled down the stairs to the main door. And there, just as she suspected, was Granny Moran in the tartan dressing gown spreading bread crusts, old sponge cake and bits of bacon for the birds. Sparrows hopped eagerly and seagulls swooped.

'I wish you wouldn't do that,' Jessie said shrilly.

'Do what?' Granny Moran sourly replied. She knew very well what Jessie was talking about.

'Feed the gulls. Look. They shit all over my car.'

The old lady looked over at Jessie's splattered car and sucked her gums the way she did, making time, gathering her thoughts. 'Have you ever thought that they just plain don't like your car?'

'No,' said Jessie. 'I'm not getting neurotic about this. They'd shit on any car. They don't just single out mine.'

'Are you sure about that? They don't like foreign motors. That's a fact.'

'They're seagulls, for Christ's sake. They can't tell where a car is manufactured.'

'But they weren't always seagulls,' Granny Moran looked at her and laughed. Didn't she know that? This strange city woman was a fool.

'Oh no.' Jessie's protest had been stopped in its tracks. 'What did they used to be before they were seagulls?'

'Well,' Granny Moran sniffed deeply. 'I don't know about your seagulls. But mine, the ones that fly over every morning, are all my friends and relatives come by to see me. The ones that've died, like.'

'Ah,' said Jessie.

'That'll be why they shit on your car. They don't know you. You're not kin. Your kin'll be back where you came from. City sparrows, chattering starlings and the like.'

You've certainly got the measure of my chums, Jessie thought.

'You're young, though,' Granny Moran patted her arm. 'You'll not know many dead folk.'

'Now you come to mention it,' Jessie shook her head. Though she knew one, and if he could be a bird – the purest bird – the whitest bird – her grief was almost bearable.

'There you go,' Granny Moran said almost cheerily. 'Nothing to fear about dying, though. Peace and freedom. First you become a bird. Flying round to see all your friends and family. See they're all right without you and letting them know you're fine, chirping a wee song for them.' She flapped her ancient arms and lifted herself on to her toes. She who longed to be up and away looked grimly down at her puffed, deformed arthritic feet swelling inside their grubby slippers. For a moment Jessie caught a glimpse of the woman who sixty years ago had driven men wild. 'Then when you've done with your goodbyes you're off to the other side where everyone who has gone before is waiting. Waiting and waving and calling your name. Ah yes,' she smiled, watery-eyed with longing, 'death's a fine thing. The time of your life.'

Then there was Annie, Magda's third child. She was a joy.

'That girl is no problem at all,' Magda said to Jim. 'She's a worry. And she's so clever. She speaks French and wins prizes at school. Where did she come from? Do you suppose they gave us the wrong baby? Look at Joe. If they had exams in training shoes and rap artists he'd get A's. And Rosie. Rosie's wild.'

It was true. Annie was popular at school with her friends and her teachers, a pleasure to teach, they said. Annie worked about the house. Helped Rosie with her homework. Annie smiled and joked a lot. Annie worried Magda to bits.

'It's not right. How can she be so constant? I actually like the child. But I don't understand her. I understand the others –

stealing cars, not wanting to look like your mother. That's all teenage stuff. But she's so calm. So nice. I tell you, Jim, no good'll come of it.'

The last customer had gone, Jessie and Magda sat at the bar drinking. Nirvana's slow angst howled from a car parked outside the café.

'Listen to that,' Magda said. 'Oh, don't you remember being like that? Raw and misunderstood. God. Sometimes I still feel like that. Don't you?'

'I was never like that. Looking back I realise I was the perfect daughter and perfect pupil. I spent my adolescence sitting in my bedroom studying.'

It was probably true. Whilst Magda had spent her late teenage out on the point, enthusiastically discovering sex, smoking dope in a fug of rock'n'roll, Jessie had been busy doing what she was told.

'Ha,' cried Magda. 'Don't boast to me. And don't go thinking you've escaped being raw and misunderstood. You don't have to be sixteen to be adolescent. It can strike at any time. It's one of life's recurrent phases.'

'You've seemed pretty mature to me,' Jessie swallowed some whisky.

'Oh, it'll be back. I'm not cured of teenage tantrums. I'm just in remission.'

'What are we going to do?'

Jim shook his head, 'There's nothing to do. It's over. They'll sell off my stuff. Pay some debts. That'll be that.' He put his face in his hands, rubbed the bridge of his nose with his fingertips. 'There you go.'

Magda stared at him. Hello, Jim. How are you feeling in there? Are you coping? He rarely showed emotions. She said nothing.

'It was just a knock-on sort of thing. This bastard owed me money and another bastard owed him and another bastard owed him and so on. And when one went, we all went.'

He had signed on today. Unemployed. He had sat for three hours in the Social Security office listening to piped music, surrounded by welfare families. Children had run around squealing, desperate mothers tried to control them vocally, yelling deranged orders, anything rather than actually get up out of the safety of the plastic seat and move centre stage to the middle of the waiting area. They felt vulnerable enough without doing anything that might get them noticed.

It was another world there. He'd hardly spoken since he got home. Magda dreaded this silence. He came and he went, he moved about the house and he said nothing. He sighed.

'Oh shut up,' Magda said.

'What d'you mean shut up? I didn't say anything.'

'You didn't have to. What you're not saying is enough.'

He rose, sighed again and left the room. Magda ran after him, beat his retreating back with her fists. 'Will you shut up being silent and say something?' And for the first time he did not knock her back, did not even grab hold of her arms and stop the blows. He stood, slightly bent. Taking it.

Magda stepped back. 'Oh don't be like that. Don't.' She ran from the house. Her children watched, shocked.

'What's going to happen?' Rosie asked. Janis bit her nails, didn't reply. Joe's mind temporarily flooded with horror stories to horrify her. He loved to watch her face fill with fear. They'll take the house and we'll have to live in a cardboard box at Shore's End. They'll sell off all your stuff, your Lego and Game Boy and send you to a children's home. But no. He said nothing.

Annie put her arm round her. 'Everything's going to be fine,' she said. 'You'll see.'

Magda, watching guiltily through the window, chastised herself. 'God,' she thought. 'My daughter's a nicer person than me.' She kicked the wall, hurt her toe and stumped off back to the café.

Chapter Ten

'So,' said Non-existent Dave, 'do I have to go through all the motions to get into your bed?'

Jessie almost said no. But that would mean he would get into her bed without going through any motions. And if she said yes, it would mean motions then bed.

'What do you mean motions?' she asked as she put a whisky before him.

'I mean a date. Dinner, stuff, whatever. Then bed.'

Jessie smiled. She wasn't going to get involved in this conversation. 'Only Black Harry gets into my bed.'

'A cat. Probably more reliable than me anyway.' He sipped his drink and smiled at her. He was going to have her.

Before coming to work, Jessie had phoned Alex and told him she wanted a divorce. 'And I want my share of the money you emptied out of our account.'

'Why. Can't you hack it as a waitress?'

'It's mine. I earned it. You have no right to it. You bastard.'

'You're getting coarse, Jessie. This is a side of you I never knew existed.'

'It's my adolescence. I'm having it late. Best time, you enjoy it more.' She heard his exasperation steaming down the line and laughed as she hung up.

Looking at Non-existent Dave, she let her new-found adolescence roll. He had all the qualifications to be on the receiving end of a teenage crush. He was intriguing and quite nice-looking. And, if she was going for full brainless superficiality – he wore the right sort of clothes: 501s, boots, a leather jacket and white shirt. He had what Magda's Janis would call a serious haircut. Cool was the word she would use if she were sixteen.

Somewhere in the depth of me a sixteen-year-old is wildly waving, trying to get out, she thought.

'Yes,' she said suddenly. 'You have to go through all the motions. Dinner, gifts, flowers whatever. Flash car if you can work it. All the motions you can think of, as many motions as you can get.'

'Then . . .' Dave raised his eyebrows – hopefully.

'Then nothing. I'm fickle and unreliable,' Jessie folded her arms.

'Come on, Jessie. Gimme something.'

'Then maybe. Maybe's it with me now.'

'Maybe's fine.'

Dave smiled. He could work on maybe. He rarely failed.

The bedroom had been redone. Mary tried to make it look like the shop. 'The dress'll feel at home,' she said.

'It's a dress,' John told her, no emotion in his voice. None left. 'It doesn't notice where it is.' He was deeply perturbed. This dress was more than a dress. It was the enemy. It brought discontent. His wife was no longer happy with the life they had, the life they worked for – she wanted more. She was abandoning her very roots looking for a life she couldn't have.

Still they redecorated. Deep green walls, pale gold woodwork. Suddenly the bed seemed inadequate, then the wardrobe and the dressing table. Mary replaced them both, along with the bedcovers and the curtains. At last she felt the dress had a proper setting. Now it needed a worthy owner.

'I'll need to get my hair done,' she said. 'Something special.' She patted her chest. This frock was giving her indigestion too.

'We can't afford it,' John said. 'And if you do get your hair done. Then what? When are you going to put the damn thing on? And where can we go? We've no money left.'

Annie discovered the letters. They lay wedged and crumpled

at the bottom of Rosie's schoolbag, along with a collection of chewed crayons, pencils, a ruler, half a cheese sandwich, banana skins, an apple core, empty crisp bags and sweet wrappers. Annie's face distorted in horror each time she dipped her hand into the bag. What was it going to bring out next? The letters.

She smoothed them out, decrumbed them, and through the stains of melted chocolate and coke, read. Deeply concerned about Rosie. Behavioural problems. Unable to cope with the set work. Worryingly behind. Disruptive in class. She showed them to Jim.

'Have you ever seen the like?' he said. 'Some of these are months old. Who does little Rosie remind you of?'

Annie nodded.

'Does the world need two Magdas?' Jim asked.

Annie shook her head.

Still, next day it was Magda who went to see Rosie's teacher, though the very smell of school still filled her heart with horror and fear.

When Jim told her about the letters she had summoned little Rosie to the kitchen to explain. 'Why didn't you show them to us?' she asked.

Rosie shrugged, 'Dunno.'

'Dunno,' Magda chastised. 'Dunno. Where would children be without dunno?'

'Dunno,' Rosie said. Magda glared at her.

'Also,' Rosie squeakily complained. 'I have the Lego scheme to work on. It takes me all my time.'

'The Lego scheme?' Magda asked. 'Is this something you're doing at school.'

'Yes. See,' Rosie folded her little arms and explained. 'Every time you do something good with the Lego, Miss Frazer puts it in the cupboard. So . . .' Her eyes brightened. Plainly the Lego scheme was filling her with enthusiasm. 'I'm really good at Lego and every time I make something it gets into the cupboard. Well if everything I make gets put in the cupboard, there'll be none left. It'll be the end of the damn Lego. And if we don't have the Lego there'll be nothing to do at the end of the day and we'll get sent home and I can watch the afternoon soaps with Gran in her red dress.'

'No,' said Jim slowly. 'She's not like you. She's worse. She's got brains. That's a smart plan. Good on ya, Rosie.'

Joe sneered, 'God, you're thick, Rosie. They'll just buy more Lego. Or else they'll take everything apart and you'll have to build it all up again.'

'Your Grandma sits in her living room watching soaps in that bloody red dress?' Magda found the news hard to bear. 'That's so sad.'

'But,' Rosie was devastated, 'if they buy more Lego, it'll take for ever to get it all in the cupboard and I'll never get to sit with Gran in her red dress. And I want to specially when they do up the living room so it's special just like a palace. The sort of place a red dress needs. I want to go there.'

'They just did up the bedroom,' Magda said. 'What do they want to go doing their living room? God I hate that red dress.'

'It's lovely,' Rosie protested. 'It's beautiful. Gran is saving it for good. When good comes she'll have something to wear.'

'How do you know good when it comes?' asked Jim.

'You just know it,' Rosie overflowed enthusiastic naïveté. 'Everything is shiny and you put your red dress on.'

Magda was playing her old Blondie records full blast. She was trying hard to blot out her thoughts. Life was closing in on her. A terrible silence was hemming her in and she didn't know what to do about it. Jim rarely spoke and her children had long-since disappeared to some private place in their heads. The Ocean Café did not bring in nearly enough money to support them all. In fact if it wasn't for Edie she doubted the café would make any profit at all. Edie saw to it that Magda kept her flamboyant cooking methods under control. Edie did all of the buying and all of the pricing. Edie knew what was in the freezer and what was in the cellar.

Magda confronted herself with a set of what-ifs? What if Jim couldn't get work? What if he lost his beloved *Sad-Eyed Lady* and never set sail in her? What if Rosie never learned to read and write and ended up like her? What if Edie died – the café would go down hill. No boatyard, no café – it would be the end of them all.

Magda didn't worry constructively. She presented herself with a series of potential dire events and let her feelings roll. Magda worried with her gut, nerves constantly shifting in her stomach. She bit her nails, clattered pots, threw ladles and lifters into the sink. She picked fights.

Edie knew to keep a low profile. She hid in the office, out of Magda's way.

Jessie still had things to learn about people who lacked the kiss on the cheek and how-are-you-darling veneer. 'I'm going out with Dave,' she said. 'I'm taking your advice. Doing the teenage thing. Listening to my instincts, going with my heart.' She was proud of herself.

'If you must,' growled Magda. 'If it works for you. It's not the bit most folks go by. The heart is the second most important organ.'

Jessie said that she wouldn't ask what the most important organ was, but presumed Magda didn't reckon the brain.

'Go with the groin, baby,' Magda started shaking her pan on the burner. 'This omelette pan isn't working. Someone's been using my omelette pan. Do you hear me, Edie, somebody's been touching my omelette pan. And when I find out who . . .' she banged and raged. 'I'll kill them. No I won't. No killing's for wimps. I'll cut off their most important organ.'

Magda in the schoolroom, Rosie's hand in hers. Schoolrooms still smelt of schoolrooms. After all those years seeking enlightenment in education, they hadn't sorted that out.

'Your daughter has learning difficulties,' Miss Frazer said, leafing glumly through Rosie's maths jotter.

'You don't have to tell me. I know all about it. She's dyslexic.'

'We haven't ascertained that as yet.'

Magda felt a sudden rush of childish defiance. She was a big girl now, she could be rude to teacher.

'Surely it crossed your mind that something of the sort must be wrong. She gets all her numbers the wrong way round for a start,' Magda said.

'It could be carelessness.'

'It could be. But it isn't. She's a bright wee thing. She deserves a chance. She should be seeing a specialist.' Magda didn't want to get angry. Getting angry didn't help. But the blood was starting to hurtle through her veins. She was clenching, unclenching her fist. It wasn't this teacher. It wasn't this school. It was her past visiting her. The misunderstanding she'd suffered, the bullying. She now knew it would always be there. She didn't want that for Rosie. She gripped Rosie's hand so tightly that she whined and tried to pull it free. 'Why haven't you arranged for her to see a specialist? Why didn't you phone when you got no reply to your letters?'

It hadn't been a good day for Miss Frazer. A child had been sick on the floor in the morning, another had taken the class scissors and cut off her best friend's hair – trouble brewing there. Someone else had lost her packed lunch and another had gone home in the wrong shoes. Miss Frazer was dreaming of a hot bath and a huge gin and tonic. Magda Horn was the last person in the world she wanted to see. But then, even on a good day, Magda Horn was the last person in the world she wanted to see.

'I want to know,' Magda's voice cut insistently through her end-of-the-day mental and emotional fuzz, 'why Rosie hasn't been sent to a specialist?'

This time Miss Frazer got the rush of childish defiance. 'I don't know,' she countered shrilly. 'She just hasn't. So sue me.'

'Sue you,' Magda fumed. 'Sue you! Who do you think I am? This is the lower classes you are dealing with, pal. You won't find yourself in a pleasant, sunny little courtroom with some LA lawyer looking after you. Oh no. We don't do nice things like sue. We put shit through your letterbox. We pour sand in your petrol tank. We're nasty.'

Rosie's teacher looked amazed. She knew teaching had been a mistake. She should have gone into computers. 'Are you threatening me?'

Magda sank awkwardly into one of the tiny kiddie's desks. 'No,' she said. 'No, I'm not. I'm just still shouting at the old bag that stood in front of me all those years ago, trying to teach me. I think I've been shouting at her all my life.'

The room was silent. The silence getting thicker all the time.

'See,' Rosie, too young to recognise the nuances of quiet, turned to her teacher. 'See, that's why I'm the way I am. My mother's really embarrassing.'

Chapter Eleven

Ginny Howard was the Mareth Improvement Group. She bustled daily up and down the narrow village wynds, thinking only of improving and maintaining Mareth. She moved, bent double, along the shore in the evening glow, moving between the trees as the dying sun spread light on the water and eiders gently cooed and warbled, a gentle gossipy call, scooping up rubbish. Tutting loudly about litter-bugs she would pick up empty crisp bags and chocolate wrappers and pop them into the plastic bag she carried everywhere, for proper disposal later.

It was Ginny Howard who had organised the planting of a thousand daffodils either side of the village. The Mareth Improvement Group had eagerly waited for the fabulous drift of yellow that spring would bring to its roadside. But the fabulous yellow had appeared not at the roadside but in most of the gardens. There had been a deal of midnight trowelling of bulbs.

'Well,' said Ruby at the Spar, arms crossed in indignation. 'Why should all the visitors get the good of the daffs? It's those that live here should get the pleasure of them.' This seemed very plausible. More midnight trowelling till all that was left of Ginny's Wordsworthian vision was a few scrawny blooms blowing feebly.

It was Ginny Howard who had organised the Mareth Outdoor Music Festival when Edith Howell the local music teacher had trundled her piano out on to the harbour that had for the occasion been garlanded with bunting. But the heavens had opened and the Steinway ruined. Edith had stoically tried to play some Schubert, her favourite. But really, above the wind and the rain, nobody could hear a thing. She was still trying to get the Improvements Group to stump up for the damage to the piano. Solicitors letters were being exchanged, but no money was forthcoming.

It was Ginny Howard who decided that Mareth could easily win the Prettiest Village competition, if only they had hanging baskets. She had organised baskets overflowing with geraniums, lobelia and nasturtiums to be placed strategically throughout the village, high on lampposts and shopfronts. 'Keep these plants safe from vandalistic hands,' she warned.

Her improvements group had been hugely excited by this. Until the watering detail came to be organised. Suddenly people had urgent things to do – such busy lives. Walter, a retired librarian, had obtained at a substantial discount, he told the group, a piece of rather special watering equipment. It was a tank that was strapped to the waterer's back. On one side of the tank was a hand pump, on the other a hose. By cranking the pump, the waterer could create enough pressure to send a formidable spray upwards through the hose.

'And thus,' said Walter, 'water the plants without actually having to carry ladder and watering can about the village.'

The group nodded approval, then spent time considering their shoes. Actual eye contact with Ginny somehow always ended in having to perform some vile chore. In public.

In the end, Ginny strapped the horrendously heavy tank on her own back and went lumbering through the village at dawn, looking like a Martian from a kitsch fifties B-movie. She set off at dawn because she didn't want anybody to see her. But of course they did. And they remarked upon it joyfully to her husband Jarvis, the local bank manager. There were no secrets in Mareth.

Feeling his standing in the community was at risk, Jarvis forbade Ginny to do any more watering. 'The plants can die,' he said. 'Stuff the Prettiest Village competition. You have become a laughing stock.' So Ginny caught Walter with some viciously piercing eye contact at the next Mareth Improvements Group meeting, and he found himself unwillingly appointed official waterer of the hanging baskets of Mareth. Ginny didn't think he was up to it, and spent mornings leaning out of her upstairs bedroom window with a pair of binoculars watching Walter's laboured progress through the streets with the tank of water on his back.

'Never thought water was so heavy,' he groaned, wheezing in dismay.

And Ginny, looming dangerously from her window, could be heard to cry, 'He's not doing it. He's missing the flowers. The spray is going right over the top of them on to the milk van. Good heavens, he's watering a cat on a windowsill now.' Hanging precariously from her window she yelled, 'Don't pump so much. Easy. It's an art.'

Recently Ginny had been composing a letter to the council pointing out that the harbour wall seemed to be constantly under repair. And why was that so? And was it some danger to the public? And if it was shouldn't they be told about it? But her concern about the harbour wall had been put on hold by the news sweeping through the village that Jim Horn's boatyard had gone into liquidation.

There could be a way here to get rid of that dreadful Ocean Café. She had to think about it carefully.

'Who owns the actual yard?' she asked her husband. 'Did Jim Horn lease it?' And more subtly she hoped, 'Does that Magda actually own the Ocean Café? Will she have to sell to pay Jim's debts?'

'Doubt it,' Jarvis said. 'She rents the place.'

Ginny said hmmm. Jarvis didn't want anything to happen to the café. He ate Magda's crêpes there most days. He was Mareth born and bred. The Ocean Café was part of his youth. He could remember being five years high, sitting on the dark red and chrome stools at the bar, little legs swinging. He had stared deep into the Alpine scene painted on the wall, imagining himself standing on the highest mountain top. He had stared so long, imagined so hard, he could smell the icy air. In his dream he spread his arms, stepped from the mountain top and flew into the deep deep blue, high above the peaks. He didn't want anything to happen to Magda's café. If it did he might even have to deal with Magda. And nothing, nobody terrified him more than Magda Horn. The woman had hairs on her armpits.

So, the living room wasn't up to snuff. John was past protesting. He mildly hoped that, if he complied, the strange malaise, the discontent would leave his wife and the old singalong lady would return.

They choose a red wallpaper with a gold fleur-de-lys pattern. 'Not the sort of thing you usually associate with small bungalow rooms,' the sales lady said breezily. The doors, skirting and ceiling were all white. The turquoise and pink swirling patterned carpet seemed suddenly inadequate. It was replaced and a leather chesterfield replaced the pink three-piece suite. Mary looked at it thoughtfully. Yes, she thought, the lady who sold her the frock wouldn't mind it here. It would do.

Mary had long stopped going to the pub. It was lonely, yes, and she missed her old pals. But singing in the pub wasn't on any more. It was cheap and she knew the lady who sold her the red dress was not the sort to drink half a dozen vodkas, link arms with her mates and sing 'Bye Bye Blackbird'. She had reached out to a new world with her red dress. It had no sequins, no frills, no buttons or buckles – none of the usual fripperies Mary demanded of party frocks. This was a dress for fierce social climbing. It would not take to Mary's old hearty round. Conga lines and karaoke were beneath it.

They had dipped deep into their savings to accommodate the frock into their household, but still John thought that if Mary wore it for at least one evening, she might get it out of her system.

'Why don't we book at the Captain's Table and have a really good night out? Dinner, wine, the works. You can wear your dress,' he said.

Mary nodded. 'Perhaps,' she said, knocking her chest with the side of her fist, wondering what the lady in the dress shop did for indigestion. She had considered phoning to ask but knew they'd think she was insane.

She was looking a bit better. Her hair was done and she was plastering her face with liposomes and vitamin E, hoping that a miracle might happen. 'Soon. We'll go soon.'

'When's soon?' John asked.

'Just soon,' Mary said. Soon was when the liposomes fulfilled the promise on the side of the little jar and some of her wrinkles smoothed out. She worried about actually wearing the dress on an outing. It would mean a trip in John's car. And could she be seen getting out of a ten-year-old rusting Ford with fluffy dice hanging in the back window? True, she conceded, the dice had come with the car and John just hadn't bothered to remove them. In fact they'd been a family joke. But still, fluffy dice and her in her red dress? She didn't know how to tell him. So she sat in her newly palatial living room with her red dress on, watching soaps.

'Why did you buy it?' Magda demanded when she came round to view the new living room.

Her mother had opened her arms, adoring the revered garment. 'All my life, all my bloody life I have never had what I wanted. Then I saw this. And I wanted it. I got it. And now it's mine. And now nothing can hurt me. I have this dress and I'm ready for anything.'

It wasn't easy stripping off. Jessie doubted her body. It had been over a year since she had let anyone see it. She had stretchmarks and her breasts sagged since her pregnancy. Back in her other world she had visited the gym twice a week. But here in Mareth she thought she had achieved a new understanding with her metabolism. She thought that the weight she put on eating Magda's cooking she took off again rushing around waiting tables. Recently, though, woefully considering her thighs, she'd come to the conclusion that Magda's cooking was making more inroads on her body than the rushing around serving tables could cope with.

Dave picked her up just after eleven when she finished work. The night was still and warm.

'I don't like the looks of this date,' Jessie complained. 'I wanted a posh dinner, wine. That sort of thing.'

'You're in Mareth and when in Mareth . . .' Dave said.

They drove along the coast beyond the village and turned down a rutted track leading to the sea and came out at Ardro Bay. Huge cliffs black in the night, white sand and a glassy sea. Jessie was stunned.

'This place is beautiful. I never knew it was here.'

'You have to be local,' Dave told her. They left the car and walked over the grass, rabbits scudding away as they passed. He carried a couple of Tupperware boxes.

'Is that dinner?' Jessie eyed it suspiciously. 'I was hoping for something grander.'

'Grander than what?'

'Grander than anything that can be carried in a plastic box.'

'Ah, the things that can go in a plastic box.'

He spread a rug on the sand. They sat together, leaning against a rock. The breeze softly hit her face. His presence almost overwhelmed her. She played with the neck of her T-shirt. She knew she had a nervous rash on her throat. 'This is where I used to come in my youth,' Dave told her. 'We all did. Magda too. Did our courting here.' He smiled to himself, remembering. Jessie slipped off her espadrilles and dug her toes in the sand. She started playing with it, lifting soft hand-fuls, watching it run through her fingers.

'We were a tortured lot, except Magda. We were going to change the world. We played guitars and wrote poetry. Crap. All crap. Only Magda got it right.'

'But she wouldn't have written poetry,' Jessie said.

'No. She just said her thoughts out loud and some of them were in verse. Nothing written down, ever.'

A boat chugged out to sea, masts lit; the sound of its engine echoed and reverberated round the bay. A seagull cried. Dave picked up a pebble and threw it into the sea. It hit the water with a hollow plop.

'We all went on to university. Magda stayed. We were all Bob Dylan or Jim Morrison or Joni Mitchell. Only Magda was Magda. She didn't know who else to be.' He sighed. 'God I envy that woman. Take off your clothes.'

'What?'

'We'll swim. Skinny dipping at Ardro Bay. I'm a boy again.'
Jessie pulled off her T-shirt. Felt vulnerable.

'What sort of thoughts in verse did Magda have?'

Dave stood up and undid his belt. 'We wrote all that jingle
jangle tumblin' twistin' leavin' in the mornin' farewell to the
man who stands alone on the hill stuff and congratulated each
other on how wonderful we were. Long-haired girls in flowy
dresses, skinny boys in blue jeans, all aching to escape. And
Magda'd come mincing by, the way she does in her tiny skirt,
wiggling her hips and laughing at us. Arty farty arses, she'd
say.'

Jessie took off her jeans. Sat in her knickers.

'Then she'd start. She did these absurd little verses to irritate us.'

He took off his jeans. No boxers, nothing. Jessie tried not to
stare. This was cool. She did this all the time. She was cool. No
she wasn't. The nervous rash on her throat was spreading.

'I bet,' Dave said, 'that every one of these people have forgotten the pretentious crap they wrote and I bet every single one
of them remembers Magda's poems.'

'Tell me then,' Jessie cried. 'I need to know. I need to know
everything about Magda.'

Dave put his arms round her. Strange, a new man. A person,
thought Jessie, gets too used to one lover. Different skin, a new
smell. A new routine. He ran his hands down her, slowly pulled
off her knickers.

'I'll tell you one of Magda's more memorable poems,' he
whispered. He put his hands on her bum. She shivered. A
poem by young Magda the rebel. Little boats out on the water,
late gulls calling and the sounds of the sea, the earth was about
to move.

> 'Tell me now, tell me now,
> What do you see
> When the Invisible Man goes for a pee?'

He laughed, 'Isn't that great? Doesn't it just slay you?'

Jessie was never so surprised. She laughed – but only at Dave laughing. Somehow she'd expected some rage, some emotional turbulence from somebody who had something to be angry about.

Dave couldn't stop smiling. 'I haven't thought about that for years. Did she up us all or what? She'd be down at the shore throwing off her clothes, yelling that stuff at us. Oh, she was always the best.'

'Tell me now. Tell me now. What do you see when the Invisible Man goes for a pee,' Jessie repeated it. And thought about it. And laughed. 'Were there any more?'

'Lots. Tell you later.'

They went together into the water. The cold hit their chests and the breath rushed from their lungs.

'It's all right once you get used to it. It's not that cold at all,' Dave gasped.

From the rocks jutting into the sea, a seal cried. A long low lonely howl drifted into the dark. A baby crying? Someone lost?

'Just a horny old seal,' said Dave. 'Oh God gimme some action. Howl howl. Got de blues.'

'It's beautiful,' said Jessie. A fulmar, always curious, came by swooping low. Who's this swimming in my sea? The chill eased. Jessie let go, sank into the water and moved with it. Let it wash over her, through her. She soaked her hair, and swam through the dark. The seal called again. They swam together. Said nothing. If she even mentioned how perfect this was she would spoil it. He did not touch her. They floated side by side, watching stars. He left her, ran back up over the sand and came back with his box.

'Food,' he said. He handed her a cheese sandwich.

'Is this it?' A hunk of cheese in huge slices of bread.

'Plain cheese, clean and strong. Not mascarpone with tomatoes or brie with bacon. Magda is spoiling you.'

Dave floated the picnic in a plastic box between them. Her fingers were wet and salty and nothing ever tasted so good.

'And now, this,' Dave said. From his second floating box he

brought out six more boxes, each fitting into the one before, and a dozen candles. 'You can only do this when the sea's like this, glassy calm and friendly.' One by one he lit the candles, melted the end, dripped wax to make a hot pool in one of the boxes and stood the candle in it. He floated the boxes, flickering light, dancing on the water, round them. Their circle of lights in the water. The horny old seal slid off his rock to swim by and watch. Huge gleamy head, silky eyes.

Dave opened a small round silver flask and handed it to Jessie. Whisky burned down her throat, she coughed and wiped her mouth with the back of her damp hand.

'Lagavulin. Your favourite.'

'How did you know?'

'I know.'

They paddled the water, handing the flask back and forward. And when he kissed her, whiskied lips on hers, it was almost too much to bear. She curled her legs round his waist and held on to him. Whisky. Cheese. Mouthfuls of sea. His hands moved down to her bum and he slid into her. They sank. Underwater kissing. On each other, in each other and still not close enough. Breathless they broke apart and struggled up to the surface. Rose foaming and gasping. They shook the water from their faces, pulled air into their bursting lungs and started over.

Afterwards, they sat together watching the night, saying nothing. He pulled the rug round them.

'Ah well,' Dave was miffed, 'I used to be able to do it in water. I must be getting old.'

Jessie, busy desanding herself, didn't answer.

'That's the problem with beach sex.' Dave lent a wiping hand. 'Bloody stuff gets everywhere.'

'Everywhere,' Jessie agreed.

'Everywhere,' Dave said softly. Turned her to him. Started over.

Magda had drowning times of the day. Times when she would be doing chores she had done a million times before, that had become automatic enough to no longer need any thought. It was then her mind would drift and her past would flash before her and she would look up suddenly, gasping for air and furious.

She would be stirring a béchamel gazing soulfully into the pot, waiting for the slow white mass to turn glossy and her reasoning and logic would wilt; she'd only have her memories and instincts. She'd be drowning in the béchamel. Why did she have a mother who dressed in a hideous gold shirt with shiny sequins in a butterfly pattern across the tits and who sang 'Jailhouse Rock' in the pub? And why was that mother now sitting in a depressed heap in the living room she considered to be palatial waiting for life to catch up with the absurd promise of a red dress?

Stirring furiously, Magda would look up, 'Bloody cow,' she would yell. 'Arse.' And she would throw her wooden spoon across the kitchen. If the fury was especially bad she would hurl her pot of sauce too. The far wall was pock-marked with Magda's drowning times. Environmental Health Visitors eyed it suspiciously, 'There may be germs.'

'Stuff germs,' Magda told them. 'My life's on that wall.'

Chapter Twelve

Granny Moran waved her ancient arm in the direction of the harbour.

'Used to be a forest of masts,' she said. 'A forest.'

Jessie said oh and did it? And sipped her tea.

'See now,' Granny went on. 'Only four boats. Five if you count Jim's *Sad-Eyed Lady*. But that'll never see the water now. Will it?'

Jessie sipped her tea. She was shagged out. Could hardly walk and still had sand where she didn't want sand to be. She shifted itchily.

'Y'can't sit still, can you?' Granny said. They were side by side on the doorstep. 'Of course in them days there were fish. Now look, the fish've gone. In them days a man was away at the fishing four maybe five days. They'd be home for the weekend. Now look, they've got to go further and further to find the fish. They're gone weeks at a time. It's not right. Look at them young ones . . .'

Jessie stared at her mildly.

'They're all noise and running around getting into trouble. That's 'cos the men are away. Then the young ones won't stay. They'll leave Mareth looking for work. The fish go then the folk go.' She sighed.

'I remember the herring used to come by. The sea turned silver. Silver. Used to be someone waiting out on the point there by Ardro Bay and when he saw them come he'd ride along the coast ringing a bell. And we all knew the herring were here. Course there were boats then. Proper fishing. That was over seventy years ago. I've seen the changes. That harbour was a forest of masts.'

'Was it?' said Jessie. 'Must've been a sight.'

'That it was. And I'll tell you people weren't the same. There was more caring. If a captain knew one of his crew was drinking all his money, he'd see the wife got the pay. Young Jim Horn, his dad was an awful man,' Granny Moran shook her head. 'Ooooh an awful man. Drinking! He could drink. Well, his mother used to send young Jim down to the harbour when the boats came in and Captain Bowman used to give him the money to take home. See you wouldn't get that now. It was different then. A forest of masts it was. There wasn't a family in Mareth didn't make a living from the boats. When the fishing prospered everyone prospered. And if it didn't, everybody felt it. Folks stuck together then. Freddie Kilpatrick has the garage now. But he used to do the engines. Wasn't a thing he didn't know about engines. Taught Jim Horn all he knows.'

'Yes,' said Jessie, discreetly slipping her hand down the back of her jeans to scratch and ease her sandy bits, Granny Moran put her liver-spotted hand on Jessie's knee.

'He's a fine boy, Jim Horn. A fine boy. Magda's fine too. A wee bit wild. But her heart's in the right place.'

Her heart is not the bit she's interested in, thought Jessie.

'Even if she can't do batter,' Granny Moran said.

'Batter?' said Jessie.

'Yes batter. She can't do batter. Oh, she can make them pancaky things, but she can't make a good battered fish like me. Like I used to make when I had the café.'

'You had the Ocean Café?'

'Oh yes,' said Granny Moran. 'Still do. It's mine. Just let Magda cook in it. She rents it. But she can't do batter.'

Well fancy that, thought Jessie. It took her mind off her sandy bits.

'When I had it, all folks wanted was fish and chips. Came for miles. Things were simple. But then I could do batter.'

'Right,' said Jessie. 'Batter matters.'

'Yes. Now I bought the café from an Italian couple. They had it first – did fish and chips like me. And it was them gave me the secret of batter. But I had to promise not to give it away. And I haven't. It's with me yet.'

Magda had pleaded for the secret of batter. But Granny Moran considered her promise to be sacred and wasn't letting go of it. Batter bothered Magda, but then she knew that most cooks were bedevilled by something. George at the Captain's Table for example couldn't do sponges. They never rose for him. And George told her that the chef who taught him couldn't do omelettes. Still she worked on her batter and her failures contributed many a mark on her drowning wall.

'Oh yes,' mused Granny Moran, 'in them days I just crossed the road and bought the fish straight from the boats. Filleted it and gutted it myself out the back and you never tasted better. Then – ' she drifted into her own musings – 'when the herring came they laid them out on the harbour wall and it turned silver. Silver with the scales. It was different then . . .' she waved her ancient arm towards the harbour. '. . . It was—'

'A forest of masts?' suggested Jessie, looking wistfully out at the horizon.

'Yes,' Granny looked at her in surprise. Now how did she know that?

Jim didn't know what to do. It's over, it's over, my life's over, over and over, the words spun through his head. It came out of nowhere and haunted him. When nobody was looking he shook his head wildly to get rid of it. But it kept coming back.

'It's over.'

At first he walked. He walked through Mareth round the harbour right out to the end to stare at the sea, watch seals passing. When he was done staring he walked back into the village along the shore out the other side past the new clifftop bungalows that only incomers were daft enough to buy – the gales hit them full-blast come winter – and for miles along the beach till he was exhausted. Striding, striding. It's over. It's over. It's over. He recognised a dementia creeping within him. He was facing emotional collapse. He stopped striding.

He stayed home and watched daytime television and only stopped when he caught himself and Lipless seriously discussing the sleazy ethics of the bitch in the afternoon soap who replaced her wheelchair-bound husband with a blond dude with perfect pecs. He might have cooked had not Magda's prowess overawed him. He read but he wasn't an indoors sort and headaches plagued him. He was alone, moving by day through a nervy nightmare and couldn't wait to get to bed at night to get away from it. He slept deeply, dreamlessly. But in the morning there it was again, the ache.

'It's over. It's over. My life is over.'

It was a slow time for rumours in Mareth. The new fancy waitress at the Ocean Café was seeing Non-existent Dave. But since, according to the rumour anyway, she was going to go away with him and become non-existent herself there wasn't a lot to gossip about. So for the moment people settled for the supermarket rumour. Jim's boatyard was to be bought by an international supermarket chain who were going to build a hypermarket. The hypermarket had started as a small supermarket but as the rumour spread the size and quality of the building had grown.

Frankie in his ironmonger's had welcomed the prospect at first. Then, upon reflection, gazing at his window display of lavatories and clay pots, thought not. He didn't think the sort of folks that would come flooding into Mareth to a hypermarket would be likely to come buying lavatories or clay pots. And furthermore he didn't want to sell any to them. He did not like dealing with strangers, not in droves anyway. One at a time was fine: you could look at them closely and make up a life for them, which helped you know if you liked them or not. Trouble with strangers – you just decided they might be an OK sort of person, someone to have a beer with at the Ocean Café – then you never saw them again. Strangers were queer folk.

Freddie Kilpatrick at the garage didn't see much profit coming his way either. Unless of course he could see his way to helping some of the incoming cars to break down in the huge car park they were going to be building. Or he could build a car wash for motorists to use on their way home. He could install new self-service petrol pumps, sell sweets and flowers and sandwiches. Get his wife to make them. Perhaps serve hot coffee and teas. Sell souvenirs of Mareth, little mugs and key rings with A Present from Mareth on them. He'd be rich. Holidays in Florida. He looked out at the rubble and bits of engine cluttering his forecourt. Plans, water rates, surveyors, then after everything was built he'd have to stay open till nine maybe ten at night to pay for it. He'd end up with a heart attack. He clutched his chest imagining the huge pain that would hit suddenly. He'd read about such things in his wife's *Woman's Own*. No. Better not bother.

Ruby at the Spar was incensed. What was wrong with your own local grocery shop? Service with a smile she yelled, thumping her fat fist on the counter. 'I even sell garlic and funny peppers for those that use them. Look,' she waved grandly at her shelves. 'Toilet rolls, light bulbs, frozen peas. There is nothing for sale at a hypermarket that you couldn't buy here.'

Jim meantime found Joe's old mountain bike abandoned and rusting in the back yard. He oiled it, tightened the chain, raised the saddle, pumped up the tyres and set off with no destination in mind. He just wanted to go. He cycled round the coast to Ardro Bay and stood for a while looking at the water, ripples. He tried not to think. Thinking did you no good at all. There was only the movement of water, the sun on his face and the shrill cry of summering terns. The air was warm, smelled salty, sea fresh. On a whim he took off his clothes and waded into the waves.

He moved strongly out to the far rocks. He'd been swimming these waters since he was a boy. A small wind ruffled the surface, cool on his face. The effort shortened his breath. To hell with it all, he thought. Moving further and further out. It got deeper, movement easier. He swam out of the bay. Away, away and away, he said, spitting out a mouthful of water.

He stopped, treading water, looked ahead. Eyes at surface level. There was only water ahead. Miles and miles of moving water. A gull circled above and he could die now. It would be all right. If he looked down he couldn't see his legs moving in the depth. He let go and sank. Soundless in the deep, shafts of light could hardly penetrate more than a couple of feet. He kicked and shot up, burst back into the world surging out of the water. The shore was miles away. Christ, I've swum further than I thought. He could see the bike lying and his clothes, two tiny misshapen heaps far far away, and in a mild panic started swimming back towards them.

Suddenly, sun on his face, sea on his skin, he was smiling. Songs from distant times in his life started humming, uninvited, through his head. Guitar riffs that played and sang through the days when he grew from boy to man. He remembered. He remembered the summer of his last year at school, his seventeenth summer. They had come here, a whole crowd of people, to skinny-dip and drink cider. They'd snuck off into the rocks and made love, first salty tasting sex and never to be so sweet again. They'd built huge bonfires and dreamed. They were going to leave Mareth and be great. Great musicians, great writers, great doctors. They were seventeen, mediocrity wasn't written into their plans. He had never wanted to leave. Even then he loved the place. It was comfortable, it fitted him. Now the great doctors and great musicians and great writers were drifting back. They were insurance men and they were salesmen and they were school teachers. They were all ordinary. When they looked at him he could see a certain envy behind the 'Great to see you again' greeting. You are the one who should be ordinary, they were thinking. What was that all about?

He remembered his mother and father. His father drank and his mother cleaned up after him. His father had not been a bawdy drunk. He drank and sang a little and apologised for being drunk and said he'd never drink again. Next day he would be drunk again and apologising again.

His mother would bundle him out, overly wrapped against the chill. He had waddled up the same wynd, little bear of the morning, to the same school his children now went to, and they sat in the same classrooms he had once sat in. But they were not sitting rigid with fear as he'd been. His teacher wielded his belt and called for the class to chant their times tables. Every single child in a sweat of fear and prickly heat from the layers of fierce clothing. Mistakes were beaten out of you, glories rewarded with a grunt. He remembered teachers incandescent with rage at the smallest misdemeanour. If they just spoke they were dragged to the front of the class and beaten.

'We were seven or eight years old,' Jim said out loud. 'We were tiny.'

What was that all about?

Now here he was. About to lose everything, when all he'd done was graft. What was that all about?

When he at last reached the shore he ran wildly through the surf waving his arms, yelling and screaming at the top of his voice. 'What was that all about. What was that all about...?'

Back home hours later, awakened muscles aching, he put the bike back in the yard and looked about. The children's old sandpit still there, neglected, weed-strewn after they'd grown and left it behind. The Horns' back yard was disgracefully cluttered: bits of things, toys, a rusting pair of shears, Magda's old washing machine that they'd been meaning to throw out for three years. There was a scrubby lawn, and blowing on the washing line the checked blue and white tablecloths from the Ocean Café, brought home and laundered every night. 'God we're messy,' he said out loud.

When Magda came home and asked him what he'd been doing all day he told her he'd been out in the yard and thought he might plant some potatoes.

It was ten o'clock on Saturday night. Shore boys were out in force. They sat in the bus shelter hollering. Their cries, a loud raw and primal noise, were incomprehensible. They passed cider around, threw the empty bottles at passing cars. They drank more and played a ghetto-blaster. Full volume, there was only noise, obliterating brain cells, obliterating thought. Songs about people being hung by their dicks and getting their arses sewn up seriously rapped out, ricocheted and boomed round the bay.

'That's not very nice,' Jessie said.

Magda looked weary, 'There you go with that N word again. Keep telling you no good comes of nice.'

'It seems to be some sort of sound trap.' Jessie pulled back the curtain to look out.

Magda nodded. 'Yes,' she said wistfully, 'good acoustics for when you're needing a sound track to your life. We used to do that. Same life. Different sound track.' She shoved aside the curtain to look out. A single shore boy had broken away from the pack and was leaping ritually on a car roof. 'But we didn't do that.'

She banged on the window, 'Cut that out,' she yelled. Shore boys didn't scare her. She knew all their mothers and their grandmothers. She lost enough money through her own rage and swearing and didn't intend to lose more through young bloods leaping on her customers' cars. She stepped out of the café, stood at the door, 'Bugger off the lot of you,' she shouted, waving them off with a sweep of her arm. They laughed at her. She steamed over to them, grabbed the car roof trampoliner by the arm, then by the collar of his Adidas sweatshirt.

'I said bugger off you little arsehole. One swift movement of my knee and I'll render you a virgin for ever, you little shit.'

Windows flew up, Shore residents hung out, bawling encouragement. 'Tell him, Magda.' 'Nut him for me, Magda.' A car moved slowly by. Inside, sitting removed from reality on velour seats, Kiri Te Kanawa soaring on the in-car CD obliterating all street sounds, Ginny and Jarvis Howard watched. 'That Magda Horn is so gross,' Ginny shuddered, but could not stop watching. Inside Kiri sang. Outside Magda raged in what seemed like silence.

The boy sniggered. They all sniggered. There was something. A movement of the eyes, a leaning of skinny teenage bodies towards the men's lavatory on the quay. Magda shoved her captive away. Without thinking she shouldn't she stormed through the door marked Gents. Inside was covered with graffiti. She recognised one word – Janis. She didn't have to be able to read, the walls spoke. They spoke dirty. She returned to the café.

'Jessie, come with me. Come see this.'

Jessie followed her. 'I can't go in here. It's the men's loo.'

'Just come,' Magda said. 'You have to read this and tell me. I need to know . . .' Jessie followed her in.

Janis is a hole, was sprayed large and red over one wall. The place smelled foul. Water ran, a tank gurgled. Janis is a great fuck was sprawled on another wall. She turned. I've shagged Janis Horn written hugely on the wall opposite the Janis is a hole wall. Underneath the shagging boast someone else had written so have I and another had added me too. And someone else asked, who hasn't?

'I don't think you need to tell me,' Magda said. 'I may be stupid but I'm not that stupid. I know these words. You don't have to be able to read to know these words.'

Jessie apologetically read the walls out loud. Magda felt sick. Her knees were weak. She could hardly breathe. Her hand flew to her mouth. 'Oh, Janis,' then, covering her face with her hands, shook her head. 'Oh no, Janis.'

Slowly they went outside. Shore boys scattered, laughing. Magda stood, arms by her side, breathing deeply. 'I need to go home,' she said.

Janis was slumped on the sofa watching a video, cars over-turned in flames, guns roared and beefy men shouted mutha-fucka. Magda stormed over to her and slapped her hard. Her head reeled. It was a vicious blow. She gasped. 'What was that for?' she cried. Her hand flew to the battered, swiftly reddening cheek.

'You know,' Magda shouted. 'You know damn fine what it's for.'

'No I don't,' Janis shouted back.

Magda put her face close to her daughter's. 'Yes you do,' she hissed. 'You can't hide it from me. I know everything. I've seen it.'

Janis went quiet.

'You slut,' Magda yelled. 'You slut.'

Janis sulked, 'If I am I got it from you.'

Magda lifted her hand again. Janis didn't flinch, stared defiantly at her mother, 'Didn't I?' she said.

Magda lowered her hand. Her rage had lost its edge.

'What have you seen?' Jim wanted to know.

'The filth written about this one in the men's on the shore.'

Janis winced.

'Janis Horn's a great shag. I've shagged Janis. Janis is a hole.'
Magda threw up her arms in despair. Janis flushed scarlet.

'For Christ's sake, girl, what have you been up to? You know
what people are like round here. You'll be a slag for ever.'

Janis no longer met her gaze.

'You can't go by what you read on toilet walls,' Jim protested.

Magda rounded on him. 'Oh yes you can. It's the truth isn't
it? You've been shagging all these blokes, haven't you?'

Janis shrugged and nodded.

'See,' said Magda. 'I knew it. People write the truth on toilet
walls. If you're ever going to write any sort of truth, where else
are you going to write it?'

Chapter Thirteen

It was inevitable that Jessie's old friends would seek her out. It seemed to Magda that they came in batches. They did not venture to places as far flung as Mareth alone. They needed support. But curiosity gripped them. They were compelled to see where Jessie was living and find out why she had abandoned them.

Trish and Lou arrived in Lou's Beetle convertible. They slammed the car doors and gazed about them, blinking. Such light, such space – hard to deal with. Staring out to sea they could almost feel their pupils shrink, coping with the dazzle. So this was the place. It was stark and simple, a row of houses facing the sea, a café, and they led such complex lives. Mystified, they looked around.

'What do people do here?' Trish said to Lou. They shook their heads, mutually baffled. Tentatively they climbed the stairs to Jessie's flat and knocked at the door. She let them in. She wasn't sure if she wanted them here. Her old life would not easily overlap and blend in with her new one. She didn't like her flat when she saw it through their eyes and shrank from their unspoken criticism. Plainly they were working hard at not commenting on the smell – unwashed agoraphobics – gosh, she'd forgotten about that. She'd got used to it.

'Oh yes,' Trish said. There was a long silence and she raked through her mind for something reasonable to say. At last she came up with, 'Cosy.' Jessie knew they would talk about her when they went away. She tortured herself imagining what they'd say. She opened a bottle of Australian Chardonnay. Lou was surprised that you got such a thing here.

'What did you expect, Newcastle Brown and Irn Bru?' Jessie snapped. 'Actually, Magda has quite a good cellar.'

'Ah, Magda,' Trish smiled secretively. She'd heard from Alex about Magda, was planning to meet her, to look her over and report back. Jessie knew that when she left the room to fetch glasses from the kitchen they'd exchange looks, mouth surprise. She hated that. They'd be raising their eyebrows at her sideboard, hideously large, darkly wooden, filling the room. And her carpet, Jessie grinned. Yes her carpet was truly loathsome. You could work up a lather hating it. She'd come to terms with it months ago, in fact was developing a fondness for it.

'So you're working as a waitress?' Trish asked as Jessie came back into the room. There was a stiffness in her tone. They were concerned for Jessie and the turn she'd let her life take. It seemed to them that Jessie hadn't forsaken her old life, she had forsaken them, their friendship. Jessie nodded.

'Why on earth?' Trish wanted to know.

'Need the money,' Jessie said. 'And there's not a lot of call for book editors round here.'

'I could believe it,' Trish agreed. 'You could of course go back to your old job.' She crossed the room and kissed Jessie on the cheek the way she would have if they were meeting in some city bar. She'd been so surprised at the flat she'd forgotten to do it when she arrived.

'We miss you, Jessie. When you left we phoned and phoned. But you didn't answer. Where were you?'

Jessie sat down, stuck her hands in her pockets, leaned back. 'Somewhere inside my head or striding maniacally round the harbour,' she said. 'I can't come back yet. Can't face it? Need a change? Too far to travel from here? Pick your answer. Actually I quite enjoy waiting on tables. There's something totally physical about it. And mindless. There's a freedom . . .' She drifted off, explaining her decision more to herself then either of her friends. 'But why travel? Why live here anyway? I mean, what do people do here?' Lou needed to know.

'They eat. They watch television. They drink. They think

about things. They chat. Mostly I suspect they gossip and ...
what do people do anywhere?' Jessie asked.

'Well darling,' Trish smiled. 'If you don't know ...'

'They have relationships,' Lou interrupted.

'Oh that,' Jessie curled her lip. 'Been there. Done that. Read
the book. Saw the film. Didn't buy the T-shirt. Got pregnant. It
didn't fit.' She pulled up her knees, heaved her sweater over
them and stared morosely ahead.

She had thought she was over it. It was weeks since she had
been swamped with sudden rage, or found herself motionless
in a torpor of overwhelming sadness. She thought her grieving
was over. She no longer mourned the child she knew so well
and hadn't got to meet. She now realised that she would never
stop grieving. Maybe it wouldn't hurt so much.

'Oh bugger it all,' she said. 'Bugger everything.'

'Alex is well,' Trish said, pointedly refilling her glass.

'Oh him,' Jessie sneered.

'You know, of course, that he's seeing somebody?' Lou said.
Jessie nodded.

'She's a lot like you,' Lou went on.

Jessie nodded again. 'That figures. Every shirt Alex buys is
blue. Every pair of shoes is brown. Every suit is charcoal grey.
He had a rackful of polka-dot ties. If this woman looks like
Jessie, you can bet the woman before me looked like Jessie too.'

Lou considered this a moment and considered Jessie a
moment. Was she up to any sort of banter? Then she said, 'You
probably all look like his mother.'

Jessie grinned widely then pulled the neck of her sweater
over her head, hiding herself, the shame and disgrace of being
a nice, respectable person in a torridly self-seeking world.

'Oh God,' muffled cry. 'I do believe you're right.'

'Yes,' Trish joined in. 'Every time we went out you always
complained that men thought you were nice.'

Jessie grinned, remembering nights they'd had, bars they
haunted, conversations and confessions. She thought they
mattered more to each other than their husbands or lovers did.
They worked up huge phone bills swapping tales. Even when

there was nothing to say they could talk for hours. Every upset, every embarrassing moment was drawn out and discussed. Jessie sometimes thought that she lived her life not for the moment but for the pleasure of talking about the moment afterwards with her friends. She missed them, and she forgave them in advance for the horrible things they would say later about the sideboard and carpet that were, after all, not her fault.

'You were always complaining you were a failed hussy. All the men you ever met wanted to take you home to meet their mother,' Trish said.

'And they always liked you,' Lou grinned.

'True. True,' Jessie smiled amiably. 'But now I'm working on it. I'm working at being a cow. It's hard, but someone's got to do it.'

Jessie took them downstairs to the Ocean Café. They stared in disbelief at Magda. Trish smiled triumphantly and remarked that she thought people stopped looking like that in 1966. 'Before I was born,' she added, smirking even more triumphantly. She lit a Marlboro and watched the door Magda had disappeared through. Magda served them monkfish with olives, tomatoes, and a side dish of spaghetti with courgettes. Afterwards she brought them strawberries with a jug of ice-cold vanilla cream. She would have flavoured them with balsamic vinegar, but had peered into Lou's car and seen the mess. Twix wrappers, Marlboro packs, a gin bottle, a chequebook, three coats and a jacket and umpteen folders heaped on the back seat. There was even a coffee cup on the floor by the driver's seat. Clear evidence of a ludicrous life. 'Coarse, bottom feeders,' she said to Granny Moran. 'Secret chocolate eaters, stress and not enough good sex.'

'Right enough,' the old lady agreed. 'A bit like yourself these days.' Magda said something like hymph and shrugged. But she refused Trish's money. 'Friends of Jessie's,' she said, 'and the eavesdropping was too good to charge you. All that relationship stuff. And speaking about other people's problems.'

'A glimpse of our busy city lives,' Trish patronised. Magda, who had heard the 1966 remark, waved her off. 'Oh, I think I know your life. Didn't it used to be a movie with Jacqueline Bisset?'

'Hardly,' Trish said. Lou watched. Watching was Lou's forte. She was a skinny skinny bottle blonde with a serious Marlboro habit. She looked out of place on her brief self-conscious walk through Mareth, from car to Jessie's door. But then she looked out of place anywhere but in a darkened bar, drink in hand. She didn't engage in conversation much, spent her socialising time looking round making sure there was nobody skinnier, more weirdly dressed than her. She was expert at the city bar game of dismissive glances and instant judgements. She could do little else.

They drove several miles in silence. Then Lou said to Trish, 'God that woman can cook. And in such a place. Waste really.'

And Trish replied, 'Jacqueline Bisset. Cheek. I'd have thought early Katharine Hepburn or Jeanne Moreau at least.'

It had been a while since the Horns had gone out as a family. But here they were in force, scrubbing the walls of the men's lavatory on the shore. Rosie stayed with Edie in the café.

'I don't want to answer any awkward questions,' Magda said.

Rosie, however, told Edie she knew what shagging was. 'I'm special,' she said. 'I've got a special teacher. And now I can read some bits of the magazines under Joe's bed.'

'I'll bet you can,' Edie said. 'You'll have to bring me one.'

Janis hung her head and muttered darkly to herself. She vowed to leave Mareth. When scrubbing with Vim and bleach didn't remove Janis's disgrace, Jim and Lipless started to paint over it, cursing about the match on television they were missing.

It was too humiliating for Janis. She took off, running out of the small utilitarian building fast as her Doc Martens could carry her, her crochet jacket flapping behind her. She was crying so much she could hardly see. There was a bus waiting at the stop. She jumped on it. She would leave Mareth now. She would never come back. Ever. She didn't care what happened to her, she just wanted away. She sat shivering on the back seat.

Mascara'd tears streaked her cheeks, her nose ran. She could hardly breathe.

Magda, stepping out for a minute, leaning on the wall, saw the bus leave, saw Janis cowering in the back, and opened her throat, 'STOP THAT BUS!' When the bus didn't stop, Magda took off after it, running full tilt along the road, ignoring cars coming towards her.

'Don't you think you can get away from me,' she bellowed. The bus gathered speed. And so did Magda.

Lipless and Jim came out to watch, paintbrushes dripping. Jessie stepped out of the café and Granny Moran leaned out of her window.

Magda caught up with the bus and began to batter on the back with her fists. 'Stop this bus.' It lumbered slowly on, ignoring her. Magda at full steam, ran alongside banging furiously on it. 'You are not going to run away. You are not.' Janis sunk low in her seat, sniffing and choking, wiping her nose with the back of her hand. Oh please let this not be happening. Oh please bus gather speed and leave this dreadful woman behind.

'GET OFF THIS BUS,' Magda screamed. 'Get off. I won't let you leave. There's too much to do.' The driver, at last realising something was happening, slowed down. Magda didn't. She carried on running beating the side as she went.

'What about me?' she yelled. 'What about me?'

The bus stopped. Janis emerged slowly, sheepishly, looking round, checking that none of her friends had been witness to this bizarre event. She walked up to her mother. 'What do you mean? What about you? This is about me, who cares about you?'

Magda stared hard at her daughter. 'I bloody care about me. And so do you.'

The pubs in Mareth rarely closed. They pulled the curtains so that no chink of light showed to any patrolling late-night lawman. By midnight the place looked lifeless, but behind closed doors the bars were lit and busy. It wasn't really that important to hide illicit drinking from the police. Off duty they joined the secret drinkers behind the curtains. But hiding the goings-on was a mark of respect; local police did not want to arrest people they'd gone to school with, and perhaps see them heavily fined. People had to live and let live.

Over the years Magda had curbed her drinking habits. 'There is a time in your life,' she said, 'when you realise that even though you're still young, your digestive system isn't. Know what I mean?' She slugged her vodka and coke thoughtfully. 'You're out late, drinking. And you get this slow shrivelling feeling in your stomach. It's like once you pass forty your digestive system becomes unionised. It demands regular hours, won't function before seven in the morning and after eight at night. "You can do what you like," it says. "But I'm knocking off. Drink what you want, eat what you will. But you're on your own, pal." '

Tonight Magda was on her own. Life was getting gruelling, something tangible to darkly whine about, and a huge amount of vodka might ease the ache. Edie and Lipless were drinking at the bar. Magda and Jessie sat at a table, a bottle between them. Magda poured.

'I used to drink whisky. But I thought I was going to die from it.' She raised her eyebrows. It was the nearest to shame she ever got. Considering drunken moments past she brushed some crumbs from her skirt stretched taut round her stomach bulges. Then played with the collar of her pink denim shirt unbuttoned to mid-cleavage, a little distracting fidget to take her mind off the atrocious moments that were flooding back to her. The sweat of her evening's cooking had left her with little make-up. There was no concealing the lines round her eyes, or the unkindnesses time and life had done to her skin.

'Malt. Drink it and it's like drinking silk. You don't get drunk, you slip into a world where you are invincible and understand everything. Know what I mean?'

Jessie looked at her. 'Why did you give it up if it's so wonderful?'

'Open pores. Foul breath. Decaying liver. Loss of brain cells.

Black holes in my memory. Waking up in the morning wondering how did I get here into this morning and knowing from the feeling in the back of my throat that I've been snoring loudly, mouth wide open, saliva dripping. Looking across the pillow, seeing someone sleeping beside me and thinking who the hell is that? Know what I mean?'

Jessie looked appalled. Couldn't hide it. Magda's heart swelled. There was nothing so gratifying as shocking someone, especially someone so extravagantly full of her own rightness as Jessie.

'No,' Magda continued. 'I don't expect you do know. Too much control.'

Jessie put her feet up on a chair and said that she didn't think she had too much control. And anyway what was wrong with control? 'I mean I try to plan my life to get the most out of it. Don't you?'

Magda spread her arms. 'I'd like to. But my planning usually comes to nothing. My life has to be elastic-sided to allow room for the unexpected.'

'Elastic-sided life,' Jessie said flatly.

'You know what I mean. When life smacks you in the face and your plans disintegrate . . .' She held out her hand, fingers spread open. Her planned life disintegrating through them.

Jessie sniffed.

'Things just happen,' Magda went on. 'Look at all these people here. Do you think they were planned? Most of them just happened. Right now Jessie Tate, in some council bedroom on some divan bed some teenage girl is getting screwed for the first time, looking up at the posters of her nonsensical heroes and thinking "is this what it's all about? – I don't reckon this much." And in nine months' time another little unplanned person will come into the world. Right now some old lady is lumping up some long road carrying a bag full of Safeway fast food and she's thinking, "How did this happen to me? This isn't what I wanted." Don't get me started. Planning, what good does planning do?'

'It's just after midnight, Magda,' Jessie scoffed. 'I don't think any old lady is lumping anywhere with a bag of fast food from Safeway.'

Magda refilled her glass. 'So c'mon. What just happened to you?'

'When my life stopped going as planned? I had a stillborn baby. I needed a little bit more than an elastic mentality to cope. I fell apart. Now, though, I wonder if it hadn't been that, would it have been something else? I was due to fall apart.'

'Me,' said Magda, 'I fall apart a little more every day.' She swigged her vodka, looking over the rim of her glass at Lipless and Edie. She could tell they were talking about her.

'She's getting worse,' Edie said.

'I've noticed,' said Lipless. They both whispered.

Magda poured another drink. She shut her eyes and let Aretha Franklin drift through her. If she got it right, every corner of her mind would be taken up with that voice and . . . And she would not worry about her mother hiding from the world in her newly palatial living room. Or her daughter who seemed to be screwing just about every male in Mareth. Though recently Janis had seemed to be returning to the world. Yesterday she had actually smiled and this morning . . .

'Janis ate a bit toast this morning,' Magda said suddenly. And Jessie nodded.

'Yes,' Magda nodded. 'With honey. I think she even kept it down.'

Jessie nodded again. And reached for the bottle. She was past feeling good. The room wasn't yet reeling, but she didn't trust her legs. 'Honey,' she said. 'Honey's good.'

Then there was Jim. Magda snorted, Jim. He had been seized by some sort of hyper-activity which unnerved her. He had planted their back yard with potatoes and other vegetables. Magda was sure it was too late in the year to get a crop and had told him so.

'Rubbish,' he sweepingly dismissed her. After the great planting he'd started on the house, polishing, scrubbing, wiping, cleaning out cupboards. It was hell. Magda no longer knew where anything was. Not that it mattered. She spent so little time at home anyway.

'There's not a lot of sex going on in this house these days,' she complained to him. Then, wondering where exactly Janis got up to whatever she was getting up to, 'At least if there is I'm not getting any of it.' Jim told her to bugger off and did she think he should paint the hallway white again or would she like a colour this time?

'Why are you painting when you could be in bed with me having sexual intercourse?' Magda wanted to know. 'Stuff painting.'

Jim burst out laughing. Formal language didn't suit Magda; when she said sexual intercourse it sounded like some polite afternoon activity to be accompanied with tea and scones. Magda was offended. After that they stopped speaking. After that they avoided eye contact. After that they moved aside when they met in the hall, in the living room, in bed no touching. No contact at all.

Magda was horny. Life without sex wasn't easy. The less sex she had the more she thought about sex. She shifted from foot to foot whilst she cooked, she crossed and uncrossed her legs when she sat. She sighed. She snorted. She snapped. When Jim had been away at the fishing before he opened the boatyard, she had relieved her ache. Men were easy. There was always one at the café interesting enough to take home. Only now her children were old enough to see what was going on. Besides, Jim was home all day. Damn the man, she muttered icily. And across the room they were still discussing her.

'Her omelette pan,' Edie raised her eyes. 'If I hear any more about that bloody omelette pan . . .' She didn't finish, couldn't conjure up anything dire enough.

'She hasn't thrown it, though?' Lipless asked.

'Oh no,' Edie shook her head. 'She loves that pan. Says she had it perfect and someone's been meddling.'

'God help whoever it is if she finds out . . .'

'She throws other things, though. And argue.' Edie leaned forward and dropped her voice even lower. She watched, checking Magda wasn't watching her. 'Argue. I've never seen her so bad. The other day we had this really loud bloke in. He was shouting, waving his arms about, annoying everybody. Proper prick. And Magda comes storming from the kitchen, tells him to shut up. And he says no. And she calls him a rude, stupid fart and he says, what did you say? And she says he's a stupid fart. And he says he's never been spoken to like that in his life. She says you mean nobody's ever told you what a stupid fart you are? And he says no. So she says well, ain't life full of surprises? Then he refused to pay his bill. And he'd had lobster.' Money mattered to Edie. Her father, a newsagent, had instilled sound business sense in her. She'd put money into Magda's business planning a twelve-year burst of hard graft then retirement. Fifteen years on, retirement was drifting further and further away.

Aretha sang. Magda thought about sex, imagined kissing, being kissed. She ripped open some faceless man's shirt, licked his chest. Slid her hands round his bum. His tongue moved in her mouth and his hand pushed up her pink shirt.

'Oh . . .' she said. Told herself to stop. In a minute she'd break up the little discussion between Lipless and Edie at the bar. She turned to Jessie who was lying back now, resting her glass on her forehead, singing softly, 'What was wrong with your baby anyway?' Magda asked. 'Why did it die?'

'Die?' said Jessie. 'Why?' She looked alarmed. Nobody had ever asked that. 'He just died,' she said sadly.

'Nothing just dies,' Magda disagreed. 'Everything dies of something. Flu, a broken heart . . . something.'

'It was his kidneys, they said. And there was something wrong with his heart and lungs,' she spoke flatly. For a second she was back in the ward with the doctor poised at the end of her bed, ready to waft off, white coat floating behind him. He spoke loudly. Everyone could hear what was wrong with her baby. Everybody knew it had died. Everybody knew she had failed.

'It would have been a sickly child,' Magda said.

'So the doctor said,' Jessie agreed.

'But it's your fault. The heart and lungs and that? You did it, somehow you did something wrong?' Magda smiled slightly. Jessie winced. How did she know that? She didn't reply. She could deal with everything except sympathy.

'Never mind,' she stared into the alcoholic distance. 'There's nothing wrong with death. Time of your life.' She flapped her arms. And flew. Lying in her chair, tears in her eyes.

'Guess who you've been talking to.' Magda gently patted her arm and got up to change the tape, leaving Jessie to rearrange her face and wipe her eyes. 'We'll have to get you a huge tartan dressing gown and a bag of bread to feed the gulls every morning.'

She put on 'Let It Bleed'. Started to sing along, swaying. Outside a boat chugged noisily into the harbour. Gulls cried. Fisherman shouted as they tied up at the quay. They floodlit the deck so that they could sort out the catch. Inside Magda sang along with Mick. Lipless and Edie watched her, silenced at last. Lipless swigged a bottle of Bud.

Magda loosened up more, spread her arms, writhed. 'Oh I used to love this. Things I've done to this. Ceilings in my life and this song playing.'

Lipless stared down into his beer, feigned disinterest. Magda shook her body at him. 'I love to dance. Don't you love to dance? I could boogie the night away. Couldn't you Jessie?'

Jessie struggled to sit upright. 'No. I'm past it. Too old to dance.'

'You're never that. Besides you're not old.'

'OK. I'm too middle-aged to dance. Too sad to dance.'

'You'll do fine, Jessie. Dance if you want to. Nobody's looking. Only them.' Magda nodded to Edie and Lipless. The music roared, tumbled frenetically. Lipless, on account of his missing lip, was having trouble drinking from the bottle. Lager dripped down his chin on to his sweatshirt.

'D'you miss kissing, then, Lipless?'

Lipless snorted. He wasn't admitting to missing anything. He watched Magda dance, hip-swaying round the room. She was alone, alone with the Stones and her memories. Her head was filled with the rattle of guitars and the howl of harmonicas. Nothing else.

'She's still got a great body,' Lipless said to Edie. And sighed. 'Indeed. Ah indeed. Pity she's such a cow.' He swigged more. Dribbled more. 'I mean I wouldn't have her for my woman. Actually I pity Jim.' Drunkenly he pointed his bottle at Magda. 'Great arse. But she speaks too much. Things she says. She's not very—'

Magda, still dancing, was listening eagerly. Vibrantly amused. 'I'm not very what?' she demanded. Lipless looked at his feet. Didn't answer.

'Well?' Magda wasn't letting go. 'What . . .?'

Lipless considered his drink.

'Oh you don't need to tell me,' Magda taunted. 'I know. Magda's not very nice. That's it, isn't it? You're right. I'm not nice. Nice! Nice! I'll never be nice. I refuse to be nice. Nice sucks.' She waggled her body at him. 'Where did nice ever get you? Answer me that.'

She picked up Lipless's leather jacket, ran to the door, and threw it furiously into the night.

'Get out. Both of you talking about me. Discussing me. Get out with your nice.'

Silently Edie picked up her jacket and handbag, and moved to the door. She needed air. Lipless followed.

'Away you go,' Magda screeched, standing in the open doorway. 'You bastard needing women to be nice. Nice!' She spat the word as if she hated having it in her mouth. 'Nice!' She heaved off her shirt, tossed it down. Then her bra. She threw it into the street after the jacket. Her tits tumbled out. 'Bugger nice.'

Enjoying her fury, Magda moved back into the room, danced round the tables. Cradling her breasts, she drifted off. She remembered skinny-dipping, oh summers ago, that feeling when the water smoothed over her, icy. Jim would pull her to him. Even now she could feel the hardness of him, muscles down his neck and back. Mouth so soft, touching him, kissing him, slowly biting his lower lip. She curled her legs round him.

It had been Jim, hadn't it? She stretched her hand out through her reverie to touch his face. Was it shaven or not? Not. She chose Jim for her bed and he made it into her fantasies too.

'Magda,' Jessie's scolding voice cut into her dream. 'That wasn't very . . .'

'Nice?' Magda pointed accusingly. 'You were going to say nice.'

'Yes I was,' Jessie admitted. 'But it wasn't, was it?'

'Well,' Magda was indignant. 'Fuck are they wanting folk to be nice to them? Whatever did they do to deserve that?'

She danced. Put her hand down between her legs, candidly confessed, 'I'm not nice. I'm a shit. I'm a bitch from hell. I refuse to be nice. Stuff nice.'

Turning to Jessie she stretched out her hands. 'C'mon, be nasty with me.'

John in his living room alone staring at the fireplace. He'd just noticed the quiet. How long had that been going on? Time was Mary would be in the kitchen raw-voiced and roaring out golden oldies from her rock'n'roll days, and from upstairs the thumping bass of Magda's records. Always voices, always noise and always movement, people coming and going, doors banging. It scared him this quiet.

He remembered Magda. Little wilful child in his life, where had she come from? Nobody in his family looked like that: wild hair, extravagant nature. The madam she'd been. He smiled. The tantrums she'd taken. Magda came to mind, six years old, returning from Sunday school, feeling the heat. As she walked she'd ripped off her clothes bit by bit, layer by layer till she arrived home naked, clothes strewn in a long trail behind her. She was seeking relief from more than the August sun. Religion, discipline, sitting in neat rows with other children, tight shoes – all that enraged and stifled her. John looked up suddenly. Magda had been an extraordinary child, full of mischief, full of life. Why hadn't he realised it at the time?

Mary worked hard, yelling at Magda, smacking her, locking her in her room, trying to turn her into something she wasn't.

Boring and safe. Like him. Mary had dragged Magda screaming and kicking to school, still the girl would lie in front of the gate, drumming her feet, howling. Then she'd tear off her clothes and throw them about the playground. Naked and screaming, young Magda had been willing to go to any length to escape the classroom.

All that time, through all the screaming and all the beatings he'd turned his back. Left the room. Gone to the pub. Driven out to the cliffs to sit in the car and stare at the sea. He'd done anything rather than join the confrontation. He told himself now that he should have spoken out, done something. 'Even though she wasn't mine.'

He knew that. Had always known that. Once he challenged Mary, 'That girl isn't mine, is she?'

'How could you say that to me?' Mary was shocked and hurt. 'How could you accuse me of such a thing?'

'Because it's true,' John said softly. And Mary said nothing. Walked from the room. What he should have said, he now realised, was that he didn't care. It didn't matter to him. He loved Magda more than anybody else in the world.

Magda missed Jim. Feeling he had let her down he removed himself from her. He'd turned into some stranger and she didn't know what to do to bring the man she knew he was back to her.

Jim knew Magda, every curve of her. He could tell just by touching, spreading his fingers on her shoulders, the mood she was in. Only he, in the quiet of their night-time bedroom, knew how to take Magda apart. When he loved her she would grip his back, dig her nails into his bum and swear and swoon. Oh you bastard, you bastard. Sometimes she would laugh with the joy of it. And sometimes, only sometimes, he could make her cry.

He would take her to him, and kiss her. He would run his hand over her thighs and slip them between her legs, two gentle fingers into the dark of her. Soothing her, touching her. Kissing her. And after she'd come, he'd kiss her longingly as he had done on the first night they'd met. It was the first time Magda had been kissed. Everything before that had been mindless necking.

Magda would put her head on his shoulder. 'Oh don't do that. I can't stand it. Don't be kind to me.'

She always found kindness unbearable. It made her weep. So, he'd kiss her again. Out on the bay a heron would call, a deep rasping cry. And in the deep of their house their babes would be sleeping.

That was the Jim Magda wanted to come back to her. She wanted to say, 'Be kind to me. I hate it when you're kind to me.'

Chapter Fourteen

Stepping into a Mareth morning was like stepping into a radio soap.

'Good morning, Lipless.'

'Morning, Granny M.'

'G'morning, Jarvis. Off to rob the bank. Ha. Ha. Ha.'

'Morning, Edie. No, I'm off to look at your overdraft. Ha. Ha. Ha.'

The soft rush of bicycle tyres on tarmac. Jim Horn pedalling by on his way to Ardro Bay for his swim. 'Morning, folks.'

'Morning, Jim.'

The click clicking of Magda's heels as she came along the quay, still trailing behind her a clutch of children to feed.

Jessie lay above it, listening. She knew everything now. The scream of gulls when Granny Moran scattered her crusts and bacon rinds. The council lorry rumbling to a halt, Lipless and his work gang tumbling out, then the clatter of their tools being tossed down to them. Walter lumbering by, bent double with his watering device on his back. The squeak of his pump, the hiss of spraying water.

Jessie lay above it, listening to it, head in the crook of Dave's tattooed arm, smoking a Marlboro. A dog barked. The postman called good morning to Magda and rattled the café's letterbox. 'A gas bill for you. And that looks like another steamer from the bank.'

Jessie lay with Dave, her body curved round his. 'Do you know any more of Magda's poems?'

'They weren't poems. They were childish chants against her

arty-farty peers. Considering that they're going for shocks, why do flashers bother with socks? That sort of thing. They were taunts aimed at us. She didn't mind us being pretentious and shutting her out, she minded us shoving her separateness in her face.'

Jessie wrestled with this vision of young Magda. She imagined her standing alone, never accepted and never seeking acceptance.

'Magda's Magda, just that.' Dave sighed. He was sick of Jessie's constant questions about her new heroine. 'She doesn't let anybody away with anything. That's why she likes you. She trusts you. She thinks you're nice.'

'Nice?' Jessie was horrified.

'Yes, Jessie. Face it, you're nice.' He took Jessie's cigarette and stubbed it out and pulled her on top of him.

'You like it best on top.'

'Absolutely.'

'Why?'

'I like to see what's going on.'

The eight o'clock bus rattled by. Dave moved into her. The milkman stopped his van at the door of the café and called out, asking how many pints today?

'Christ knows,' Magda answered. 'Ten? I'd ask Edie but I'm not speaking to her. She's been discussing me with Lipless.'

The bed creaked. Dave watched her face, did not touch her. Did not put his fingers on her nipples or on her bum, underneath it, centre of it. No. He watched as Jessie moved against him, and as she slipped off on her own, pursuing her moment.

The children in the café laughed and ate and threw bits of bacon sandwich at each other. They were not Magda's. They came because she offered food in the morning. She believed in breakfast. At first she offered cornflakes to kids who took to the streets early because their mothers worked at the canning factory or the fish shed. Then it was eggs and bacon, now favourite was scrambled eggs with ham, peppers, tomatoes and garlic: piperade, though none of them called it that. The multicoloured morning children sat round the table discussing soap plots, football, videos, and if oak-smoked bacon was tastier than old-fashioned thick cut and the fluffiness of the perfect omelette. Jessie breathed and whispered and moved. And lost control.

'Oh God.' And, 'Yes.' And, 'Touch me . . .' She beat him, little ineffectual fists flying.

The bed groaned and shuddered. It was not up to all this activity. Dave laughed at her, was tempted to leave her till she was screaming at him, swearing at him, letting go at last. But he put his arms round her and moved into her harder. Jessie cried out. Magda leaned against the café door drinking coffee.

'Grand day,' Lipless called.

'Grand indeed,' she agreed.

The bed moved into the wall. Banged and thumped against it. Bomp bomp bomp. Jessie howled and Dave laughed. Magda got a broom and banged its handle on the ceiling. Jessie heard it.

'There are children down here,' Magda called. Jessie knew the life's philosophy of such a woman could only be – if I'm not getting any, nobody gets any. She came. She came like she hadn't in years, let go and yelled. A cry from the deepest hollows of her. Just pleasure, just instinct. Felt that shudder move up through her entire body and oh she cried out more.

Later, when she went down to work, Dave, bare-chested, leaned out of the window watching her go. The crew on the quay clapped and cheered at her. Good one, Jessie. She blushed. Dave lit a cigarette and laughed. In Mareth everybody knew everything about everybody. Sometimes Jessie found that hard to cope with.

Thirty-four years ago when Edie McCormack was eight and standing in the school playground, her best friend Isobel Hargreaves turned to her and said, 'You know, Edie McCormack, if you don't mind my saying so, you'll never amount to anything in life. You're too quiet, my daddy says.'

It had been a turning point in the life of young Edie. Until that moment it had never occurred to her that she had to amount to anything. Her *Girls Bumper Book of Nature*, cuddly stuffed dog Willie, her wooden-handled skipping rope and her dreams of riding the range with Calamity Jane had been enough. She had thrown her skipping rope down, walked slowly to the bench inside the wooden shelter and sat, legs stretched straight out before her, staring, at her black lace-up school shoes. Life had never been the same again. She worried a great deal about amounting to something.

If she only knew what it was she should amount to. Her gym mistress had once solemnly told her that all girls should have a heroine, someone they could secretly look up to, someone they wanted to be like. For years, when finding herself embroiled in life's little situations – the first sweaty twelve-year-old hand to clumsily reach for her breast, the delicious illicit pleasure of it; coming to school with no PE kit; starting to menstruate; being caught smoking in the school lavatories – Edie had coped by sweeping her fine straight hair from her forehead, whispering to herself, thin lips moving as if in prayer, 'What would Doris Day do now?'

Then her father had bought the newsagent's business in Mareth and moved his family there. Then Edie had met Magda. One swift glimpse of the wild one moving through Mareth High tossing her hair, and Edie had abandoned Doris for ever. Here was a real heroine. The things she could learn from Magda. That night in front of the mirror she had held a tight fist in front of her and slowly she had let her middle finger stand up alone. 'Fuck off,' she said slowly, lovely lovely new word. 'Fuck,' jerking the defiant finger up and down. It was the first thing she'd learned from watching Magda from afar. Edie knew there would be more. Magda knew everything that school wouldn't teach her.

When the family sold up their business and moved on, Edie stayed in Mareth. She did the accounts and was receptionist at the Captain's Table. She watched Magda. There was not a day passed when she did not wish she had the courage to do the things Magda did, say the things Magda said.

In time Edie married. Her husband Fred had been killed in

a car crash. He'd been with another woman at the time. Edie bowed her head, the shame of it. But there had been a few thousand insurance money. For months Edie had considered her new bank account, weighing up her new situation. At last she'd worked up enough courage to go to Jim Horn and tell him that word in Mareth was Granny Moran was giving up the Ocean Café. If she leased it, could he get Magda to come cook?

Jim had stared at her. Magda in her own café? No way. But the proposition plagued him. If Magda was in Mareth and away from the Captain's Table, her secret sexual doings would be curtailed. He could keep an eye on her. He matched Edie's money, signed the lease with her and took out a loan to revamp the kitchen.

'Edie?' Magda said. 'Little wimpy Edie? Her?' She couldn't believe it. But her own café? It was more than she'd dared hope for. She couldn't help smiling. 'And it's still got the Alpine scene?'

'Oh yes,' Jim nodded. 'Would we dare get rid of that?'

So Magda took over the Ocean Café. First time she went there she stroked the bar and the tables and the chairs. 'Mine,' she said. 'All mine. Well, mine and Edie's and Jim's. But mostly mine.'

Now Edie knew that it wouldn't be Magda's for long. And Magda wasn't even speaking to her. Though of course that absurd hostility wouldn't last long. Magda's sulks never did. But now that Jim was bankrupt the bank was about to turn nasty. Edie could not meet the loan payments without Jim's help. It was likely the café would go bust too. She moved her thin and innocent lips as if in prayer. 'Now,' she whispered, 'what would Doris do about this?'

'So,' said Magda suddenly, 'how are things with Dave?'

As if she didn't know. But other people's sex lives were always interesting.

'Fine,' Jessie said. Silence, thinking about the fineness of it. Then, 'Yes fine. But we don't actually talk much. We do other things. But we don't talk. He isn't the sort you could confide in.'

'Confide.' Edie and Magda looked at each other, shared shock. Without any negotiations or retributions they were speaking again. Hallelujah.

'You can't confide in men,' said Magda. 'They're not for that.'

Jessie stopped laying the tables – blue and white check cloth, knives, forks, salt and pepper and daisies in blue jars – to think about this.

'What are they for then?' she wanted to know.

'Making babies,' Edie told her. 'And doing jobs that need going up a ladder.'

'Rubbish.' Such . . . such . . . She was stuck for a definition. Such sexism. Yes, that was it sexism.

'If you were honest with yourself,' Edie said, giving Jessie her best serious gaze, 'you'd admit men aren't for telling your troubles to. They're just not for that.'

Jessie shook her head in dismay. She wasn't admitting to this. Though a small voice somewhere in the back of her head reminded her that she thought men were for carrying heavy luggage and telling bad jokes to. However, she told them indignantly that what one should look for was a full relationship. When she, Lou and Trish had discussed the perfect man, they all agreed he'd be, 'A friend and a lover. He'd listen, and talk – discuss stuff. You'd be able to tell him your troubles.' She repeated the notion to Edie and Magda now.

'You can't tell men your troubles.' Magda hooted derision. Did this woman know nothing? 'You can't confide in them and you can't tell them your troubles. You tell your troubles to a woman. She'll listen and sympathise. She'll let you get it all out. If you tell a man he'll *do* something about them. Men are like that. They *deal* with situations. Women watch them marinate, wait whilst they stew. They keep an eye.'

Jessie shook her head. No, this wasn't right. 'You think men and women should lead separate lives, then?' Jessie asked.

'They do in Mareth,' Edie said. 'Here we have three sorts of human being: men, women and incomers.'

'Oh yes,' Magda nodded. 'Incomers can be men or women. Mind you, I like men. They're one of my favourite sorts of human being. I'd let my daughter marry one. But I wouldn't want to be one. A woman's the best thing in the world to be.'

On Thursdays Magda took her mother's shopping list to Ruby at the Spar. 'That's an awful lot of indigestion powder Mary's buying these days.' Ruby scanned the list critically. Magda agreed, and added that Mary had changed since her trip to London.

'Don't know what to do with her,' she worried. Lately Mary had sunk deeper into herself. She daily cleaned her bungalow, wiped the sink unit, dusted the mantelpiece, vacuumed the floor, made the bed. She did it all the way her mother had taught her years and years ago. Dust your surfaces before you do the floor, then vacuum up the fallen dirt. Carry clean cloths and polish with you. Put polish on with a circular movement, take off same way. Living room and laundry Mondays, bed-room and ironing Tuesdays, lavatory and change bed Wednesdays, kitchen Thursday. Friday would be hallway and shopping, but she didn't like going out these days. People looked at her. And recently she felt uncomfortable with that.

She drank tea. She watched soaps and went through to the bedroom to look at the red dress. It was still wonderful, but its presence hanging on the back of the door no longer thrilled her. She did not know where to go with it on. So she saved it for good. Good would come along one day, something really special and she'd be glad she'd waited. Sometimes, though, thinking about it, her heart hurt and she couldn't breathe. She'd sink on to the bed, banging her chest with her fist, cursing herself for eating too many digestive biscuits instead of proper food.

John came home from work every day at six-thirty and they'd have something hot properly at the table, not on their knees in front of the television which was how people who didn't know better ate. Poor things. John would clear the dishes and she'd wash up wearing pink rubber gloves to protect her hands.

Sometimes little Rosie would come by and they'd get the best china out and drink tea together. On Thursdays Magda

139

brought in the shopping. Usually she'd pop something special she'd made in the fridge, saying, 'Try this tonight.'

There'd be chicken cooked in red wine with tiny onions and mushrooms, or sea bass rubbed with sea salt and green peppercorns, olive oil and lemon, a grape tart shiny and perfect, gâteau plithviers – melty almond paste, noisettes of lamb in a redcurrant coulis.

'Noisettes,' Mary said to John across the table. 'What a funny word. Noisettes. Fancy our Magda knowing a word like that. Fancy her being able to cook a noisette.' Their Magda who lay naked and drumming her heels at the school gate. 'How did she learn that? Noisettes. Noisettes. Noisettes.'

She would run the word over her tongue, marvelling at the wonder of it. Oh life was lovely. Full and lovely, waiting for good.

'Ah, ladies,' said Jarvis, waving an arm towards Magda and Edie. 'Come in and sit down.'

The two stepped cautiously into his office and slowly and in unison lowered their bums on to the seats on the customer side of his desk. They were, Magda noticed, slightly lower than his. There was something horribly headmasterish about this. Magda refused to acknowledge the tremor in the pit of her stomach. This man was not going to frighten her.

'Well,' Jarvis smiled at them. 'I thought it time we had a chat. Um, certainly before things go too far.'

He played nervously with his pen, tapping it on his desk as he spoke. Jim Horn had taken out a substantial loan to refurbish the kitchen of the Ocean Café. There hadn't been a repayment in six months, more. Head office was badgering him for action. Some movement on the account. Ginny was more than hinting at him closing the café down. Why, for heaven's sake, did she so loathe the place? Maybe she knew she'd lost her husband to it. He was addicted to Magda's crêpes and to daydreams whilst gazing at the Alpine scene.

'Thing is,' Jarvis said, trying to bring to mind the tricks he'd learned on his customer relations course. Body language, eye contact, what was all that? Now, when he needed it, it seemed to have vanished from his brain. 'We have to have some movement on your account.'

'Seems to me,' Magda interrupted. 'That there is a lot of movement on it. All of it in your favour. I mean your interest charges...'

Jarvis had tried desperately to get hold of Jim Horn. He had written, phoned and even knocked on his door. But Jim had opted out of the world. He would not open letters or pick up the phone and whenever someone came to the door he hid.

'The Ocean Café's overdraft isn't all that healthy, I'll admit. But I'm prepared to let that go for the moment. No. It's the loan we're worried about.'

'Loan?' Magda knew nothing about a loan.

'Ah, yes,' said Edie quietly. 'Jim took out a loan to cover costs when we took over the café.'

'Loan?' said Magda again.

'Yes,' said Jarvis. 'I have actually tried to get in touch with Jim. But he seems to be constantly unavailable.'

'You can say that again,' Magda agreed heartily. She looked around. What a boring office. Polished wooden desk, phone, green carpet.

'You should get a few pictures up,' she waved at the walls, 'brighten up the place. A nice Alpine scene,' she grinned. She'd noticed.

Jarvis sucked in his breath. 'I don't know if you are aware, M... M...' did he call her Mrs Horn or Magda? He always avoided names when addressing her, 'Um. But Jim used your house as collateral.'

'So?' Magda took some gum from her pocket, unwrapped it and put it into her mouth. Edie watched in horror.

Jarvis tightened his lips. Nobody made him uncomfortable the way Magda did. Her presence on the other side of his desk irritated him greatly. There was something uncompromisingly female about her. She was all woman, and he didn't know how to handle her. Thus far in his life his dealings with women had been primal. Primal and nothing but. Women had bedded him, fed him, schooled him, scolded him, bathed him, tucked him up at night, kept him in his childhood place, spanked his bottom for being naughty. He couldn't cope with them.

Looking for some minor activity to distract him from the rage he felt gathering within him against this particular member of the female species, he raked about in his mouth with his tongue for bits of leftover lunch caught between his teeth. It didn't work. He grabbed a pencil and pointed it at Magda.

'We are going to have to see some sign of movement in your account,' he barked. 'You don't seem to understand. Unless we get, and get soon, some repayment on this loan, we could have your house.'

Edie reached over to pat Magda's arm. 'Please, Magda,' she was pleading for Magda to keep her mouth shut. But never in her life had Magda held her tongue. She was not about to start now. She looked at him coolly. How dare he try to scare her? Him with his suit and tie and manicured nails. And her with four children to clothe, feed and house. 'So who are you?' she said. 'The testosterone kid?'

Chapter Fifteen

There are pictures in Magda's head. They are of other people's lifestyles. They come from magazines. Houses, rooms with white carpets and long sofas, rooms with stripped pine floors and tumbling plants, women with perfect haircuts, wearing suits and high heels sitting in bars, climbing into cars. The pictures are of the life Magda imagines people live in the huge world beyond Mareth.

Sitting at her kitchen table three o'clock in the morning, drinking tea, she flicks through these pictures saying yeabut. 'Yeabut, I'll never see any of it.' It seems to Magda that nobody notices she rarely leaves Mareth. Where could she go? How would she get there? She had failed her driving test eight times. Each time with more bile and venom than the time before. She couldn't master the Highway Code. Rules of any kind mystify her.

With Jim's help she had memorised the registration number of every car in the street outside the testing office so that she would pass her eyesight test. Oh there was nothing wrong with Magda's eyes. She could see for miles and miles. She just made unexpected sense of what she saw. It made no difference, still she failed. This last time because she'd turned into the wrong street and when this was pointed out to her she'd done a U-turn and headed back the way she'd come.

'Why can't I do a U-turn?' she asked. 'What's wrong with that? I didn't hit anybody. There was nobody around.'

'It's against the rules,' the inspector told her. 'It's not part of the Highway Code.'

Back at the café she raged and stamped. 'God dammit. It was perfectly safe. Bloody man with his bloody rules. If a woman wrote the Highway Code it'd just be take care and don't bang into anything or run over any children. Everyone understands that. But men. Men have to have rules. Rule number so-and-so don't do a U-turn. And don't say nasty things to the test inspector and don't play any Rolling Stones tapes during the driving test. Keep a clean nose. Watch the plain clothes. You don't need a weatherman. To know which way the wind blows. Stuff it. Who wants to drive anyway?'

'Actually,' Jim carefully pointed out, 'that was written by a man. Um, Magda, you didn't play the Rolling Stones during your driving test, did you?'

'There's a problem with that?'

Jim shook his head. There was no arguing with Magda. Still, she'd failed and that was that. She was stuck. She could get the bus. But, what if she got on the wrong one? And besides, so profound was her dyslexia she couldn't read street names. She feared getting lost. Whilst taunting others about the tight control they kept on their lives, she hated losing the grip she kept on her own.

Lack of a licence did not totally stop Magda driving. She shot about Mareth in Jim's fifteen-year-old BMW collecting veg, delivering her mother's shopping, on the four days of the week the local police station was unmanned. The three days it was manned she walked. She was kept informed of unscheduled visits by the policemen who drank at the café after their shift was done.

'What's on the menu for lunch tomorrow?' one would ask, stretching. 'Might look in.' And Magda would know not to let them see her driving illicitly. They knew she did it of course. She knew they knew. They knew she knew they knew. It was a situation she was accustomed to, could deal with. Life went on.

At five, cursing and whining and saying yeabut, Magda returns to bed. She lies listening. Jim breathes noisily and outside the swallows are already swooping and crying. At six-thirty she wakes. Seven, she drags herself from bed. She showers. Clothes are never a problem. She always wears whatever is cleanest. She knows Jim is not sleeping. She knows he knows she knows. She lets him pretend and wakes her children. Seven-thirty she is on her way to the Ocean Café. The familiar click of her stilettos sounds up the empty street.

'Hey Magda,' the bin men call leaning from their lorry. They come every morning to the shore where they clean up the mess, the huge greasy spreading of carryout bags and wrappings stuffed into the litter bins by tourists during the day and dragged out by seagulls scavenging in the night. 'Who are you feeding today?'

'Who knows?' Magda calls. 'They all look the same to me.'

There are always children to feed. They appear, it seems, from nowhere, a small drift of hopeful hungrys. Sometimes her own join them, sometimes not. Schoolchildren get free breakfast at the Ocean Café, everybody knows that. Billy the egg man leaves extra most days, and the milk van puts free pints on the doorstep. After all, their own children have in their time eaten Magda's bacon sandwiches. In school it is obvious who has been to the café and who hasn't. Well-fed children do not wriggle and yawn and chatter in class. Well, not so much as hungry ones.

'Nobody ever learned anything on an empty belly,' Magda says as she moves through the kitchen, full bustle. 'And don't think any of you will get away with just eating. I'll be asking questions soon enough. I want to know how you're all doing.'

Lipless and his crew arrive as she opens up. 'Great day, Magda.'

'For some,' she shouts back.

In the back yard the Harrys sit patiently waiting for food. Now there are five; two more have turned up since Black Harry left the back yard for Jessie's bed. Ginger Harry and One-Eyed Harry. 'The hell have you been up to?' Magda asks One-Eyed Harry as she puts out the bowl of scraps: trout, salmon, lamb and chicken with wholemeal breadcrumbs and a side order of milk. 'Too much tom-catting around. What does it get you? One eye and a bashed ear. Now I've had your balls cut off. Life's a bitch.' The cat arches his back and purrs furiously.

Outside on the shore, the dustcart returns to empty the litter bins and reline them with black polythene bags. Magda hears the banter, the junk language. Then the shrill shriek of seagulls as Granny Moran shuffles across to the edge of the quay to spread, with aching, gnarled hand, crusts and other leftovers. The eight-twenty bus rumbles by, sleepy workers on their way to the fish sheds.

Magda pours coffee and takes it to the front door. She leans, clutching her cup, drinking slowly. Her stillness only shows on her morning face. As the day gathers steam, her rage takes over. This is the best time of the day. She has the world to herself – apart from Duncan the postie cycling by, and Lipless and his crew on the quay, and the ladies of the fish sheds knocking on the window of the bus, waving wildly. Everybody calls her name. But apart from all that she has the world to herself.

Nine o'clock, Edie arrives, breezing smally in. She hangs up her coat and bag through the back. In the office she phones the fish man, checking today's prices. Behind her Magda complains, 'Tell him I don't want any of that effing stringy monk. I want the good stuff, same as he sends to the Captain's Table. And,' raising her voice so that she can be heard over the phone, 'if that lemon sole was fresh yesterday, I'm a virgin.'

She returns to the kitchen. She has to make thirty little pots of chocolate for the lunchtime and dinner menus. And strawberries are past it, but the raspberries Edie bought yesterday were good. 'Get some for freezing,' she says. 'Rasps freeze. And when Jessie finally climbs out of her bed, tell her to go up to the house for the tablecloths. I forgot them.' Magda always forgets them. She bangs the ceiling with a broom. 'Get up. Are you out of bed? What are you doing up there?'

Edie pokes her head out of the office and tuts. 'Leave her alone.'

'Why should I?'

'You just don't want anybody to have fun, Magda Horn. If you're not getting any, nobody gets any.'

Magda goes grumpily to the kitchen. 'What'll it be?' she calls. 'The Stones. Great day for it.' She puts on 'Beggar's Banquet'.

Jumps around. Edie holds her head and disappears. How can someone play that stuff first thing in the morning? It's like eating chocolate first thing. Or drinking whisky first thing. But then, she has often seen Magda do both. Will she ever grow up?

Jessie passes the window. The men on the quay cheer and yell. 'Ho Jessie, how're you doin'? Who're you doin'? Come over here darlin' we've got something to show you. Ha. Ha. Ha.'

Dave hangs out of the window. 'Filthy bastards.'

Jessie does not come into the café. She's off to collect the tablecloths from Magda's house. Magda always forgets them.

She knocks gently on the back door. Jim is in the kitchen drinking coffee. He hands her a cup. He knew she was coming. Magda always forgets the tablecloths.

'Potatoes look good,' says Jessie, peering into the garden.

Jim nods. 'Yes. Good,' he agrees. Then, 'What do you think of the hall? It's a pale greeny colour.' Jessie follows him through.

'It's taupe,' she says.

'Taupe,' Jim looks baffled. 'What sort of a colour is that? I've never heard of it.'

Jessie shrugs. Jim complains, 'You turn your back for a minute and they invent a new colour. Taupe. Nobody ever mentioned it to me. There wasn't any taupe in my school paintbox.' He dips his brush and wildly starts on the wall, brushing away his indignation. Colour it taupe, which is no colour at all for indignation. Jessie takes the tablecloths and leaves.

By eleven the tables are set. Lipless and his crew come in for coffee. Magda refuses Lipless alcohol. 'You can have coffee and a croissant with bacon,' she says.

Lipless shifts bulkily from foot to foot. 'I hate fancy food. I just want a wee whisky with a wee pint of beer to follow. That's all.'

'You'll get some food before your liver goes the same way as your dick and stops working. Eat or I'll start talking about periods and my mother's hysterectomy.' Magda points firmly at the plate in front of Lipless. He eats. Across in the corner the first customers of the day, trippers in woolly jerseys and jeans with ironed seams look alarmed and ask Jessie for the bill. Edie comes out of the office. She has the menu which she writes every day in careful, perfect calligraphy. Thick strokes up, thin strokes down. Or is it the other way round? She doesn't know, she just does it.

Starters
Soup of the day: Lentil and tomato. Garlicky and good for you.
Mussels in curried cream sauce. Comforting if you're a wee bit glum.
Melon with Parma ham. Just plain tasty.
There's always melon for folks who find soup too heavy and don't like mussels.

Main course
[Edie always writes main course. Magda hates fancy names, like entrée.]
Roast monkfish in fresh tomato sauce. Lots of Vitamin C, chippers you up.
Smoked fish omelette. An Ocean Café regular, our golden oldie.
Noisettes of lamb in redcurrant coulis. Eat it and weep, white boy.
All served with today's selection of fresh veg, or salad. Or chips if you must.

Puddings
Little pot of chocolate. Thick and rich, clings to the throat all the way down.
Grape tart. Shiny grapes, cream sauce, sugar almond pastry. It's wicked, it isn't good for you – it's everything a pudding should be.
Melon stuffed with raspberries and kirsh. Fresh fruit, Vitamin C, again disguised by booze.
Coffee with mints.

Jessie looks at it.

'Isn't kirsch spelt wrong?' She no longer knows. She thinks recently her brain has been replaced with a small bit of chewed bubblegum.

Edie frowns. 'Kirsh,' she says. 'I always spelled it that way.'

'Ah,' says Jessie. Edie's writing is so positive, she makes spelling errors with such panache it's hard to spot them. 'I'm sure it's got a c in it.'

Edie stares hard at the menu. 'Do you know,' she admits at last. 'I do believe you're right.' She bustles back to the office. Reappears seconds later with the amended menu.

'Yes, definitely.' She is pleased. 'Thanks for that. I'd have looked so stupid.' She shows Jessie the new menu. Melon with raspberries and Ckirsh. Jessie stares at it. Doesn't dare mention the misplaced c.

'Great,' she hands it back, smiling. Edie puts on her coat and goes off to Neil and Young solicitor's where Shona, Pretty in Pink now into pale green, taupe?, will photocopy it. One copy for each table. Jessie serves an American tourist coffee and a chocolate croissant then goes to help Magda prepare the veg and salads.

Outside, Weasel the street-sweeper trundles his cart along the shore. He stops to pick up some crisp bags and coke tins. Trundles wearily on. In an hour he will come slowly down the other side of the street and Magda will hand him out a chicken mayonnaise sandwich.

Jessie scrubs new potatoes and tops and tails green beans. Magda will steam them to make a warm salad: beans, tomatoes, almonds, mustardy French dressing. In the evening she will serve this with pieces of chicken tossed in sesame seeds. Edie returns with the menus, puts them in their red folders. Tourist cars line the harbour. A few drift over to read the menu Edie sticks to the café window. They register surprise at such a selection in such a place.

'I mean,' a voice floats in, 'look at that Alpine scene.'

Magda peers out at them. 'There's a couple of monkfish and a little pot of chocolate if ever I saw them.'

'There's something funny about the menu,' Edie squints at

the monkfish and little pot of chocolate. 'I can tell. They're laughing at it.'

'Folks laugh at anything,' Magda flaps her hand dismissively. She puts her thumb over her wine bottle, controls the flow on to her pan. Sizzles. The smells drift out. Two monkfish and little pot of chocolate come in. Can't resist it.

Jessie takes their order. She comes back, arranges the coloured tokens on the board. 'Two monkfish, one omelette. No starters. Puddings are two grape tarts and a little pot of chocolate.' She calls out the order anyway. 'Table two.'

'Told you,' Magda prides herself on always knowing what customers will choose to eat before they know themselves. 'I wish you'd discussed the omelettes with me. I wasn't wanting to do omelettes today. I've redone my pan several times, soaked it in olive oil. Dunno.'

'We always do smoked fish omelettes,' Edie hotly defends the omelette inclusion.

Lipless lumbers in. Magda puts extra virgin olive oil in a pan, adds garlic, waits till the aroma hits her, adds a couple of ladlefuls of soup. She empties the contents of the pot into a bowl, parsley on top. Jessie takes it to him with a basket of bread. He tucks a white napkin into his collar. Eats slowly. Staring ahead.

'Hey Magda,' he bawls suddenly, terrifying the monkfish and pot of chocolate. 'This soup's got garlic.'

Magda appears from the kitchen. 'Of course it hasn't Lipless. You're imagining it. And don't you go eating just the white bread. Wholemeal keeps you regular.' She smacks his wrist.

'Everybody says my breath smells,' Lipless sulks.

'Get some toothpaste from Ruby,' Magda turns to go.

'It certainly smells very garlicky.' The little pot of chocolate joins in, sniffing the wafts of soup floating across the restaurant. Magda gives her a long withering stare.

Jessie nudges Edie, 'The little pot of chocolate got the Look.'

'Don't say anything,' Magda hisses returning to the kitchen. 'It's good for him.'

Other diners come in. Jessie moves tokens on to the board.

Table five: two monkfish with salad. One melon with ckirsh. One little pot of chocolate.

Table three: Soup. Lamb. Grape tart.

Jarvis arrives. Magda gets her crêpe batter out. Heats the pan, smokily hot. Lets a thin film spread over the surface, waits till it bubbles and firms, flicks it over, lets it brown, removes some mussels from their shells, takes some creamy curried sauce from the pot, adds mussels, folds them, with an extra dash of white wine, into the crêpe.

'Help him dream about flying off the mountain,' she grins.

She takes it out personally. Leans over him. Cheek close to his, boobs on show. 'There you are. Your favourite,' she speaks huskily. Laughs. Walks back slowly. She knows he's watching her arse. Laughs again. The three crowd in the door watching him. He eats. Jaws moving almost mournfully, he looks longingly at the scene. Magda brings him a glass of wine. Soon he will stop eating and only stare. Then he will be up in the chill mountain air, moving, arms spread, through the pristine cloudless sky. Edie sniggers.

'It's lack of sex,' Magda nods knowingly. 'He's not getting any.'

'You'd know,' Edie moves to the till as a monkfish comes over to pay. He raves. But points at Jarvis. 'Why is he getting something different?'

'He's the bank manager,' Edie says. The monkfish nods. Tells the other monkfish and little pot of chocolate. They all nod. Jessie collects plates. She has to wash them. There is not enough crockery to have it out of commission whilst a dishwasher goes through its cycle. They wash as they go, working in perfect harmony. Saying little, feeling slightly neurotic today, they listen to Jackson Browne.

Lipless leaves. He doesn't pay.

'Poor bugger,' says Madga. By the end of the evening she will have made enough profit from his drinking to cover the soup. Jessie clears the monkfish table. Removes the cloth. Shakes it. Reverses it. Puts it back on. By two-thirty the lunchers have gone.

'Not a lot today,' says Edie.

'Midweek,' says Magda. 'What d'you expect?'

Mrs Lawrence, who makes the chocolates at home, brings in a fresh batch. Magda pays her from the till. Gives her extra.

'Why did you do that?' Edie is enraged.

'Her man's not working. She needs it. Five children...' Magda is unrepentant. Edie shakes her head. The café will be in overdraft for ever. They clean up the kitchen.

'You know who I hate?' Magda says, apropos of nothing.

'Who?' says Jessie.

'George Bernard Shaw,' says Magda.

'But he's dead.'

'Just as well. I really hate him.' Jessie and Edie exchange baffled looks. Jessie eats mussels for lunch. Magda drinks coffee. Edie has grape tart and some cheese. She wants a pot of chocolate but pots of chocolate are popular with customers and they don't want to run out. Besides, Magda always knows what's missing.

At half-past three Dave stops his car outside the café. Jessie gets in beside him. They're off swimming to Ardro Bay.

'Ha,' mocks Magda. 'She'll get sand up her arse and worse. She'll suffer later.'

'Jealous,' says Edie. Magda makes to hit her. Edie laughs. Outside a bus shudders to a stop. Magda rushes to the door with her no coach parties sign. She sees Jim cycling by, going home. Jessie and Dave will have disturbed his swim.

'He doesn't like to share a beach. Likes it all to himself. I think he'd like the bloody world to himself,' she says. Edie says it must be hard for him. Magda sniffs. They are not going to change the menu for dinner, except to add the chicken. Magda pours a drink. Lately, Edie thinks, she has been drinking too much. She sees gannets flying far out past the harbour, sun glinting on them. Such white birds, whiter than the rest. What powder do they use? She goes off to make the chicken changes to the menu.

A couple, chilled after walking the length of the beach and back, come in for a coffee and a glass of brandy.

Keeping Up With Magda

'A wind's got up.' They clutch their cups, warming their hands.

'Jessie'll be back soon then,' Magda looks out to see if Dave's car is back. She lays out lamb noisettes on a tray. Brushes them with oil, scatters rosemary on top. Rubs cooked sweetened redcurrants through a conical sieve. Puts on another tape. Seagulls screech. Granny Moran spreads out their afternoon feed.

'Ah, Freddie McGregor,' she calls. She's been reading the obituaries. 'Thought you'd be round today. Some bits of fruit cake. You always liked that.'

Lipless comes in for afternoon coffee. Magda gives him a slice of yesterday's apple cake. Notices Jessie and Dave clambering out of the car. From here she can see Jessie's chilled complexion, red and goosepimply. Her jaw is chattering.

'Stupid cow,' thinks Magda. 'That's what you get.'

'Just a wee drink,' Lipless whines.

'No,' Magda snaps. Soon the bed upstairs will start. God, that woman's insatiable. Other customers look up in mild surprise. Glad really that they didn't ask for a drink too. The whole building suddenly chunters and rumbles as ancient plumbing springs into action.

'Bastards are having a bath,' Magda says indignantly to Edie.

'They're allowed.'

Annie and Rosie come to see her. They drink coke and sit at the bar.

'Has Janis eaten today?' Magda asks.

'Yes, she ate a couple of spoonfuls of cornflakes and took a banana to school,' Rosie watches everything. 'And I got my special teacher today, too.'

'Not bad,' says Annie.

'Not bad at all.'

'Joe's got a hangover. Drinking again. And Jim's still painting the hall.'

'Life goes on,' Magda muses. Upstairs the bed slowly creaks. She casts her eye at the ceiling. To hell with them.

'I'll be home at half-past four for an hour,' she tells them.

Robert from the market garden brings in fresh veg. Edie takes him into the office to settle his account. Magda considers the cherry tomatoes. Smells them. Fabulous. She takes them into the kitchen, washes them and reduces them to fresh pulp in her food processor, rubs them through her sieve. Fresh uncooked tomato sauce with just a touch of ginger and maybe some sugar. She starts preparing the monkfish.

Her father comes carefully in, head round the door, checking his welcome before the rest of his body follows. Magda pours olive oil into a pan, adds garlic and chillies some tomato pulp, basil, sugar and wine. As it heats and reduces she puts in fresh prawns. Waiting for them to turn opaque she puts pasta into a pot of boiling water. When it's ready she fills two carryout trays.

'How is she anyway?' She sprinkles parmesan on each before sealing them.

'Worse,' says her father. 'Won't go out at all. Complains about her indigestion. Sits in front of the telly all day.'

'Won't she see a doctor, then?'

'She says doctors know nothing about the human digestive system. She can cope with it herself. Bicarb.'

'You know,' says Magda. 'I think she's getting smaller.' She gives him the food. He leaves shaking his head. She's right, Mary is shrinking.

A bus squeals to a stop outside. Ladies of the fish shed dismount, cackling laughter, heated gossip. A couple come into the café for a drink. Magda serves them. 'How're you?' 'Fine. And what'll we do for tea tonight?'

'What've you got?'

'Guess,' they shout, a fish shed habit, it's so noisy there. 'Fish,' they yell, holding out their opened bags. 'Haddock.'

'Put it in the oven with some soy sauce over and lemon. Do you have garlic?'

'Garlic salt.'

'That and a touch of ginger. And a spot of water. Not much, a splash. It'll take about four or five songs on the radio in a medium oven, as long as the disc jockey's not wittering on about something.'

She returns to the kitchen. The ladies of the fish shed agree,

Magda's looking tired. 'Pale and tired,' they nod. 'Not herself at all.'

The council lorry comes by, Lipless and his crew leave the harbour. Lipless will wash and shave and come back wearing his blue evening polo shirt. Magda will feed him and then he will get a drink, 'The woman's a cow.'

Magda goes home. She kicks off her shoes and lies on the sofa. Annie brings her coffee. 'I've brought lamb for you,' Magda tells her. Annie nods. She will cook it later. Magda drifts into a sleepy' distance. She can hear sounds of her household but they are far away. Joe goes out. Jim comes in from the yard with potatoes. Rosie puts the television on and weaves herself round her on the sofa to watch.

Janis is saying, 'Meat. Disgusting. I'm not eating that. I'm a vegetarian. I don't eat dead animals.'

Annie is indignant, 'When did you become a vegetarian?'

Janis, 'Ten minutes ago. I just decided.'

'Shut up. Oh please,' Magda moans.

She returns to the café. Gives the Harrys their evening feed. Last meal of the day for them. She will not leave food out at night. Rats.

Edie does not go home at all during the day. There is nobody there. The Ocean Café is home. She takes a walk along to the postbox. Bills to pay. The phone rings three times when she's away. Three reservations. Magda remembers them all. Edie will write them up when she comes back.

'You can't turn your back for a second,' she says. Then, remembering Magda's lunchtime outburst, 'How come you know George Bernard Shaw, then?'

'There was a big picture of him in school. Remember? In the hall?'

Edie shakes her head. Jessie comes in and the evening starts. There are drinkers at the bar and five tables to serve. She serves the drinkers and carries food to and empty plates from tables, arranges tokens on the board. Edie does the bills. Magda cooks. Someone orders the smoked fish omelette. Magda swears, 'Sod this pan,' everyone hears. Jaws stop chewing, forks are poised

155

between plate and lips. Magda crashes and bangs. 'This should slide off. It should be fluffy and perfect. Golden and softly fishy inside. Sod this pan.'

At nine she stops and comes out for a drink at the bar. She has not eaten properly all day. She nibbles as she goes, a bad habit. Jessie serves Lipless, 'A man has to go through hell to get a drink here,' he says.

'I can't imagine why you've got it in for George Bernard Shaw,' Jessie wants an explanation to Magda's surprising lunchtime remark.

Edie says, 'We'll have to go through the cellar tomorrow. We're running short on Australian Chardonnay and it's really popular with these August people.'

'Yes,' says Magda. 'July folk like Riesling. Riesling and Vimto. Not together, though.'

'And you get a lot of Sancerre and Chablis folk in September,' she nods at her own wisdom. Then, 'Actually, I got pregnant by George Bernard Shaw.' She turns her little eager face to Jessie. Edie has a tiny body and a huge voice. The restaurant has hushed. Jessie doesn't know what to say.

'Oh?' says Magda, adding more vodka to her coke.

'Well,' Edie draws her breath. This is a big story, 'I used to eat all these health foods, y'know. And in the health shop there was these packets of burgers made up to an original recipe by George Bernard Shaw.'

'George Bernard Shaw burgers,' says Magda. 'Who'd've thought it?'

'Exactly,' says Edie. 'So I thought, that'll do me.' She raises her eyes, flaps her hand in dismay. 'Well. Roughage did you say? No human being needs roughage like that. And if George Bernard Shaw needed roughage like that, no wonder he looked so grim. Wonder he had time to write all them plays.' All conversation has ceased. Diners eavesdrop blatantly.

'I only had one, maybe two, George Bernard Shawburgers and my goodness – diarrhoea did you say? DIA-RR-HOEA. You never saw the like. So much so my pill went right through me. And I got pregnant. It was George Bernard Shaw did it. No doubt about that.'

'See,' says Magda. 'Told you I hated him. I'll probably do a stew with parsley dumplings when it gets colder. And some steamed puddings. What happened to the baby, then?'

'Miscarried. I cried and cried,' says Edie.

'I didn't know that,' says Magda.

'No,' says Edie. 'That was twenty years ago. More. God knows what the child would've been like.'

'George Bernard Shaw,' hoots Magda.

'Mightn't have been that bad. You don't know what he was really like,' Edie says. 'You only ever see his face. And I like to see a man's bum. I like a good bum.'

'The good thing about a stew is it improves with time. And you're not in a constant lather. It's there doing on its own, like,' Magda has nothing more to say about George Bernard Shaw.

Jessie clears a table. Edie does the bill. Diners have stopped eavesdropping, the hum of conversation resumes. But departing gentlemen are aware of Edie watching their bums. They don't know what to do about it. Magda laughs. Edie sighs. More folk who won't be back. Jessie clears the tables. Magda drinks some more.

Joe, who has been pubbing, brings some friends back to the café. 'I'll cook,' he says.

Magda hates people in her kitchen. She twitches, eyes Joe evilly. 'Don't,' she says.

'Don't what?' He spreads his hands. Innocence.

'I don't know. Just don't.'

'Can I cook?' Joe folds his arms. And Magda says yes, but don't mess up and don't use everything. And she can't think of another don't so stares at him witheringly.

'Oh the Look,' Jessie points. 'That's twice today.'

Magda doesn't know what to do. She does not want anybody using her pans in her space. But she wants to be her child's friend. In a month he will be out of her life, off to college. She shrugs.

'The thing to remember about being a parent is you can't win. You'll never win with children. In the end they'll leave you and you'll cry for the life they'll have and for yourself for missing them.'

'But,' says Edie. 'They might not leave. Some children don't.'

'Ah,' says Magda 'Then, you'll cry for the life they'll not have and for yourself for being stuck with the little buggers. You can't win with children.' The last diners leave. Edie takes their money. Clears the restaurant till. Puts the money in the safe in the office till morning. Magda pours another drink. Joe and his friends leave. Magda takes a look round the kitchen. She picks up a tomato, smells it. Puts it in the fridge.

'It's been a tomatoey sort of a day.'

At midnight the Ocean Café closes. Magda locks the door. Jessie goes upstairs to Non-existent Dave. Magda heads home. Edie, bag banging on her leg, coat buttoned, walks tiny steps, amazing speed, in the opposite direction. She stops mid-stride, turns suddenly. Opens her throat and bawls, a street stopper of a voice. Walking backwards she yells, 'MAGDA. That wasn't George Bernard Shaw. That was Captain Mareth. He founded the school.'

Magda is surprised. Fancy that. I always thought it was George Bernard Shaw. 'I still hate him,' she roars back. Seagulls gathering on the quay, hovering ready to scavenge the bins, rise in unison. Like a wave.

Home, Jim has finished the hall.

'Yes,' Magda nods. 'It's good. Good colour.'

'Taupe,' says Jim.

'Taupe!' Magda looks disbelieving. 'Never heard of it. You sure? D'you think they saw you coming?'

'Taupe,' says Jim. 'Definitely taupe.'

Magda has a bath. Soaks away the day. Then walks naked down the hall to bed. Jim is already there pretending to sleep. It's the familiar knowing routine, the silent lie. He knows Magda knows he is pretending. She leaves him to it. And sleeps. At ten past three, always ten past three she will wake. She will get up, go downstairs and make tea. Sitting at the kitchen table she will unfold the pictures in her head, and, darkly whining say, 'Yeabut. What about me?'

Chapter Sixteen

When the baby died, Jessie was taken to the maternity ward. She lay in a small side room with three other mothers and their babies acclimatising herself to the rhythms of motherhood. Every four hours bottles of formula were brought round, and every four hours Jessie said, 'I don't need it. My baby died.' Every four hours her grieving started anew. The other three mothers, all much younger than her, formed a mum's vigilante group. They had an anti-Jessie rota. Armed with gaudy tabloid information about the insanity of childless mothers, they decided their infants were not safe if left alone with Jessie. They took it in turns to stay behind on watch whilst the others ate, went to the lavatory or phoned home. Jessie felt like more than a failure, she was a person to be loathed and feared. All she wanted was someone to love her. All she wanted was Alex to put his arms round her.

When she got home he hovered round her, bringing her tea and asking if she was all right.

'Fine,' she said, sometimes six or seven times a day.

'Alex, I'm fine.' He seemed to need to hear her say it though. Her reassurances released him from guilt. They allowed him to run away back to work because the sadness at home was too much for him to bear. They should have clung to each other and cried together. They should have shared their grief, then maybe Jessie would not have felt isolated in guilt.

She remembered desperately wanting her mother. She longed for her to be there to talk to, stroke her head, touch the sore bit, make it better, tuck her up and tell her to never mind. But her mother didn't come. She found life difficult when it did not move seamlessly, smoothly from one day to the next. Upsets upset her. If a spilled jug of milk caused her to flap her dishcloth and fuss, a dead baby was more than she could bear. Besides, confronting it meant confronting, in some measure, her daughter's sex life. How could she do that when Jessie was in her mind always, six years old in a pretty blue dress, bow at the back, ribbons in hair running across the lawn – a butterfly cupped in her hands?

Jessie was a precious child. She spent her perfect suburban childhood being doted on by two people who thought they would never be parents. She had everything – and a rocking horse too. Her father, a quiet balding man, came and went. When she was ten she wrote a poem about him: Here comes Jack in his hat and mac, he says good evening every day and good morning when he goes away. Her teacher had written 'a nice concise poem, Jessie.' But her mother didn't like it at all.

'I don't think this is very nice, Jessie. Not at all what we should be letting your teacher see. And we do not call our fathers Jack.' Jessie, however, was proud of her poem.

She couldn't remember much about her childhood. Other children came round to play and looked at her things with envy. She had almost every toy imaginable, but the thing that caused most resentment was her Mickey Mouse luminous alarm clock. She remembered crowding with several others into her parents' wardrobe and shutting the door so that they could marvel at the glowing green face and hands. Her mother discovered them.

'Jessie, we do not go into wardrobes with these children, boys especially. It is not done.' Jessie had asked why but no satisfactory explanation was forthcoming.

Now Jessie puzzled over her childhood. She tried to bring to mind specific events, but couldn't. Something must have happened. They had a colour television set, but she couldn't remember it coming into the house. Where had the Mickey Mouse luminous alarm clock come from? Who had given her it? She couldn't remember. Her mother and father must have argued from time to time, but she couldn't remember a single cross word ever being uttered. All she remembered was the politeness. They said dear a lot. Yes dear. No dear. Dear dear. Oh dear.

Her father left the house every morning at seven-thirty and returned at half-past six. Good morning and good evening. She left for school at eight and returned at four-thirty. Bye Mummy and I'm back, Mummy. Homework, supper then bed. Was that it? No arguments, no dirt, no sex, no laughter? Had they come as a family to the Ocean Café they would have been August people, Chardonnay or a nice Burgundy.

'Shall we have a nice Burgundy, dear?'

And had Magda misbehaved, shouting and swearing, they would all have stared deep into their lemon sole and pretended it was not happening. That's the sort of folks they were.

Jessie remembered seasons. Building a snowman in winter. Borrowing coal from the bucket by the fire for eyes and a carrot from the vegetable basket in the kitchen for a nose. And the summers of her childhood were sudden. That escape from school and there it was, warm weather. All she could remember of them were small things: squatting low in the flowerbeds, the brown smell of earth, watching a worm, putting captive caterpillars in a jar and thinking they'd take for ever to turn into butterflies, sitting on the back doorstep shelling peas. But there must have been more to her life than that, surely there must.

In Mareth there was that same childish joy in summer's arrival. She woke one morning in May and there it was, summer. August and it was still there. It seemed to lie in the bay. It turned the air soft and silky. Every day Jessie walked through it, felt it on her arms and bare legs. She felt strong. So strong, so different she sometimes forgot her old life. But it was there in her head and it wasn't going to go away.

It came back to her in a series of flashbacks. A moment from her past would be with her, vividly with her. Every colour, every movement, every word spoken was so much more clear than they had been when they actually happened.

When Alex went back to work she watched him painfully going through his shower, shave and clothes routine. He moved stiffly, his suffering spread through his whole body. They exchanged silent distress signals, saying nothing about their pain.

'I have to go now. Will you be all right?'

'Yes. I'm fine.'

'Do you want me to bring you anything when I get back?'

'No, Alex. I'm fine.'

She wanted her mother to come with armfuls of flowers. But of course she hadn't. She hadn't even phoned. When Jessie phoned her she said, 'Well, dear, how are you?'

'Fine,' Jessie lied.

'I thought you'd cope. You always muddle through, even when you were little you muddled through.' There was a long silence. Neither knew what to say. Jessie didn't want to ring off; by hanging on she still had her mother there in some sort of contact. But that was that, the tragedy had been discussed, Jessie's mother moved on to talking about the weather and their new car. When she rang off, Jessie sank deeper into her tunnel. Now she was really alone.

She thought she had come to Mareth and left her despair behind. These past days, however, she felt the blackness returning. She was beginning to stare again. She would come home from work, sit in her chair by the window and gaze out to sea, saying nothing. If Dave asked her what was wrong she would wanly reply, 'I'm scared.'

'What are you scared of?' Dave asked.

'If I knew that, I wouldn't be scared.'

Dave told Magda. 'Jessie's gone all funny. You couldn't speak to her, could you?'

Magda looked at him witheringly. 'Speak to her. Make her better. Bring back the woman you first fancied.'

Dave shrugged. 'I don't know what to say.'

Magda went upstairs to Jessie's flat. The door wasn't locked. Locking doors was not the Mareth way. She found Jessie lying curled on top of her bed.

'What's wrong with you?' she asked. As if she needed to ask.
'There's nothing wrong,' Jessie lied. 'I'm fine.'

'Here we go, thundering into your middle class politeness.
Of course you're not fine . . . Look at you. Look at your face,
it's crumpled like an old potato. You've been crying.'

'I don't know.' Her sigh shook her entire body. 'I thought I
was getting better. But I keep thinking about the baby. It would
have been ten months now. Would it have been walking and
talking?'

Magda shook her head, 'Not quite. He'd have been on his
way, though.'

'I can't stop thinking about it. It keeps creeping up on me.'

'You thought it was going to just go away? It comes back
and back and back and it hurts a little less each time.' She sat
on the bed, stroked Jessie's hand.

'The wound never goes away?' Jessie was surprised.

'You don't see much, do you?' said Magda. Jessie looked at
her sharply.

'Most of the world,' Magda said, 'has been poleaxed at some
time or other. You see it in the café, everyday people who've
been hurt. You can see it in the way they drink too much too
quickly or the way they drift away from the conversation
around them and sink into themselves, or stare out to sea, or
laugh too loudly at some pathetic joke. Now you've been poleaxed too. You've joined the walking wounded. Welcome to the
human race.'

Jessie didn't know what to say.

'You're building up some emotional immunity. Life won't
hurt so badly next time it hits.' Magda was matter of fact
about poleaxing.

'Is this why you're the way you are?'

Magda didn't let go her hand. Reached out to gently push
the hair from Jessie's eyes. Sometimes, though she fought hard
not to be, Magda was momma to the world.

'And how am I?' she asked.

Jessie searched for the appropriate words, 'I dunno. Loud.
Brash . . .'

Magda laughed.

'See me? When I was at school and I couldn't read or write, everybody used to laugh at me. The teacher hit me. Every single day she would call me out to the front of the class and hit me. My mother beat me. My father hardly spoke to me. Jessie, when I grew up I thought so little of myself, I was the town bike. Know what I mean? I had two miscarriages when I was still in my teens, before Jim took me in. Oh, I've always had a mouth on me. But one day when I was working at the Captain's Table, the boss started on me. I was useless, I was this. I was that. And he would. He would what? What could he do to me? I'd had so much pain I couldn't hurt any more. I was invincible. Know what I mean?'

Jessie gazed at her. Tears still streaming from her.

'Wash your face,' Magda bossed. 'Come to work. Have a drink. Join the walking wounded at the bar. You'll get better this time and next time you'll get better quicker. And maybe one day you'll be invincible, too.'

Jessie heard Magda going off down the stairs, shouting back at her, 'Oh yes. Invincible. I don't cry. I don't hurt. Not me. I am woman. I am invincible.'

She heard Magda enter the Ocean Café. 'Invincible,' she shouted. 'I am Invincible Woman.'

There were moans and groans and grumbles of disbelief, snorts of derision. 'Here she goes. Will you listen to that? Invincible. Ha. Ha. Ha.'

'Invincible,' Jessie whispered. And joined in the laughing. 'That'll be right.'

It was true. Mary Lomax was getting smaller. She was moving into herself. Shoulders hunched, head bent and looking thinner and thinner as the weeks went by. The red dress hung loose on her. But Mary didn't think so. This was natural thin, proper thin. The same sort of thin as the woman with the lovely accent and soft eyes in the dress shop. She admired herself in the mirror. Yes the red did something for her, lit her face. She moved stiffly down the hall and into the living room. John was sitting watching football. He did not turn as she came. He did not like to look at her these days.

'Look at me, John,' Mary commanded. 'Look at me.'

John turned. The room was dark but for the light from the television. It was unbearable to look at her, this small shrivelled woman he had loved, drowned by the dress that had driven her crazy. The crowd roared. 'Oooh,' the commentator snapped 'surely that was a penalty. But the ref hasn't seen it.'

'Look at me,' she said again. 'I'm gorgeous.'

It wasn't that Ginny Howard was frigid exactly. She just forgot about sex. Day to day there was so much to do, by the time she lay down in bed at night it didn't occur to her. Jarvis didn't like to remind her. He thought he might get used to it. But knew he wouldn't. He dreamed of someone charming and, well, nice, who'd be like Magda, or like he imagined Magda to be, in bed. He was fascinated by Magda, and terrified of her.

He had one abiding memory of her. She had been in his class at school. Once, in a chemistry class, after the teacher had been horribly scathing about her work, Magda had stepped to the front of the rows of desks.

'Get back to your seat, girl,' her teacher demanded.

Magda shook her head. 'What sort of way is that to speak to somebody?' she asked.

'I'm tired of you and your messy attitude.'

Magda shrugged. 'I just don't understand,' she said.

'Well, I can't explain it any better.'

'Do you always speak to people like that? Does it make you feel better? Do you feel good making people feel terrible about themselves? Is it 'cos you're a man? But you're such a bully I don't think you're a man at all. I think you're a coward.'

And before the hushed schoolchildren she had reached forward and gripped the poor fellow right between the legs. The surprise and shock on his face was something none of them would ever forget. 'Just as I thought girls,' she said. 'Nothing there.'

For days the class had waited to see what retribution Magda

would suffer. Nothing happened, but the mockery stopped. Jarvis had been misty-eyed in admiration for the girl – just so long as she kept her distance and didn't come near him.

It wasn't just sex he missed. He wanted someone to chat to. Someone who wouldn't clear the table the instant he stopped eating. Someone who didn't think it wicked to leave a coffee cup on the floor beside the sofa. Who would sleep naked, go to bed Sunday afternoon when the kids were out, who would make love outside the bedroom.

Last week Ginny had risen at five-thirty to clean the house, and this week she had told him she was thinking of doing it in the evening before she went to bed to save her doing it in the morning. He winced. How had this happened to them? And where was the nubile, willing woman he'd married? The one who'd willingly wriggled beneath him in the back of his Ford Cortina all those years ago after the golf club Christmas party.

The silence woke Jessie. It took her a while lying staring at the ceiling to realise why she felt alarmed. Eight in the morning already and there were no gulls crying outside.

'Granny Moran,' she said, urgently getting out of bed. In T-shirt and knickers she stood on the landing, banging on the old lady's door. No reply. Trembling Jessie tried the handle. The door was open. Only incomers with their city fear and loathing locked their doors.

Inside the flat was dark, smelled musty. Jessie moved slowly down the hall. The thick chenille door curtain swished behind her. She tiptoed and gently called on Granny Moran. 'Hello-o.' Spindly, uncertain voice moving through the awful silence.

The living room was dark, thick red curtains drawn. Jessie heaved them back and stepped back as light flooded the room. She looked round: several overpoweringly large pieces of dark mahogany furniture, a table with a bowl of wrinkled fruit dead centre, a beige velvet straight-backed chair in front of the biggest television she'd ever seen, but no Granny Moran. Heart pounding, oh God please don't let me find a dead body, she crept through to the bedroom.

Granny Moran was in bed. Her head lolled on the pillow, long grey hair spread out, mouth open, she stared wordlessly at Jessie. She was pale, pale, grey pale. Her glasses, false teeth and gold bracelet watch lay on the dresser beside the bed. Jessie fetched Magda.

Magda took Granny Moran's cold hand in hers and reached out to touch her cheek. 'Fetch Dr MacKintyre,' she said. 'Edie'll have the number.'

Jessie ran downstairs to the café. The workers on the quay watched her go and did not whistle and stamp. They knew when something was wrong. The morning children eating their breakfasts cried 'woooooo' then stopped. The air today was different, foreboding. Somebody was dying.

Dr MacKintyre came and went. He listened to Granny Moran's failing heart, took her pulse and shook his head. 'There's not a lot I can do. I don't think I even know how old she is,' he said.

Magda rubbed her eyes, 'I don't think she knows herself.' They looked at the old lady.

'You're not moving her. She'd want to go here at home. It'd kill her to die in hospital,' Magda insisted.

'You must think me more insensitive than I do myself,' the doctor said stiffly. He'd had recent dealings with Magda. Last year she'd found a lump on her left breast. It turned out to be a benign cyst. He'd looked at her over his half glasses and asked what she expected at her age? Magda's survival depended on never letting anyone get away with anything.

'At my age I expect to get patronised by doctors who look at me dismissively over the top of their specs reminding me of my age.'

He left, promising to look in later. Meantime, was there anybody who could sit with the old lady? They took it in turns. Magda, Edie, Ruby from the Spar and her oldest daughter, then Jessie after lunches were finished. She felt privileged and terrified. What if the old lady actually died when she was there? She didn't think she could cope.

Granny Moran's bedroom was dark and cool. The old lady's laboured breathing scarcely touched the silence that spread outward beyond the airless, stuffed room to the street. Cars crawled past and the workmen on the quay whispered when they swore. At four the old lady stirred, her rattling chest eased. Moving her hands painfully, she signalled Jessie over.

'Magda,' she croaked, the word barely coming out of her throat. Jessie ran downstairs, knocked on the café window. In baseball cap and apron, Magda sat on the bed, leaning her ear close to Granny Moran's lips. Jessie hovered in the doorway. She didn't know what to do. She shouldn't be here, turned to go.

Magda stepped back, shaking her head. 'No, stay. It's all right,' she grinned hugely.

Granny Moran sighed, lifted her worn translucent, liver-spotted hand and waved. Did Jessie hear her say, 'Bye, Bye'? There was a gleam in her watery eyes. She was off. Time of her life.

Magda put her arm round Jessie when she cried. Stroked her hair, kissed the top of her head. And Jessie loved the smell of Magda, sweat and raspberries and garlic, and that deep unfathomable smell of being a woman.

'It's all right,' Magda said. 'It's what she wanted more than anything. She was tired of waiting for it. She'll be flying round the bay right now, calling out to her old pals.'

'Fuck, fuck, fucky fuck,' choked Jessie. 'That's what it sounds like you all say to me.'

'Oh,' Magda stroked her hair, 'we're not nearly as witty as that.'

Jessie wiped her nose. 'What did she say to you anyway?'

Magda let out a breathy laugh. She was pleased. 'Gave me her batter recipe.'

'She didn't.' Jessie couldn't believe it. 'On her death bed? Heaven's sake.' She didn't know if she was crying or laughing. 'What was it anyway?'

'I'm not telling you,' Magda shook her head. 'Oh no. It's a secret.'

Chapter Seventeen

Jessie dreamed she was giving birth in the Ocean Café lavatory. She cleaned the lavatories a couple of times a day, a job she loathed. She was being tended by a blond man who'd flirted with her over his watercress soup a couple of nights before. He told her to push and she swore foully at him, said she was pushing. He said he could see the head, and she said she could feel it and didn't want to push any more, fearing she would break it. She complained that the yellow knobbly carpet was vile and a person in labour should have better quality soft furnishings. The pain woke her. She breathed deeply, scarcely able to believe she was not in pain at all, and ran her hand gingerly over her stomach – just in case. The relief to find it flat, or flattish. She still felt embarrassed at being so intimate with someone she scarcely knew.

'What's wrong?' Dave asked gruffly. He did not want to be awake yet.

'I dreamed I was giving birth,' she told him.

'Christ.' He turned over, keen to get back to sleep.

'You don't understand. It was sore. I was in pain.'

'You were dreaming.'

'I was in agonies in my dream, giving birth.'

'Never mind. Here you are in bed, and the baby you had is still in your dreams. Best kind of kid. It won't grow up to demand cash and slag you off to his chums.' He snorted at his joke.

Telling him he was a stupid bastard who didn't understand, Jessie got up to light a cigarette and smoked it staring out of the window. The depth of her upset shook her; she felt as if she had been crying her eyes out.

'Who the hell do you think you are,' Dave demanded, 'calling me a stupid bastard? Saying I don't understand? I understand. I understand plenty.'

'I don't think you do.' Jessie sounded caustic.

'Babe, you'll never know.'

'Oh you patronising shit. Babe, you'll never know.' She curled her lip, strutted some, imitated him again. 'Babe, you'll never know. What is it I'll never know? The meaning of life? All the butch macho things men know? How to drive a fast car . . . in reverse? How to drink a pint of beer in a oner? How to use big shiny power tools? How to shout louder than anybody else with your big deep voice . . .'

Dave got out of bed, moved across the room to where she was, by the window, put his face up to hers and, using his big deep voice, yelled, 'How about how to take responsibility for yourself?'

She was stunned. 'The hell do you mean by that?'

'I mean what exactly are you doing here, Jessie? Working as a waitress in a seaside café with your money, your education. Are you enjoying yourself mixing with the lower orders? Do we amuse you?'

'No,' she shook her head. 'It isn't like that.'

'What is it about?'

'I'm trying to sort myself out.'

'I get the feeling you're floating above us, Jessie. Looking down, being slightly amused the while. I think we're not really real to you. Just a little distraction whilst you do your running-away-from-life thing.'

'Who the hell are you to criticise people for running away? You're the great Non-existent Dave.'

'Yeah. And when I ran away I made a job of it. You're dealing with a master here. And like I said, you'll never know babe.'

'Oh for heaven's sakes, Dave. Of course I know. You run away all the time . . .'

'If you say, "Where are we going with this relationship,

Dave?" Or "I want some kind of commitment, Dave", I'll ...
I'll ... throw you out the bloody window.'

They stared at each other in surprise. This was absurd; not
only would he never throw her out the window because he
wasn't the type, the window was too small anyway. More,
though, it came as a mutual revelation that neither of them
wanted any sort of commitment. And neither of them really
cared where they were going with the relationship. Oh the
relief. They went back to bed.

They carried Granny Moran to the graveyard. Six pall-bearers
in top hats and tail-coats walked slowly along the shore with
the coffin on their shoulders. Most of Mareth followed. It was
an exquisite day, that summer stillness lay in the bay.

The whole village had come to bid the old lady farewell. In
church Reverend Borthwick smiled and nodded. Fourteen years
Mareth had been his parish, never before had he seen the place
so full. People had come to Mareth from across the world to
say goodbye to Granny M. Magda pulled Jessie back as she
headed for a seat near the front.

'Front rows are for relatives only.'

Relatives filled the front ten pews. An extraordinary amount
of them looked just like her. But then, looking round the faces
in the rest of the church, half of Mareth bore a resemblance to
Granny Moran. Maybe the tales they told about her voluptuous
past were true.

'Are you related?' Jessie leaned close to Magda's ear, whispering her question.

'Nah,' she shook her head. 'The Lomaxes are a whole different breed. Though ...' Though, she was not really a Lomax.
She didn't know who her father was. It wasn't her mother's
husband, that was for sure. 'You'll not see a funeral like this
again,' Magda said.

'They don't take everyone to the graveyard on their
shoulders, then?' Jessie asked.

Magda shook her head. 'It's Granny's way. All her friends
would have had that. But then most of them went about thirty

171

years ago. She's been a long time alone.'

Jessie looked round at the mourners, barely a dry eye. This was alone? These people know nothing about alone. She could show them alone.

They sang the twenty-third psalm.

Reverend Borthwick said Granny's name, 'Euphemia Maureen Moran, Granny M., Mareth will be an empty place without her . . .'

Jessie watched the grieving faces. She had never seen communal crying before. The church was filled with flowers people had brought from their gardens. Every flag in the village was at half-mast, every curtain was drawn. Visitors to Mareth would find the village closed for the day.

'Mareth does a good funeral,' she said.

'We're good at death,' said Magda. 'Drinking and death.' Freddie Kilpatrick sang 'Yesterday', Granny's favourite song. His rich tenor surprised Jessie. He came and went to and from the Ocean Café in oily dungarees and cap. Who would have thought such a thrilling voice lurked inside him? After the sermon they sang 'Onward Christian Soldiers', hardly funereal, Reverend Borthwick smiled. But Granny Moran always liked it. And when at last they went out into the graveyard, everyone agreed that Granny M. would be well pleased to have her gravestone finished at last. It was a weathered stone.

'Been up twenty-five years,' Magda said. 'Had it put up herself. She didn't trust anyone to do it right.' She nodded, smiling. 'Granny M. had it all figured, did she not?'

'She did that,' Jessie agreed, looking wistfully at the stone.

Euphemia Maureen Moran, 1898 –
Time of Her Life.

'Time of her life,' Jessie read. Magda nodded. The envy they felt at Granny Moran's departing glee. Death scared the shit out of them.

The café was closed to the public for the day. Family and friends squeezed in and drank to Greasy Mae, a legend in her time. They had to put away fourteen bottles of whisky, one more than had been drunk at the funeral of Granny Moran's best friend twenty-eight years ago. To fortify the drinkers, Magda brought in a huge platter of battered fish and chicken. Ruby from the Spar held a piece between her fingers and, weeping still from the song and Onward Christian Soldiers, cried, 'Oh, Magda. She passed on the recipe. Now that was grand of her. She was a grand old lady.'

At four o'clock seagulls gathered on the quay. Jessie took some scraps to spread for them. They swooped and fought round her. There you go, there you go. Some for you and some for you and let the little one through. She needs some.

The place was still. Not a car moved. No children played. No ghetto-blasters on the harbour. There was only the aching thrum of Granny's Australian grandson's pipes. A lonely pibroch at the end of the pier.

The first storms came in September. Early, Magda said. They usually came a month later.

'There'll be no more nudy swimming for you.' She wagged her finger at Jessie.

Huge waves galloped in and smashed against the quay. The spray flew across the street and hit the Ocean Café window. Passing cars were drenched, and the fish shed ladies scattered squealing when they clambered from the evening bus.

For two days, four tides, waves boomed, and spray hit the café window. Hardly anybody came, only Lipless and Jarvis for his crêpe and mountain stare.

The wind was incessant, a constant howl. Upstairs in the flat Dave lit a fire, sat staring at the flames. Storms unsettled him. Seagulls rode the waves or lined the quay. Morning and evenings Jessie fed them.

'Come on now. Some for you. Here you are Granny M., chocolate doughnut. Can't resist it, can you? Come on then . . .'

The wind whipped round her, flapped her coat. Gulls snatched and gobbled. 'Now you, that's enough of that . . .'

Dave watched from the window.

'Here little one . . .'

'Jessie?' A familiar voice.

She turned. 'Alex.'

'Dare I ask what you're doing?' He came close, shouting above the storm.

'What do you think I'm doing? Feeding the gulls.' She was soaked. Her hair was plastered to her head, mascara ran down her cheeks. There was so much rain she could hardly see.

'But it's lashing rain. Won't it wait?'

'No.' She continued tossing lumps of bread and doughnut.

'Can we talk?'

She was deeply tempted to say no again. But nodded toward the café.

'No. I want to talk,' Alex insisted.

Reluctantly, fearing a confrontation with Dave, she led him upstairs to the flat. Her espadrilles squelched as she walked. She'd been standing in a puddle. Dave wasn't there. No sign of him at all. She looked round for him. Seconds ago he'd been at the window, now he'd vanished. He wasn't keen on confrontations either.

Alex hung his damp coat in her hall then sat in front of the fire. 'Cosy,' he said, trying to hide his horror. He still found cosy offensive. Jessie nodded. So it was.

'I'll make some tea,' Jessie offered.

Alex nodded, 'That would be good.' He pulled out his wallet. Handed her a cheque. 'I've brought you some money. I would have had it transferred to your bank account but I don't know if you have one.'

'I have one at the local bank. It's got less than a pittance in it.'

'Well here's half the profit I made on the house. A bit more as a matter of fact. It'll see you through for a while if you don't go wild. But I'd invest it.'

'Yes. You would.'

They stared at each other. So much to say, but how to start?

'Jessie. I can't bear to see you living here. I can't bear it.' He was a knight in a shiny little sports Mazda. He could rescue her. He gripped her arms, 'We could go back to Italy. Take the car. Fill the boot with decent wine and olive. We could visit old haunts. Lucca.' He was enthusing, convincing himself as much as her that this would solve everything. He took her hands as if they could just run out into the night, get into their little red car and drive into the night, forgetting everything. 'You always used to complain that we never did anything on impulse. I always planned too much. Think of it, Jessie. Italy. The light. The smells. The shoes . . .'

He was a man for buzz words. Shoes got her.

'Italy.' She remembered. 'The shoes. Oh the shoes . . .' When had she last shopped for decent shoes?

'Visit the late-night street markets. Buy books.' He was getting carried away.

'Alex, stop it. You're doing what you always do. Building up a glowing picture . . .' She sighed, 'Let's drive to Italy, Alex. Let's get caught up in the traffic in Rome, Alex. Let's get hysterical yelling at each other. Let's fight over my map-reading. Or my driving. You know, with you stamping the floor shouting brake, brake. Let's get sick eating squid . . . Life is not a series of perfect moments, Alex, no matter how hard you try.'

'You could still come back. We had a marriage.'

She shook her head, 'No we didn't and you know it. We had a shampoo-ad relationship that got soured by reality.'

That hurt. He let go of her and turned away. 'If we're talking superficial, you're the one turned on by shoes.'

'You of course don't need accessories. You're so perfect, you're your own accessory.'

He shook his head. 'What's happening to you, speaking to me like this? Standing out there in the rain talking to the gulls?'

'I don't know,' said Jessie. 'Why don't you leave me alone? Please go.'

Without a word he rose, took his coat and made for the door. 'If you're passing the café, would you go in and tell Magda I won't be back tonight. I don't feel well,' Jessie called, then considered the state of her health. 'Actually, I really don't feel well. I think I'm going to be sick.' Alex hovered in the doorway. If she was going to be sick he should do something. What?

'Please,' Jessie said.

He needed a drink. Went into the café. Edie and Magda stopped their conversation and looked at him.

'Sorry,' he said. Aware that he was not wanted. 'Could I have a whisky? And Jessie says she won't be back she's not well. Actually, she's sick.'

Lipless hoped she'd be better soon. 'I like Jessie,' he told Magda. 'She's got manners.'

Magda laughed, 'Not like me. Well, you know me, Lipless. Manners are a pain in the arse. They'll always get you exactly where other people want you to be.' She handed Alex his whisky. The wind battered the windows, waves crashed against the quay, a great wall of water heaved into the air, battered to the ground and sucked back, leaving a debris of pebbles, dulce and sand.

'Some weather,' Alex said, staring out. It was warm here, windows steamed, somehow the world seemed far away. He sat in the far corner and asked to see a menu.

He had cream of potato and tomato soup and a bottle of Sancerre, and did Magda know what was up with Jessie? Edie nodded. Sancerre, typical September visitor.

'She's sorting herself out. Leave her to it.'

Alex shook his head. 'So much pain,' he said.

'Yep,' Magda agreed. 'Life's a bitch. Mind you,' she never could resist making judgements, 'if you ask me, and I know so far you haven't, if there's pain going about you caused a fair bit of it.'

'I hurt too. It was my baby too,' Alex said. Speaking about it always made him grumpy.

'Tell me about it. You lost interest after the conception,' Magda said, removing his empty plate. 'There's only steak on the menu.'

'I'll have it. Nobody asked me if I wanted a baby. I'd only just got used to the idea of being a dad when it died.'

Magda nodded. 'You felt guilty when it died too, then?'

Alex nodded. 'Yeah, of course I did.'

Magda glared at him intently. 'Why are you staring at me?'

he asked, wincing under the scrutiny. 'I just came in for a drink. I didn't ask for this.'

'That's OK,' Magda assured him. 'I don't charge extra for criticism. Or for sorting folks out.' She sat down and gave him the full piercing, all-seeing look. 'You didn't want a baby. You didn't want to share Jessie. You didn't want the mess. When it died for a moment you were glad. It wasn't a big moment, but it was there that moment. And after it you couldn't bear to be with Jessie, you felt so bad. You couldn't stand it. That's it, isn't it?'

Alex stared out the window. 'Could I just have my steak, please?'

Magda rose and went to the kitchen.

'She's a cow,' said Lipless. 'She does that to everybody. She feeds you. She figures out your life. Then she gives you the bill. Don't know why people put up with it.'

'She dishes up food and the truth. Who could resist it?' Alex reflected.

Magda stuck her head round the kitchen door. 'Lots of men feel like that,' she said. 'You can congratulate yourself on being normal.'

She liked his suit. Mareth men didn't wear suits, except for weddings and funerals, or unless they were the doctor, lawyer or bank manager. Or unless, she continued her muse, they were off to see the bank manager for a loan. She thought she would have Alex. She always wanted something of Jessie's. Alex no longer felt hungry. Hated to be reminded of when the baby died. Looking back he had a vision of himself running around for weeks with his palms spread, mouthing incoherently, lips opening and shutting, like a goldfish. He remembered himself as wearing a permanent bewildered and pained expression. The weeks immediately after the death had been the worst in his life. He thought he behaved quite well but didn't dare ask what other men did in the same circumstances lest he discovered he'd been a prat.

Magda brought him a peppered steak in Madeira sauce. She leaned on the bar watching him eat.

'I see you looking at him,' Lipless muttered into his beer. 'City shite.'

'Oh yes, he's that,' Magda agreed, and went to fetch a tarte tatin. Alex ordered another bottle of wine. It was funny, folks here thought city men to be wankers.

'Blokes like that,' Lipless said, 'are just women. Can't hold their drink.'

'What do you mean, just women?' Magda said. She sounded glum. She could feel an argument coming on and didn't feel up to it. This storm was draining enough.

'Just women. They can't do much, can they? Like hold their drink. City shites are women when they drink.'

'I can drink you under the table any night, Lipless,' Magda sneered.

'Yes, I'll give you that.'

'And I can cook, run a restaurant, care for a family and—'

'Oh I know, 'cos I'm a wooooooman,' Lipless burst into song. His flat, lifeless singing was surprising.

'Oh, I can't stand that stuff,' Magda scorned, before singing her own life's song. 'I get up five in the morning, scrub miners' backs in the tub outside, feed the bairns, discover a cure for cancer, do a milk round, take hot meals to housebound old folks, give my man a blow job and never give a sod about myself. 'Cos I'm a wooooooman . . .' Her song stopped. In the light of not being able to think of a single thing to say, Lipless made a dismissive face.

Magda's song went on, 'Or should it be, 'Cos I'm stooooooooopid?'

'Still think city shites can't hold their drink,' Lipless muttered. He glared at Magda triumphantly. As far as he was concerned he'd won the argument.

But this city shite could hold his drink. He could hold quite a selection of alcohol. He'd had one and a bit bottles of wine and several whiskies and was still standing. Well, Magda thought, he's not going anywhere tonight.

At nine Edie went home. She needed an early night and she wasn't needed to look after two customers, only one of whom was eating. Lipless drank on. Alex drank whisky with his coffee. Magda cleaned the kitchen. Outside the Harrys complained about the weather. 'You're not coming in here,' Magda told them.

Lipless left at ten, 'Where is everybody? It's dead in here tonight.'

Magda smiled. She was wondering when to charge Alex – before or after? Before. It would be easier to take his money before sex; there was something lurid about after even though he owed her for the meal.

Upstairs Jessie lay in her darkened bedroom sweating and nauseous. She'd caught a chill feeding the gulls.

She visited her past. She saw it so clearly, her old house, the Smallbone kitchen with french windows leading to the garden where she'd walked serenely pregnant. She reached out into the dark, as if her life were out there to be touched, waiting for her to come back to it. But the house was sold, husband sent packing; everything was gone. Nothing left, she said. Nothing left. Outside the wind blasted relentlessly.

Magda locked the café door. 'Enough's enough,' she said. 'If anybody wants fed tonight they can go somewhere else.'

'They're missing a lot,' said Alex.

Magda brought a bottle to the table. But only half-filled his glass, 'You've had enough already.'

He kissed her. His tongue in her. She moved her hand on the back of his head. Liked the short hairs against her palm. He pulled her to him, knocking over her chair.

'I have to switch off the lights,' Magda said. Before she did, kissed him again. Let her body move against his. He pulled her to him, lips on hers. She loved the feel of mouths. Unbuttoned his shirt. Not wanting to stop, each scared lest the other came to their senses and say no, they collapsed to the floor. Mauling each other, pulling off clothes. Kissing. Moaning. He took her breast in his hand. Sucked it. She wrapped her legs round him. Another chair toppled. Above them the bottle on the table fell over, vodka poured out, flooded the floor.

'Please,' Magda thought, 'don't let that put him off.'

'Please,' he thought, 'don't let her stop to clean it up.'

Love oh love oh clumsy love. Afterwards they moved to the bashed sofa in the office. Magda threw back her head and laughed and yelled. His face twisted with ecstasy. He pounding into Magda as if it would dispel the guilt and pain of the rest of the evening rather than add to it. Neither of them thought about Jessie.

They lay afterwards amidst the mess, nothing to say. After a while Alex got up, stuffed his shirt-tail into his trousers and collected his coat. He did not look at Magda. As he left he laid money beside the till. 'For the meal,' he said shortly. 'I owe you.'

Magda nodded. She was sitting at the table. Head bowed as she ran her fingers through her hair. She did not look at him. When he finally walked through the door they did not bid each other goodbye.

'You shouldn't have done that, Magda,' she said out loud. She thought of Jim and her children at home sleeping whilst she got up to mischief. She was too old to behave like this. When she set out to seduce Jessie's husband, she hadn't considered how guilty she'd feel afterwards. Sometimes she was like a child stripping off her clothes and rushing into the sea, sometimes she was like that with sex. She didn't stop to think she was getting in too deep.

'You stupid cow,' she chastised herself. 'Stupid. Stupid. Stupid.'

She picked up an ashtray and threw it at the wall. But she was tired. It sailed weakly for a short distance, trailing ash and cigarette butts before sinking to the floor. More mess. She hated herself. But checked herself for bites and scratches, though she knew a man like Alex would be incapable of both. She tidied her hair and went home.

Jim was up. 'Where have you been?'

'At the café.' She feared she smelled of sex.

'What have you been doing till this time?'

Magda shrugged. She wasn't going to answer that. 'What's the point of coming home these days?'

Jim didn't answer that. 'They're selling me off in three weeks. Everything in the yard has to go.'

Magda reached for his arm. She should have been here earlier.

'Magda, I feel like they've stripped the skin from my bones and snipped it into little bits to feed to anybody that's passing.'

Magda's eyes filled with tears. She hated seeing him like this. 'They can't touch you. Not you.'

'They're taking my life and selling it off. Just like that. Have this, two pounds, take that fourteen pounds fifty. That's me they're fucking.' He turned away from her. He was crying.

'No,' Magda said. 'They can't do that. They can't ever do that.' She cradled his head against her. Could feel his tears dampen her shirt. Her favourite pink denim too. He unbuttoned it, took her nipple in his mouth. Such comfort. She sat on him. Hoped he wouldn't notice she'd come home without knickers. Opened his fly and moved him into her.

'It's all right,' she said. 'Everything will be all right. I won't let them hurt you. I won't let them.' And he gasped, slow pleasure. Thank heavens for good old-fashioned well-made sturdy kitchen chairs.

Edie got to the café first. She looked round and knew what Magda had been up to. And disapproved.

'You're a bitch, Magda Horn. A hussy and a bitch . . .' she blistered when Magda arrived.

'Oooooh,' Magda wasn't going to let her shame show.

'That was Jessie's husband you did that with.' Edie pointed at the mess on the floor, overturned chairs, spilled booze.

Magda dismissed the accusation. 'So what? They're not getting back together.'

'Makes no difference.' Edie shook her head and set about working off some of her shock cleaning up. Magda laughed. Didn't mean to but Edie's moral stand amused her. Aggression passed Edie by. She didn't carry anger well. Magda always wanted to cuddle her when she raged, which always made her angrier.

'Don't you go laughing at me. You did a terrible thing last night. And you know it.' She pointed at the ashtray. 'You took a little tantrum and you threw that. You always throw things when you're mad at yourself, Magda Horn.'

Magda smirked at her. 'Oh well done, Sherlock. It was almost worth it, though.' Disapproval brought out the worst in Magda. 'In fact, he was quite good. Better than some of the blokes round here ...'

'How are you going to look Jessie in the eye?'

'... But then, what's sex to them? A swift twenty-second blast followed by ten hours' sleep and a plate of Cocopops ...'

'She'll know.'

'... And foreplay ...?'

'You can clean up your own mess in the office.'

'... Brace yourself, lass. That's foreplay round here ...'

Edie threw down her duster, 'That's enough of that.'

Magda put on The Rolling Stones full blast. A jangle of guitars and harmonica roared out. Boomed from the café over the bay.

'What do you mean, look me in the eye?' Jessie walked in.

Magda smiled. Edie looked guilty.

'What's going on?' Jessie looked at the mess on the floor and immediately understood. She sat down, stunned. 'You've shagged Alex,' she said. Magda nodded.

Jessie took her time considering this. 'How was it for you?' she asked.

'Not bad. Better than some I've had. Not as good as Dave.'

'Oh come on, Alex has his moments.' Jessie was surprised at how little she cared. Or how she was giving the impression of caring little.

'He had one last night. In fact I'd say he had quite a moment.'

They laughed. Shrieked together. Women are such bitches.

'I'm shocked. The pair of you, listen to you. Poor bloke,' Edie went off to the office tutting, shaking her head, a can of Sparkle in one hand, a bright yellow duster in the other. Her ineffectual rage made Jessie and Magda laugh even harder.

'Tumblin' Dice' howled out. Jagger hollered loud enough to let Mareth know Magda had been up to no good last night.

Alex woke. He was crumpled and sore. Last night, after Magda, he had driven down the coast road. Fearing he was still drunk, he stopped in the clifftop car park in the neighbouring village and fell asleep crumpled in the driving seat, face pressed against the window.

He leaned on the steering wheel. He was shattered, raw, utterly alone and very cold. The damp seeped into his bones. It hurt to move. His head ached. He felt as if a layer of skin had been ripped from the back of his throat. The light seared against his eyelids. Soon he would have to open his eyes. He dreaded the moment.

The sun came exquisitely up, black against a glowing sky. Seagulls laughed, tumbled freefall. Alex had tears in his eyes.

That woman, the sort of woman he would normally dismiss out of hand – too fat, too common, too honest, too tiring – had taken one look at him and had seen his secret right away. When the baby died, for one small spark of a moment, before the grief set in, he'd been relieved. He could have Jessie to himself again. After that betrayal, what did it matter if he slept with another woman? Or two?

He snorted. There was no doubt that Magda would tell Jessie what had happened. He'd lost Jessie now for sure. There was no going back.

'A shampoo-ad relationship,' he muttered, starting up the car. The sky turned from night to day, white where the chilled haze met the sea. A cormorant keened across the top of the waves.

'Shampoo ad,' he said again, and shrugged. He put the car into reverse and screeched back across the car park, skid marks in the grit. He shoved it into first, swung out into the road, snapped some Verdi into the cassette deck and, gunning through the gears, roared away.

'Shampoo ad. There are some pretty bloody good shampoo ads out there, baby.'

Chapter Eighteen

John Lomax could hardly bear to touch his wife. She was more than just thin, she was frail, suddenly old. When he reached for her in bed it was bones he touched. When he took her hand as they climbed the stair at night, it was a skeletal thing he held – long fingers, deep veins. It looked as if her very skin had given up on her. He called the doctor.

'Dr MacKintyre,' Mary blushed when she opened the door to him. For goodness' sakes, surely he had more important things to do than come to see her. 'What brings you here?'

'John's worried about you.' The doctor came in.

'About me? For crying out loud. That man . . .'

'We don't see you about these days.' He watched her face.

Mary dismissed this. 'I'm just biding my time. When things are right . . .' She tailed off.

'But you feel well?'

'A touch of indigestion. What else can you expect at my age?'

Dr MacKintyre brought out his stethoscope. 'Can I listen?'

'If you must. But I don't know what you mean about not getting about. Only the other week I was in London. All that way. Went to see *Cats*. Lovely. It was lovely, Doctor. Oh you should go . . .'

He gently listened to Mary's heart. A pale and ailing thing fluttering in there. 'I think you should drop by the surgery sometime soon, Mary.'

'And I got the loveliest of frocks. Beautiful. Of course it's not the sort of thing you can wear anywhere. Not for everyday use. I'm saving it for good.'

'I think we'll make a wee appointment for you to see some-one. A specialist. Would you do that, Mary? Put on your red dress.'

'I can't wear it to a hospital. Hospital's not good.'

'When is good then?' Dr MacKintyre was intrigued.

Mary looked at him. Couldn't answer. When was good, then? She turned pale wondering. Damned if she knew.

'You could close down the café.' Ginny Howard's eyes gleamed. Power. 'You could shut the café and you could have their house, too.' She got wet thinking about it. She hated Magda Horn. 'They'd have to leave Mareth.'

'Where would they go?'

Ginny didn't know. Didn't care.

'Ginny,' Jarvis sat back in his chair. 'Where would Mareth be without the Ocean Café?'

'Oh food. Who needs it?'

'Why do you hate the place?'

'It's horrible. Full of old drunks. That Lipless. And it needs refurbishing. I mean, that Alpine scene. And Magda Horn is always mincing about in those shoes of hers. And her skirts are too short. You can see her knees. I ask you – knees on a woman that age.'

'She brings in tourists. She feeds children.'

'She's a whore.'

'Cats, she feeds cats.'

'She's a cow.'

Jarvis had never seen his wife so animated. She was luminous with loathing. He had thought the tragedy of his life was that the lustful willing woman who had moved, shuddered under him all those years ago had turned into an overly motivated bossy shrew. All that passion had been denied him and sear-ingly redirected into a series of petty causes. He knew her passion scared her. She denied it. But here it was in the living room with him. He saw again the torrid woman he'd fallen in love with. And saw that the true tragedy of his life was that she'd turned into a bitch right under his eyes. He'd done nothing about it.

Now that he had something she desperately wanted, he could have her. Right now he could take her upstairs to bed. She would writhe again for him and scream for him. He owned the lease to the Ocean Café and she wanted it. He got up, poured a drink.

Granny Moran was his aunt. Granny Moran was auntie to half Mareth. But she had left the lease of the Ocean Café to him. He could close it down.

'We could open a shop. We could sell paintings and souvenirs. Tasteful things, of course.'

Oh but Magda made such crêpes. And as her landlord . . . well . . . he could get the best. He didn't want to fuck Magda. But power over her – that was something else. A small, and unheeded voice told him that nobody had power over Magda.

He imagined himself being brought the best. Salmon with balsamic butter, or maybe dill sauce, warm wood-pigeon salad, a plain perfect steak with Madeira sauce, chocolate Bavarian cream. Oh yes. Lovely. He'd sit by the window and demand that Magda keep the Alpine scene for ever.

'Granny Moran asked me to try to keep the café going.'

'Granny Moran's dead,' Ginny enthused. 'We could . . . you could . . .'

Yesterday on the golf course – Mareth had a golf course; the golf curse, they called it, nine hellish holes (anybody wanting a full round had to go on twice) – Dr MacKintyre had given him the works.

'Frankly, Jarvis, if you close down the café, you close down Mareth. Or at least a very important part of it.' He had selected a five iron, swung wildly at his ball, hit it and sent it singing into the sea. Small splash. 'Bugger.'

Jarvis whacked his ball and it whistled through the air, easily easily on to the sixth green.

'Nice one, Jarvis,' the doctor nodded in admiration. 'You've certainly got the hang of the course.' Then, as they strode together towards Jarvis's ball, 'It'd be a pity to see it close down.'

'Close down?'

'Well, if the tourists stop coming – ' he let Jarvis have a few minutes alone with his imagination – 'if the café closes, if the children stop getting their breakfast, if the school starts showing the results it would have with unfed infants, if the Ocean Café's reputation didn't bring in odd gourmets and ... well, just if ... Jarvis ... let me see. Now my ball went into the sea. Will you concede that it might have landed here. And I'll try and get it up from the beach?' Jarvis nodded. 'Good man. I think I must owe you a lunch. Where do you want to go? Is there anywhere else you'd consider going, Jarvis? Can I treat you to a crêpe?'

'You don't have to let me win to make your point,' Jarvis said. 'Someone with your handicap. You're so bloody obvious. Did you know that?' He whacked his ball, watched it rise, clear against the blue and tumble into the sea.

People were getting at him. He couldn't stand it. He could almost convince himself that he held the future of the village in his hands. But he knew that wasn't true. He'd lived too long. He'd seen too much. Mareth would survive. The people would live on. Their children would still grow up here, on hot days they'd jump off the harbour wall into the sea, on cold days they'd wrap up, walk, bent against the wind, up the cobbled wynd to school. He could die tomorrow and life would go on. That was the way of it. Life would go on with or without Magda's crêpes. He'd prefer with. Crisp and perfect batter, creamy hot insides, oh yes. And an Alpine scene to gaze at, dream into. That was for him.

So, Magda had slept with Alex. Well, not slept exactly. They had done it. Jessie sat at the window table of the café drinking coffee.

'I have been betrayed,' she thought. 'Betrayed.' Sometimes she tortured herself with it, and sometimes she dismissed it. If she thought of the act as a swift bonk, she could live with it. A bonk, nothing more, nothing less. I've done that. They probably hardly took their clothes off, didn't touch, didn't even really look at each other. I'm mature, I'm sophisticated. I can handle that. She would shrug, things happen.

But if she thought, 'They made love. They touched. They

whispered each other's names. He stroked her face and kissed her. They moaned in exquisite pleasure and afterwards lay talking in quiet voices ... about me. I hate them. How could they?' If she thought that she felt her throat tighten. She wanted to defend herself against the hurt they were causing her. Or at least do them some damage. She gripped a fork. Alex was long gone; she could not stab him. She dared not stab Magda. She thought she might plunge it savagely into her own wrist. That would show them.

She thought she was alone. But Edie was across the café emptying ashtrays into a pink plastic bucket and wiping them out with deft and vibrant movements. She watched Jessie clutching a blunt fork, staring wildly at her arm. 'That'll do it?' she said. Her voice was clipped, eagerly correct.

Jessie looked up, alarmed. She was abashed that her stupidity had been observed.

'That'll do it every time,' Edie went on, waving her fingers at the fork. 'That's a well-known cure for adultery, stabbing yourself in the arm with a fork.'

Jessie put it down. 'I was ...' She could not think of anything to say. 'I was ...'

Edie watched. Jessie's embarrassment interested her. 'You were just realising that your husband has been with Magda,' Edie guessed.

Jessie nodded. Been with? Yes, she could live with that. It sounded more social than passionate. There was something dutiful about it. Yes, yes, they'd been with each other.

'It's hard to bear,' Jessie said.

'I know,' Edie nodded.

'My Fred was a terrible one for women. He was a terrible trouser-dropper, if I say so myself. I felt such a fool. I was inadequate. I wasn't enough for him.'

'Oh no,' Jessie rushed to comfort Edie. 'Not you.'

Yet, she felt that if she was inadequate, Magda would now know it. Didn't matter what word she used – screwed, had, made love, humped – it was all the same. Magda knew Alex now, and knew something deeper and more secret about her than she knew about Magda.

'I'll tell you what it is,' Edie offered. 'You're jealous.'

'Jealous?' she wondered. 'Me. Oh no. Jealousy's not in my life's remit.'

'Oh rubbish,' Edie flapped her hands, shooing away this sophisticatedly ludicrous claptrap.

'Of course you're jealous. But you're not jealous of Magda having your husband. You're jealous of your husband having Magda.'

Edie busily took her bucket of cigarette stubs and ash through the kitchen to the bins at the back door. Jessie heard her enthusiastically mulling over her analysis of the situation.

'Yep,' she said, bang of bin lid. 'Hmm-hmm. That's it.'

She came back. Started clearing a table, removing the cloth and shaking it feverishly. 'Oh yes. You want Magda to yourself. You don't want your husband to have any part of her. She's your friend.'

Jessie turned pale. Edie's deftly delivered truth stunned her.

'And if you ask me – and it's only an opinion, mind,' Edie's active little face became briefly earnest as she spoke, 'none of it is worth jabbing your arm with a blunt fork for. Of course, that's only what I think. And who listens to me round here?'

Eleven o'clock in the Ocean Café and the last customer had long gone. Magda was sitting with Jessie listening to Aretha Franklin.

'She's the best.' Magda tipped her glass toward her tape deck.

'Absolutely,' Jessie said. 'Nobody better. Nobody.'

Joe burst in, grinning wildly, smelling boozy. He had with him four drunken, baggily clothed friends. They all wore baseball caps. They looked like a group of pleasantly maladjusted youths out on day release. They moved sheepishly behind Joe, avoiding Magda's eye. Joe pointed to the kitchen and raised his eyebrows. Could he . . .?

'OK,' Magda said. 'Only . . .'

'I know,' Joe smiled. '. . . Only don't.'

Magda looked at him. Somehow along the line, and she was sure she hadn't taught him this, he'd become charming. He knew if he smiled in such a way, people, especially female people, would let him do anything.

'That's the thing about men,' Magda said to Jessie, 'they seem to know you want them to like you. I hate them for that.' She went for a pee. In the lavatory she looked glumly at her face, 'This is me,' she told herself. 'Old face, hello old face.' Vodka swirled through her brain. And from nowhere the mystery of the omelette pan came to her.

'I know,' she yelled out. 'I know who did my pan.'

She burst out of the lavatory and hurled herself into the kitchen. Her sudden intuition served her well. Joe had her best pan on the burner. It was filled with fat, mushroom, tomatoes, eggs and bacon.

'My pan. You little shit,' Magda howled. 'My best pan.'

Joe shrank back. 'It's only a pan,' he weakly suggested. 'You have others.'

Magda reeled and raved. Joe thought in horror she was going to burst or have some kind of fit.

'It came to me,' Magda shouted, 'truth always dawns when you're not thinking about it. You're using my pan. Have you any idea? Any idea . . .? This pan took years. Years. You don't just get a pan.'

Saying nothing, Joe approached Magda slowly, hands spread. He had some simplistic notion he could calm her down.

'Enough,' Magda shrilled. 'Enough. You have taken enough.'

Joe laughed. 'What do you mean?'

'I mean enough. That's all. Enough.'

Joe cocked his head sideways, indicating that he didn't understand. He did, of course, understand. He was just testing Magda. How far could he go?

'It's only a pan,' he suggested again.

'Don't be boring,' Magda said, tired voice. 'You know what I mean. You rummage through my clothes to see if there's anything you fancy. And if there is, you take it.'

'Oh,' said Joe. He didn't know she knew he did that. He put

his hand guiltily on the pink denim shirt he was wearing. He was a fool to think she wouldn't notice.

'You take clothes, records, money, anything. Enough. Leave me something. You know me. Me. Me. Me. You think you can do anything. But you can't. Just because your mother loves you doesn't mean you can bugger up her pans.'

Joe stepped back, sensing another outburst. Did Magda know about the moisturising cream he plastered on when he shaved and the money he took from her purse? Magda picked up the pan. Hot fat and food tumbled out on to the floor. She held it a moment, viciously eyeing her son. He seized a knife.

'Oh that's right, protect yourself with one of my good knives. Ruin that too.'

'What do you expect me to do? Get bashed with a pan?'

She quietly picked up a potato peeler. Handed it to him, 'Use that.'

He took it from her, turned it round and round in his hand. Then left, still holding it.

Magda waited, eyes shut. 'Me,' she whispered. 'Me. Me. Me.' Every time she said the word, she said it louder. 'Me. Me. Me,' shouting now. She beat her chest, fists clenched. 'Me. Me. ME. ME.' Yelling, eyes bulging, throat throbbing, voice cracking. '*ME.*'

Out in the yard the Harrys scattered. When she returned to the café to finish her drink, everyone had gone.

'Oh,' she said. How strange. She had forgotten people were out here, hadn't realised they could hear her. Besides, it was her anger, why should other people be so bothered by it?

Everybody knew about Jarvis. It was the rumour of the moment. The bank had told him it was reconsidering its position on rural managers. The new policy was to invest in young people and at forty-three he was considered too old . . .

'What does it mean?' Ginny wanted to know.

'I've been made redundant,' Jarvis told her flatly.

Out in the village the news spread wildly. It started with Duncan the postman, but the clerks in the bank had already guessed.

'Irony,' Magda said. 'That's all there is to it. There's always irony.'

Jarvis took it well. He worked a month's notice, giving as many personal loans as possible. He walked round the harbour to tell Willie Patterson and Joe Boyle who worked the creels bringing in lobsters to come in and borrow the money for their next tax payment before he left. The new policy from head office was not to lend money to fishermen to use to pay taxes. During his final fortnight, Jarvis stopped wearing his suit and tie. He sat at his desk, feet up, swigging cans of Bud in jeans and a sweater. His final week he spent at the harbour, chatting to Willie and Joe and finally worked on their boat with them.

He could remember what it was like to be a boy. The smell of it. Sitting on the harbour wall clutching his knees. He stood staring at a cormorant flying low across the surface of the water. If he reached back far enough into his past he would remember the smell of his knees.

He had known every rock round the bay where the lobsters hid when the tide went out. Once he was able to go to their secret crevices and hook them out, a triumphant boy in short pants taking lobster home for tea. They were beautiful beasts, dark blue and brown before cooking turned them red. And they were sweet, so sweet. He put his hands to his face, remembering like this shook him. When he was a boy, Willie Patterson's dad had fished these waters. They'd brought in crab and lobsters in such quantities local kids got tired of them. 'What's for tea? Aah Mum, not lobster again.' 'What've you got in your lunch box?' He'd had a Lone Ranger lunch box – where was it now? 'Lobster sarnies.' 'Oh no, not that. We want meat paste.'

'I think I'll get a boat,' he said to Willie Patterson. Willie said, 'Oh aye.' Jarvis smiled hugely. He knew Willie would get up before him in the morning to rob his creels. Willie caught the grin. He knew Jarvis knew he would get up before him to check the creels It was the Mareth way.

'Well, that would be fine.'

The rhythm of not working at the bank was easy. Jarvis took his boat out, laid down his creels and waited for the next tide so that he could go out again and haul them up, take in his catch, bait the creels again and leave them. Between tides he sat in the Ocean Café drinking coffee and whisky. He only sometimes looked over at the Alpine scene.

'No need of it now,' Magda said. 'You took off and flew.'

'I was pushed,' Jarvis told her.

He had his pay-off from the bank, and his rent money from the Ocean Café and Granny Moran's old flat. He was giving the flat a deal of thought. Jessie would hear him go to it. Stay a while. When he went back down to the harbour, Lipless and his crew loading the council lorry on their way home always called to him and he always called back. It seemed to Jessie he said, 'Fuck. Fuck. Fucky. Fuck.'

Magda shut her kitchen door and stood quite still, feeling the atmosphere. Something was wrong, it was in the air. She didn't know what it was, this wrongness. But she could smell it.

She wandered through the house. There was, it seemed, nobody home and nothing was missing. She stood motionless, felt the hairs on the back of her neck rising. Yes, something was going on in this house. A long low swoon drifted from her bedroom.

Magda looked up, fiercely peering at the ceiling. If she peered hard enough she might just see right through it, see what was going on. Not that she had to do that, she had a very good idea what was going on. She just wanted to know who was doing it and with whom. She climbed the stairs, holding her breath as if her very breathing would disturb the noisemaker. Though she knew it wouldn't, the swoons were getting longer and louder. Furthermore she recognised the voice. That was Janis in her bed. She was, no doubt, with one of those horrendous shore boys.

Even before she burst into her bedroom, Magda could see the scene vividly. They'd be naked, the pair of them, in her bed writhing and tumbling, skinny white teenage bodies; and on the floor by the bed there'd be a heap of clothing, grubby jeans, bashed trainers, T-shirts, socks and discarded underwear. She'd kill them.

She quietly opened her bedroom door. Janis lay sprawled on top of the bed, a slow smile on her face; she gazed dreamily at the ceiling. One hand was spread over the pillow, the other held the head between her legs. Magda recognised that bum, that back, that head . . .

'Dave. You bastard.' Magda was shocked. 'How could you?'

He turned to her, grinning. 'Easy,' he said.

Magda slammed the door and went downstairs to the kitchen. She was sitting at the table staring fixedly at the oven when Dave came down. She did not look at him. Her anger scared her.

'She's only a child. Sixteen,' she said. 'What sort of pervert are you?'

Dave looked past her, 'Oh come on, Magda. She's a big girl now.' Then he said, 'Don't give me any crap about ruining her. She ruined herself long ago.' He stuck his hands in his pockets. 'I won't say town bike . . . but . . .'

Magda got up. 'How dare you speak about my daughter like that? How dare you?'

'Because it's true. Like mother . . . like daughter.' He grinned at her. 'Huh?'

Feeling for the first time in his life he had the edge over Magda, Dave went on. 'Such a sweet young cunt. I love it.' He leaned forward, nudged Magda. 'She loved it too. She's not a goer like you. You're still better. But oh boy, give her a year or two . . .'

Magda hit him so hard she felt the blow jar right up her arm. Her hand hurt for hours after. Dave's head reeled, for a moment his vision blurred. He rubbed his cheek, looked at Magda, said, 'Yep.' And left. Magda covered her face with her hands.

'Oh Janis. Janis. Janis,' she cried for her daughter.

The roup was held on 15 September at ten-thirty at Jim Horn's boatyard. It had been advertised in the local press. Most of Mareth went. They gathered early to stop strangers getting near the front, though the view had been the day before.

Jim refused to watch. He went swimming at Ardro Bay, then

came shivering back to Magda at the café. She gave him whisky and sat with him and Janis at the table furthest from the door. They didn't want to hear the goings-on.

Janis was, at Magda's insistence, working at the café. 'I have to keep an eye on you. You stupid bitch.'

The three sat in silence. Jim drumming his fingers, Magda staring ahead, Janis twirling a fork.

'You were sick again this morning, weren't you?' Magda said. Janis nodded glumly.

'You're pregnant, aren't you?' Magda accused. If things were going to be bad, they might as well get it all over now. Janis sniffed and said she thought so, in fact she knew so. Yes. Yes she was pregnant.

'Christ,' said Jim. 'I don't believe it.'

'You better,' Magda told him. 'It gets worse. It's Dave, isn't it?' Janis nodded.

'I'll kill him.' Jim looked wildly round. If Dave was about he could do it now.

'How long have you been seeing him?' Magda asked.

'Dunno,' said Janis. 'Since he came back.'

'I thought Dave was seeing Jessie.' Jim was incensed. The intricacies of people's affairs amazed him. He was Jim. He lived with Magda. He used to go to the fishing. Now he fixed boats. That was him. He and Magda exchanged despairing glances and sank privately into themselves. When they worried, they worried alone.

Along the quay the sale went on. A couple of the boats Jim had renovated went to visitors. Then the locals took over. Jarvis bought the remaining boat. Freddie Kilpatrick took up the bidding for Jim's tools and eventually got them. Edie bought the computer he'd bought recently to do his accounts. Ruby from the Spar surprised everyone by buying Jim's trailer and winch. And so it went on: the local people moved in, stopping outside buyers from bidding successfully.

The auctioneer had seen it before. It was protectionism. People looked after their own, and in the process looked after themselves. If locals got together to buy up the boatyard they could keep Mareth the way they wanted it, the way it had been all their lives. When the news spread that Jarvis had bought the yard, others came forward to buy whatever they could afford. Now the boatyard at the harbour would stay a boatyard at the harbour. Nobody would build a supermarket, or a hotel or a block of flats. Mareth would continue to be Mareth. Nobody would undercut Ruby's prices at the Spar, or Freddie Kilpatrick's or Frankie's at the ironmonger's. There wouldn't be a new restaurant in opposition to the Ocean Café. Life went on.

The *Sad-Eyed Lady* came up. Fishing boat, built 1958, currently under renovation. It had been undergoing renovations since Jim bought it fifteen years ago. Jessie brought her chequebook along, intending to buy it. But she couldn't bid. Couldn't buy Jim's dream and hand it sweetly back. That would tarnish it. Jarvis bought the boat. He would work on it with Jim. Jim would add bits, then Jarvis. In time they wouldn't know or care whose it was. And maybe they'd take it out, catch fish for the café. And maybe they wouldn't. Only the chat and the planning mattered.

'Would buyers please settle up and collect their goods before leaving?' the auctioneer called, disappointed the *Sad-Eyed Lady* hadn't gone for more. It was always the same in these little towns. Local people stopped serious buyers by moving in front of them. Today the person most interested in the *Sad-Eyed Lady* had been bidding well when someone had pointed out that his Mercedes was slipping slowly off the end of the harbour. God dammit.

Freddie paid for his tools. 'I'll just leave them here for now,' he said. 'I've no need for them at the minute.'

Ruby laughed out loud at the suggestion she remove the trailer and winch. 'I can't be working with stuff like that. Oh my no.' Edie refused to take the computer. 'I've my eye on something a bit bigger. Something with a really, really big memory.' She spread her arms wide, explaining.

'I thought for a moment you were going to buy the *Lady*,' Jarvis said.

Jessie shrugged, 'I'm not local enough for that. Or rich

enough. No matter what I do, I'm going to need all my money. If I stay in Mareth, or go back where I came from, I'm going to need all my money.'

It was over by noon. Everything was sold and, apart from a couple of boats and odds and ends, everything lay untouched.

Three days later, Jarvis asked Jim in the Ocean Café if he'd do some work on the boat he'd bought. Jim said why not? They'd gone back to the yard, picked up the tools and started.

'Did you know I'm to be a grandad?' Jim said.

'I heard,' Jarvis nodded.

'Bloody children,' Jim said.

By the end of the week, Jim Horn's boatyard was back in business. This time it wouldn't close, couldn't close. Who the hell owned it?

Dave disappeared slowly. He did not just go. He went away in stages. His first vanishing was the night Alex came to see Jessie. He was away a week.

'Where does he go?' Jessie asked Magda.

'Who knows? We used to wonder if he had another life somewhere else. A wife, children. But I don't think so. When the weather's good he walks. He just walks and walks. He takes his tent, sleeps out. In the winter . . .' she shrugged.

Wiping himself off the face of the earth had been a wheeze for Dave. Then when it was done he couldn't cope. He had to move, movement helped. Hitching rides was OK but actual movement was best. Walking. The last Jessie heard of him was after he had walked his first hundred miles away from her. He phoned to see how she was.

'Fine,' she said. Would she ever say anything else? 'I'm fine. How are you?'

'Great. I saw an eagle today, really close. Huge bugger. You should come. I'll show you.'

But he never did say where he was.

Chapter Nineteen

The year moved on. Janis worked at the café and got fatter. Jessie watched, not knowing if she was jealous or relieved. She had for a while ached to be pregnant again. She longed for a baby.

Recently, though, she had been feeling vulnerable. If she had a child now, she had a child on her own. More than that, she did not feel able to cope with the nine months of worry a pregnancy would bring. She would, she knew, be constantly monitoring her body for signs of life, waiting for the child to move. She would be thrown into a panic if there was too long a pause between little kicks and dunts from within, imagining all sorts of dire things if they didn't come. No, she was not ready to brave any more pain. But one day. Definitely one day.

October evenings were busy. Jessie had no help with the tables. Edie had gone on holiday and Janis wasn't allowed out front for fear of what she might say. She wasn't taking her pregnancy well.

'I hate this,' she whined, slumping into a chair, legs apart. 'It's horrible. Look at me. I'm horrible.' Then turning on Magda, 'You bitch. You didn't tell me having a baby was like this. You think it's funny. I hate you.'

Magda, resigned to Janis's outbursts, said that a little bit of hate gets you through the day. Not getting the reaction she wanted Janis screamed, 'It's all your fault that I'm expecting a baby.'

'Don't be absurd,' Magda said. She had been accused of many things, but this was a first.

At the end of every working day, Jessie's legs ached. Her feet swelled. She soothed them by sticking them out of the window. The chill evening air was wonderful. Night after night Jessie sat, feet jutting one floor up into the night, drinking vodka, smoking Marlboro Lights and considering her fate.

She wasn't good at decisions. The only time she had instantly made up her mind about something was when she decided to come to live in Mareth. Usually she pondered, she debated with herself, squirming at any sort of commitment. She even went through this tortuous routine when in the baker's shop, choosing between a slice of carrot cake and a fudge doughnut.

She thought about the life she had left behind. Trish and Lou would be there now in bars, at dinner parties, laughing, flirting, sitting in each other's kitchens complaining about their love lives, making judgements about other people and other people's lives. Here she was sitting alone in this God-awful flat with her feet out the window swigging vodka straight from the bottle. This wasn't right.

Trish and Lou were her friends and she missed them, their chat. She just didn't know if she missed them more than she would miss Mareth and Magda if she went back. Trish ran her own press-cuttings business; recently she had moved into video. She scanned the world's media on behalf of several huge corporations. If they were mentioned anywhere from Bangkok to Birmingham she would find it, repackage it glossily, send it to the corporation in question and charge them a huge amount of money. She employed six people including a p.a., and had the messiest private life imaginable She'd been married twice, and had a child that lived with her mother, 'I'm just not good at the maternal thing, darling.'

She kept a shifty eye on the door in bars and restaurants, there were so many people she had to avoid. Mostly male, mostly because she'd slept with them and, that done, didn't want to see them again.

'One day she's going to run out,' Jessie said aloud to the empty room. She knew Trish had slept with Alex and for a couple of months afterwards she too had been on the avoidance list.

'What it is,' Trish once explained, 'is I dread meeting a man I like. I can cope with love. It only breaks your heart. But if a man you like rejects you then he's not just rejecting your body and your sex, he's rejecting all of you. I can't face that.' Trish had been hurt a lot.

People had long since stopped going to Trish's flat. Not that they didn't care for her. It was the dysentery aspect kept them away. It was no longer a joke that the mould in Trish's bread bin and fridge should be donated to science. Trish had loaves that were into the fifth or sixth degree of growth. 'Look,' she enthused. 'It goes green, then brown, then it has wonderful spindly stuff like a spider's web. It's quite exquisite.'

Jessie disagreed. 'It's quite revolting.'

Mould infestations in Trish's life were a sign of broken affairs. The only people that brought food into her kitchen were lovers. Trish would fall on the supermarket bags with childish glee.

'Look bacon. And eggs. How super, we could have breakfast.' Men fussed over Trish. Once Jessie had been in her kitchen when a rancid egg exploded.

'How long have you had that?' Jessie asked.

'Oh,' Trish looked at it mildly. 'These eggs were Steve. He was four months ago.' Dysentery looms, Jessie thought. But oh she envied her.

Lou was the opposite. Her flat was perfect, everything painstakingly chosen and placed. Lou had been engaged to the same man for ten years. She saw nobody else. Her weirdness was skin deep only. Ordinary weird, Jessie thought. Black fingernails, pale skin sort of thing. Lou was the first to bleach her hair and have it cropped. Lou worked in an art gallery.

Jessie wondered what she and Trish were doing now. Sometimes she longed for the city. That boozy waft from pubs, swift blasts of this week's hero in the pop charts humming from shops, international smells – Italian, Chinese, Indian – oozing from restaurants. She missed the noise and clatter, the rush and hum. Then again she didn't miss it at all.

Realising her feet had become numb with cold she shut the window and crawled into bed. She dreamed the dream that had been recurring since she was twenty. Recently she'd been having it once, sometimes twice a week. She lived in a large house. In the middle of the ground floor was a wide staircase, yet she never climbed it. It was carpeted with plush green Wilton. One day she went up the stairs, into a huge room filled with shiny treasures in glass cases. She moved among them in wonder; all this was hers, yet she hadn't as much as visited any of it and couldn't understand why. In the morning, feeling as if she hadn't slept at all, she went to work.

'Do you know,' she said to Magda, 'I was thinking about my friends last night and I realised they're just ordinary. Just like anybody else.'

'It's taken you a while,' Magda said. 'What a pressure you put on them to be more than that.'

Jessie said nothing. Later she phoned her mother. She wanted to ask her what to do. She had forgotten about the tiny world her mother inhabited. Her only decisions were if she should put on her blue blouse with the pink floral print or her plain navy. Or if she should make an apple crumble for supper. Or not. 'How are you dear?' her mother asked.

'Fine,' Jessie couldn't say anything else. In her entire life she'd never answered anything other than fine to that question. She wondered how to broach the subject of her dilemma.

'Your father fell down on the garden path yesterday and has such a big bruise on his leg. He tripped on the step. Oh I don't know. What time is it? Goodness me. I've missed lunch. I think I'll just have a banana. I had a cheese sandwich yesterday and it gave me indigestion. I have to be careful these days . . .'

Jessie listened. She had forgotten, too, how her mother had turned small talk into an art form. She remembered her father's business friends coming for dinner and having their discussion on South African politics interrupted by her mother. They listened, frozen by suburban politeness, as her mother took half an hour to tell them how she'd seen a weed growing amongst her pansies and had kneeled down to pluck it out.

'. . . I only had a bit of toast for breakfast, I thought I was feeling a bit hungry.'

Jessie felt her neck stiffen. She rolled her head around to loosen it up.

'. . . I'm not making jam this year. Well, I didn't last year come to that. Or the year before. It's just your father and me now and we just don't eat the stuff like we did when you were home . . .'

Jessie held the receiver away from her ear, 'I don't know what to do,' she whispered. 'I don't know what to do.'

'Mrs Thomson across at number ninety-four makes it all the time. Goodness knows what she does with it. You're awfully quiet, Jessica. Is anything wrong, dear?'

Jessie said that no nothing was wrong. She was fine. And rang off. Put back her head. And screamed, 'Aaaaaaaaaaah.'

As her pregnancy developed, Janis got grumpier and grumpier.

'I thought the baby moved,' she complained, bent over clutching her stomach. 'This isn't moving. This is boogying. This is jumping around. I hate this baby.'

Magda said she shouldn't read romantic literature usually written by poetic men about pale winsome women being with child. Janis told her to bugger off what the hell did she know about having a baby? Magda gave her the Look. Ignoring it, Janis continued to complain, 'It feels like it's having a party. What's it finding to do in there?'

'It has invited all the other foetuses from the ante-natal clinic round for a rave,' Magda offered.

'Another thing.' Janis was whining so much she was beginning to permanently speak through her nose. 'I thought babies lay in the foetal position. This one is lying diagonally, leaning his elbow on my ribs and spends all day idly kicking my bladder. I hate this baby. I hate him. And I don't want him. I'm going to call it Wayne. Serves him right for kicking about inside me.'

They decided Janis was expecting a boy. Dave, it was agreed, could not possibly have a female chromosome in him.

'It'll probably come out with a tattoo on each arm,' Jessie said.

'And needing a shave.' Magda sighed. 'If only it was non-existent.'

On the day the first geese flew over Mareth on their way to the marshes past Ardro Bay, clattering and honking, V-ing across the sky, Mary Lomax died. She was walking across the living room when the pain hit her. She went white, turned to John, said, 'Oh my God.' And dropped dead before he could reach her.

Magda was in the Ocean Café at the time. She turned to Edie, said, 'Oh no.' She dropped her best knife and ran out into the late autumn chill wearing only her thin blouse, absurd skirt and baseball cap. Even though it was a non-police day in Mareth and Jim's BMW was at the door, she ran all the way to her parents' house and found her father on the living-room floor cradling her mother's head, crying, 'Oh no. Oh no. Oh no.'

They buried her three days later. Magda cried as she stared bitterly into the grave, 'The silly bitch. Silly silly bitch. She broke her own heart. Bloody stupid cow, she'd no right dying.'

John put his arm round her. 'Maybe she's happy at last.' He sighed deeply, 'She's got on her red dress. First time she wore it was to her own funeral.'

The first fistfuls of earth rattled as they hit the coffin.

'Now she won't ever take it off,' Magda said.

Mary Lomax lay in her coffin, first peaceful expression on her face for months and months, wearing her red dress. She had something to wear when good finally came.

Friends and relatives gathered in the Ocean Café after the burial. John did not eat. He drank. It was hard when someone you loved ached and finally died for something you could not give them. Achingly, then, as the whisky in his glass dwindled, his slow tuneless voice seeped through the afternoon's small talk and expressions of sympathy and grief.

'Put on your red dress, baby.'

'I didn't know my Dad knew any blues,' Magda looked shocked. Sometimes it was hard even at Magda's age to realise that parents were, after all, only folk.

And still in childish revolt, she protested, 'That song isn't meant to be sung like that.'

Jim put his arm round her. 'Magda, you especially must know you can sing the blues any way you want.'

For weeks Magda visited the grave every day. Jessie came across her sitting in the graveyard throwing pebbles at her mother's tombstone. Mary Lomax, aged sixty-four years, beloved wife of John. Good finally came.

'Do you know, Jessie, I miss her. Who would have thought it? I want the old bag back so I can tell her what an arse she was. I feel cheated. She got away with being stupid. I'm so bloody angry with her. Christ, what a waste.'

'Her life wasn't a waste, Magda. Look at the time she had, all those Elvis songs she knew. She was fine. You should meet my mother. She and Dad bought their house in 1946, just after the war. They bought it, then they sat in it for the rest of their lives. My mother is lost in trivialities. I don't think she's ever really enjoyed herself ever. I don't think she knows how. I don't think she liked sex much. She has spent every day of her life in that house in that street of houses waiting for my father to come home. She's been alone all that time.'

'Some women,' said Magda, 'are never alone. They always have their own mother standing, arms folded, tutting and disapproving in the dark of their minds.'

Jessie said nothing. She didn't want this to be true. She was not ready yet to forgive her mother for being so trivial.

'Maybe your mother was so obsessed with her mother she wasn't able to take you seriously. Here you are, despairing, about her, but you don't feel any guilt about her. Maybe, Jessie Tate, that gives you more freedom than any of us.'

Just before Christmas, Jarvis Howard came to live in Granny Moran's flat. Deciding he was the source of too much mess, dirty socks, crumpled newspapers, Ginny threw him out. Besides, she didn't want to be married to a fisherman, she wanted to be the wife of a bank manager. Jarvis sat on Granny's chair, looked about the room at the huge bits of antique furniture, and felt the silence. There was a calming silence within the flat, heightened by the noises, cars, workmen's shouts, gulls, without. It was different from the tense silence at home which had unnerved him. He was so overcome with relief that, had he known how, he would have cried.

Next day he went with Jim to shoot geese. They got four. One for him, one for Jim and two for Freddie Kilpatrick to repay him for the loan of the gun and the new water pump he'd put into Jim's car. Magda would cook one with brandy and prunes and hand it in on Christmas Eve.

In the off-season the Ocean Café served several meals a week that were not charged. They were payment to the plumber, the electrician; anybody who had done some work for the Horns. Mareth had a healthy, seething black economy that was recession-resistant. Two meals with wine at the Ocean Café paid the electrician for rewiring Jim's garage. Lobsters and crabs kept Jarvis in crêpes, and a glass of malt of an evening helped him turn a blind eye when rent on the lease was late.

When Jarvis caught a particularly large lobster he handed it to Magda: there were three lunches at least in that he reckoned. Jim requisitioned it to give to Frankie the ironmonger for some tins of paint, Frankie had given it to the plumber for plumbing in his new washing machine, the plumber had given it to Ruby at the Spar to pay off at least some of the huge grocery bill he had run up whilst business was slow, and she'd given it to young Paula Kilpatrick to come do her hair. It was a prize, this lobster. Its life as an item of currency was long. By the time it was cracked open it was too rancid to eat.

Jarvis cooked his goose with chestnut and apple stuffing and invited Jessie in on Christmas Day to share it. She brought the pudding and a bottle of champagne which they opened before they ate. Jarvis reminded her of Alex, he was so efficient in the kitchen. Alex had done most of the cooking and cleaning. Looking round his immaculate flat, she felt guilty about her flat: the dirty heaps of laundry on her bedroom floor, unwashed dishes cluttering the sink and scatterings of newspapers and coffee cups. Shoving some pine-scented stuff down the lavatory was the only housework she did. She no longer straightened her bed, had mastered the art of making it at night whilst in it, just before she went to sleep. She arched her bum and smoothed the sheet beneath her, then sorted out the rest of the bed with her feet. It worked well enough.

'I don't expect you miss the bank,' she said.

'Of course I do,' he told her. 'I miss the respect. The order. I miss the big desk. I even sometimes miss the suit. Life isn't that black and white.' He leaned towards her, 'I miss the power.'

His honesty shook her. Of course, she knew bank managers had power. It was a surprise to her that they enjoyed it.

'You could do something else, surely. You must have qualifications.'

'I'd have to leave Mareth and that would be hard. My family's here. I was brought up here. Everybody knows me here. I belong. It's home. But yes, you're right, in time when I'm ready, I will do something else. I am the worst fisherman in the world. But for the moment it pleases me.'

He poured some more champagne. She worried him. She had what he had come to call the privet-hedge mentality, typically suburban. She thought people led separate lives in separate houses cut off from each other by a neatly trimmed boundary of privet. Here in Mareth, people's lives were grittily entwined. They were a tangle of inter-relations and shared experience. The notion of separate and secret lives would bore them witless. What would they gossip about?

Jessie was so embroiled in the absurd business of being Jessie, it seemed to escape her that everyone round her was similarly embroiled in the absurd business of being themselves. If any religion was instilled in Jessie, it was the glorification of niceness. Jessie thought that being nice mattered. Why, she was almost fanatically nice. Jessie got up in the morning and spent the day being nice to people, and no matter how nasty they were to her, she would wake next day, vision of niceness renewed. It was odd, a woman like Jessie must have examined and rejected all sorts of beliefs, but that great suburban creed of niceness, the blandness of it, was so inherent in her, so deep in there, she hadn't thought to reject it. God, he didn't want his children to be hard or cold, but he hoped they would grow up with more savvy than Jessie Tate, for if they did, that would mean they would grow up with more savvy than him. 'I do believe our goose is ready,' he said, refraining from saying that their goose was cooked.

They did the Christmas thing. Ate too much, pulled crackers, told jokes and worked hard at having a day away from the world. Only once did Jarvis ask, 'Do you know what you are going to do? Are you going to stay or are you going to leave us?'

'Yes,' said Jessie. 'One of those.'

He nodded. Decisions were a bitch.

'I have some money from the sale of the house. It isn't that much. But I could perhaps buy some place. I could get a computer and do some freelance work from here. I can't keep working as a waitress. There are things I could do. I just have to make up my mind.'

At four Jarvis left to visit his children and hand over his presents. He walked up the wynd from the shore, across the High Street then up to the large Victorian houses on top of the hill. Every now and then he turned to look back over the village rooftops to the sea. When dusk came down it spread grey over the water up through the day, a real colour, like a fine curtain; he always thought he might just be able to get a fistful of it. Smoke rose straight from chimneys. There was nobody about. In a garden a blackbird called. The sea was empty today, no boats out. A pale half moon was scratched on to the sky. That same moon had risen on these same rooftops for years and years before he was born, and would rise long after he was gone.

'Hold on to this moment, Jarvis. It's the nearest you'll get to for ever.'

He imagined the scene at home. It wasn't hard. He'd been through twelve Christmases with Ginny already, every one the same as the one before. His in-laws would be there, sitting on the grey velour sofa in the overheated living room. There would be a fake silver Christmas tree, and cards strung up on the walls. The television would be on. His children would take their presents, open them, then ignore him. Handing him a sherry, Ginny would stiffly say, 'Merry Christmas, Jarvis.' There would be no disguising how disappointed in him she was. His mother-in-law would look at him with loathing, and his father-in-law with envy. Ah well.

Jessie went back to her flat. This was the first time in her life that she had spent time alone at Christmas. She phoned Alex.

'Merry Christmas,' she said. 'I just wondered how you were.' She could hear voices and laughter in the background. He was not alone.

'I'm fine. How are you?'

'Oh, fine.' Would she *ever* say anything else? They hung on in silence for a couple of minutes before Alex asked, 'Are you sure you're all right?' He sounded as if he actually cared.

'Of course I am. I'm fine. Really fine.' She hung up.

Jessie stared into the fire. Lining the mantelpiece were cards from all her friends, old and new, Trish and Lou, Magda, Lipless and Edie. She still didn't know what to do. If she didn't go back soon there would be very little to go back to. Her friends would get on with their lives and leave her behind; they'd have nothing in common to talk about. She'd lose her place on the career ladder. Though she suspected she had lost that already. Lost ground was always hard to make up. Her home had been sold. She didn't want to go back to her folks. She sat in front of the fire, Black Harry on her knee, a comfortable weight. She contemplated her new situation. She no longer knew where home was.

She thought she might stay in Mareth a while. She could try to buy this little flat. She could redecorate. If she stayed in Mareth she'd spend time staring out the window, wondering what her friends were up to, and if she went back to her old life she'd spend time with her nose pressed against the window-pane dreaming of Mareth.

Chapter Twenty

On 25 February, with a deal of shouting, swearing and scream- ing, Janis gave birth to a boy. When the doctor laid the new- born infant on her stomach, Janis leaned forward and took it and wept. She cradled it and loved it, and was reluctant to give him to the nurse to get him cleaned up, checked and weighed.

'I'll be a better mother than you,' she said to Magda. 'I won't be off cooking and shouting and having affairs like you.'

'Well, I hope so,' Magda said quietly. 'I hope so.' She took the child in her arms and watched his tiny crumpled face, 'Well, aren't you beautiful,' she said gently. Janis watched her.

'Nobody told me this,' she complained later, not sounding in the least nasal. 'I didn't know I would love him. Not like this.' She took the baby, held her cheek against his head and crooned to him softly. Her eyes damp, voice stretched and ruined from yelling bastards at the doctor and midwife, 'Hello, little one,' she said. 'This is me, your mummy, Janis.'

It was the first birth Magda had witnessed. She had, of course, been there when her own children came into the world, but always complained she was at the wrong end to see what was going on. When she entered the delivery room, Janis was at full screech, yelling and swearing foully.

Magda thought, shamefully, 'That's what I'm like normally, never mind giving birth.' But she did not vow to change.

She saw the baby's head appear, tiny damp. Little wrinkled puckered bewildered face, waiting on the brink of the world for life to begin.

'Don't push,' the midwife bossed. 'Now push.' And here he

was. First breath. First bawl. It had begun.

'Oh God, Janis,' Magda cried in amazement. 'It's a baby.' She stood in wonderment, 'I didn't know. I didn't know.' She didn't know she would feel this rush of joy to see a new person, child of her child, enter the world.

She was shaken more by this birth, this moving on of generations, than she had been by the birth of her own children. But back then she had been too overcome with her own maternalism and pain. Now all she wanted to do was find a quiet corner, bury her head in her hands and weep.

'What are you going to call him?' she asked cautiously. She didn't really want to know. Last week Janis was going to call her baby Fast Eddie, after Paul Newman in *The Hustler*. The week before Flavor Flav after one of her heroes. She had also considered Slash and, briefly, Snake.

'Well,' Janis said firmly. 'I'm not having all this Jim nonsense. He has to have his own identity. I'll call him James.'

Edie festooned the outside of the café with balloons and put notice of the baby in the window in the menu holder. A boy, James, 7lbs 3oz, at five o'clock in the morning, adding, at Magda's insistence, mother and guilt complex doing well. It was a day of free drinks at the Ocean Café. Everybody asked Magda what it was like to be a granny.

'Exactly the same as not being a granny only older and wiser and with one more birthday to remember,' she said. But they could tell it meant more than that. She just wasn't letting on.

Six weeks later, Janis was fully in charge of her emotions once more. She dyed her hair purple, 'For a change,' she told Magda. She sat in the Ocean Café, legs seeming skinnier than ever in leopard-skin leggings, vast steel-capped workman's boots on her feet.

'They keep her from blowing away,' Magda said, looking through the kitchen door at her daughter. Janis was feeding James, tits hanging out of the collarless shirt she'd found in her grandfather's wardrobe.

'You got a problem with this?' Janis asked a couple who were eyeing her as they drank coffee and ate some raspberry shortbread. They shook their heads, 'No, they hadn't a problem.'

'Hey Mags,' Janis yelled. 'Do you think it'd spoil the baby's feed if I got my nipple pierced?'

'Does the term garden sprinkler mean anything?' Magda hollered back.

Thirty years on, Miss Clarkson's face was still terrifying. It didn't look any different. It must have reached wrinkle peak when she was teaching and stopped developing. 'Well,' thought Magda, 'is there room for any more?' Maybe, though, the eyes were more watery, less piercing. She still came to the Ocean Café every week after she'd returned her library books. She sat in the window drinking cappuccino, eating maybe a slice of apple cake, maybe a chocolate croissant. She didn't like to be too predictable.

'I know you've been overcharging me for years, Magda Horn,' she accused.

'Me?' Magda arranged her features into a semblance of innocence. 'Who, me?'

'Oh, don't do that innocence trick with me. I'm too old.'

Magda didn't know what to do. With Miss Clarkson she would always be a scared child with a grubby jotter and a spelling problem. Miss Clarkson was the only person in the world who made her doubt herself.

'What have you been doing with the money? I know you. You're a terrible woman. You have been too busy being yourself to notice half of what goes on around you. But you are honest. And I want to know what happened to my money.'

'I gave it to charity,' Magda told her.

'I won't ask which one. I don't want to know,' the old lady spoke crisply.

Jessie cleared a table nearby and took the dirty dishes to the kitchen. For a second, only a second, Miss Clarkson stopped speaking, stopped thinking to watch her go. Magda caught the look. A tiny tiny fleeting moment in their lives that was over almost before it happened. The teacher suddenly gathered her handbag and picked up her crumpled, over-used Safeway bag full of library books. 'I trust I'm donating to something worthwhile and not one of your absurdities, Magda Horn,' she said crisply. And left.

Magda turned to Edie and said, 'Well me. Did you see that?'

'See what?' Edie said. 'I didn't see anything.'

'The way she looked at Jessie, just then – a moment ago. The longing in her eyes. She's not a demon. She's just a lonely, insecure old lady. Like me.'

'Oh rubbish,' Edie dismissed her. 'You live in your head, imagining things.'

'All those years, Edie. She's been by herself all those years. Edie, I think she's even unhappier than I am.'

'The drivel you talk, Magda Horn. Unhappy. You don't know the meaning of the word. There is not a person you know doesn't care about you.'

Magda went huffily to the kitchen. Edie heard her furiously chopping some chives and parsley. Heard Magda say, Oh sod it. Sod the lot of you.

Chapter Twenty-one

March came round again. Jessie looked out, hoping to see porpoises.

'You're lucky to have seen them the once,' Magda said. 'Some folks never do.'

Jessie was looking for a sign. As a child she'd believed in signs. If I can beat the bus to the end of the street, everything will be all right, little hurtling figure in a blue dress steaming up the pavement. Bus drivers who still had some of their childhood in them knew the symptom and slowed deliberately to let her charge past the winning post. She'd grin. The joy of triumph. Everything would be all right. Jump the cracks on the pavement, step over the lines. Stand on a line you'll break your spine, stand on a crack you'll break your back. She would never risk anything as dire as that.

Hold your breath from the school gate to the classroom and everything will be all right. If it takes three hundred steps from the bus stop at the end of the street to her front door, everything will be all right. If she can do a proper handstand and hold it for ten, everything will be all right. If her mother doesn't make fish for tea, everything will be all right. If she sees porpoises out of the window again, everything will be all right.

When no porpoises passed, Jessie looked for another sign. She read old horoscopes in the dentist's waiting room, watched the sky for shooting stars. Nothing. On her day off she drove out to Ardro Bay. She was wearing her long black coat and big boots. It was cold, the sea was icy calm.

'You'd not last four minutes in it this time of year,' Jarvis told her. Gannets flew in a long line and out on the rocks cormorants hung themselves out to dry. It was four o'clock, getting dark. She strode the length of the bay, torturing herself with every step. What should she do? This was her life, she couldn't let it slip away. If she stayed she'd wonder what her old friends were doing without her. And if she went she'd miss Mareth. She could imagine herself working in some tidy office, plants and books and Apple Mac, dreaming of Mareth, a distant sparkle. Without her Mareth would carry on, no doubt about it.

She found a perfectly round flat black stone and took off her glove to pick it up. It was a good skimmer, this stone. She stepped towards the shore. If she could get it to jump over the surface four times, four bounces, she would stay.

'Ah, but,' she thought, 'I'll never manage four. Three. If I can get it to skim three times I'll stay in Mareth.'

She leaned down, took aim and threw. The stone flew out over the water, bounced. Once, twice, three times, four times.

'Damn,' Jessie said. 'Now I'll have to do it again.' She'd promised herself three skims to stay in Mareth and couldn't renege on that. She found another stone. It skipped twice on the water. The next once. Then twice again. It got darker. There was one star in the sky. One star, didn't that mean a wish? She shut her eyes: wishes don't happen for wishers with open eyes. How childish could she get, she wondered?

'I wish I could find another stone and get three skims.'

Was that two wishes? She didn't know. Maybe she wouldn't get any for being greedy. She was being silly, and knew it. But still she looked around and found another flat stone. Yes, her wish was answered. Now she could get three skims and go home. It was cold here. It skimmed one long beautiful bounce.

'Damn. Damn. Bugger and damn.'

She cast around for another stone, couldn't see one. 'Oh fart.'

She went up the beach to the stony patch on the softer sand and gathered as many flat stones as she could find. It was dark, her nose was running, her hand numb. She was stumbling about. Her scarf kept unfurling and her woolly hat fell over her eyes.

'Oh sod this. What a stupid, adolescent way to behave.'

Carrying a pile of stones suitable for skimming, she lumbered down the beach to the shore. The tide was going out. A gull called.

'Oh God,' she sighed. 'Three skims. This could take for ever.'